MW00773429

GRAVE HUMOR

A Magical Romantic Comedy (with a body count)

R.J. BLAIN

GRAVE HUMOR
A MAGICAL ROMANTIC COMEDY (WITH A BODY COUNT)
BY R.J. BLAIN

Most days, Anwen regrets working at a funeral home. With the residents no longer inclined to stay in their coffins where they belong, she's got her hands full making sure everyone follows the rules:

In the funeral home, there is no screaming, no murdering, no mutilation, no possessions, no kidnappings, no resurrections, and no cursing of any type. Be quiet and stay polite.

The day Old Man McGregor decides to take a walk and disturbs her peace, Anwen learns there's a lot more to the basement in the funeral home than a vampire and a handsome gentleman on ice.

If she's not careful, she'll learn first-hand why 'eternally yours' is the most potent of threats.

Warning: this novel contains romance, humor, bodies, shenanigans, and mythological puppies. Proceed with caution.

written permission from the author, except for the use of brief quotations in a book review.

ONE

Your funeral is at noon tomorrow.

HAD I been smarter or wiser, I never would've accepted the job offer at the funeral home. With my prospects few and far between, I hadn't had a choice, not really. Who else would hire an eighteen-year-old high school drop out?

I could type.

Dead bodies didn't bother me.

When the dead started chatting up a storm, I ignored them until the priest arrived. I almost liked the days when the corpses got talkative. The boss paid me triple the normal hourly rate per incident, and if nobody screamed, a gift card would magically appear on my desk the following morning. Without fail, the gift card would be for the grocery store, and it would offer me the rare opportunity to enjoy a luxury.

Luxuries came few and far between.

Tomorrow, I would take my gift card, fondle some honey rocks until I found the perfect pair to take home with me, and I'd crack them open and go to town on their sweet, sweet insides. I sighed happily at the thought of two perfect melons all for me.

It really was the little things in life.

"It's no fun if you don't scream, Anwen m'dear," Old Man McGregor groused. "Must you suck all the joy from my funeral?"

"Your funeral is at noon tomorrow," I reminded him. That was the problem with the newly dead. They got lost on the way, refusing to leave their bodies until someone came to lay them to their final rest. Old Man McGregor could make my life a living hell if I wasn't careful.

In life, he'd enjoyed yanking on chains for the fun of it.

In death, all he had to do was sit up to yank on the entire town's chain.

"You're still going to suck the joy right out of it," the old man whined.

I checked my watch. In an hour, Old Man McGregor's wife and grandnephew would arrive for the viewing, which was scheduled to begin in three hours. I expected half the town would show up to pay their respects while the other half showed up to partake of the drama.

The dead getting up for a final chat tended to create a lot of drama, and after the first time it'd happened, attendance at viewings and funerals had skyrocketed.

People loved a free show.

Damn it all, I couldn't afford to wait for my boss to arrive. If I wanted to get my greedy hands on a pair of honey rocks, the old goat needed to get back into his coffin where he belonged without pranking the entire town on his way to the grave. That meant one of two things. I could cut a deal with the cantankerous coot, or I could call for the priest myself.

The priest would arrive within ten minutes, as he didn't appreciate when the dead refused to abide by the natural order of things. Corpses belonged in coffins or caskets, and Old Man McGregor had opted for a coffin rather than a casket.

I figured he knew he was a pain in the ass and wanted us to nail the lid closed so he wouldn't get out once we put him in the ground where he belonged. Technically, the difference between caskets and coffins was one of shape, but generally, caskets were of better construction in addition to being rectangular. Traditionalists favored the coffin, as did many a vampire, claiming they were head and shoulders over the rest.

Every time someone cracked that damned pun, I wanted to beat them to death with their burial vessel of choice.

Personally, I liked cremation. Any urn would do, and you could store the ashes in a plastic container if an urn wasn't available, although I'd heard of a few unfortunate incidents where someone had left their loved one out where a cat might use them as a litter box.

There wasn't a whole lot anyone could do about urine-contaminated ashes, yet somehow, once a year, *someone* would stroll on in asking how to get Fluffy's excrements out of their granny.

Oy, oy, oy.

At least Old Man McGregor wouldn't be showing up again as a victim of cat pee and poor handling.

I straightened my shoulders so I wouldn't sigh at the unfairness of it all. Old Man McGregor would prove a challenge, but I really wanted my damned honey rocks, and the only time I got them was when the dead returned to their rest without breaking any of the funeral home's rules.

"You're not going to do this the easy way, are you?" I asked, careful to keep my tone pleasant and curious rather than expose my readiness to rip what remained of his internal organs out through his right nostril.

"When have I ever done anything the easy way, missy?"

With that one question, I gave up on my attempt to be the immaculate professional. I sighed. "You're going to cost me this week's groceries, aren't you?" Not only would he cost me the rest of my groceries, my honey rocks would be a dream within a dream.

It'd been so damned long since a corpse had actually cooperated with me. The last time, Mrs. Theault had been the one to do the screaming, and it'd taken an entire night of talking to her to get her to return to her casket. Everyone handled death a different way, but Mrs. Theault's problems broke my heart.

She'd been headed to heaven.

Her husband had gone to hell.

The whole town knew why, but it took death and some help from me to guide her back to the light where she belonged.

Mr. Theault was just one of the cheating, abusive bastards in town, and on a bad day, I wanted to take a pair of honey rocks and beat the assholes to death with them. The thought of ruining two perfectly good melons kept me from indulging in my desire to clean up Sunset, which probably meant I had a ticket to hell once I kicked the bucket, too.

I'd still gotten a gift card for helping Mrs. Theault head to where she belonged, but it hadn't been enough to cover even a single honey rock after I'd gotten the necessities to get me through another week.

I hoped Mrs. Theault found a better man in heaven or got a new chance at a life with someone worth her time. Of all the little old ladies in town, she'd been one of the nice ones. Despite her long years, she never forgot what it meant to be compassionate. I supposed that had something to do with her final destination.

We needed a few more people like Mrs. Theault in the world. Then I wouldn't want to do things like rip a dead man's remaining organs out of his nostril.

Why the hell was mutilation of a corpse illegal? And since the corpse happened to be able to get up, walk, and talk, not only would I be hit with a count of mutilation of a corpse, I'd also get jailed for assault and whatever other charges someone got for ripping a dead guy's remaining internal organs out through his nose.

I allowed my shoulders to slump, and I sighed again.

"That would be mean of me. All right, Anwen. I'll give this hand to you. How do you get your groceries, and what does me going back to my coffin have to do with it?" The old, dead man sat across from me, squishing as he made himself comfortable. After the first dozen chatterbox corpses, I'd convinced the funeral home director to use thick pleather cushions, which were a breeze to clean. An hour with the right chemicals and some elbow grease, and no one would know Old Man McGregor had left his coffin and gone for a stroll.

"It's simple. At your viewing—before and after, too—you don't make anyone scream. You don't scream. Nobody screams. Director Hammel hates when people scream in his funeral home. If no one screams or breaks any of the other rules, I get groceries. My current wage doesn't pay for my bills and my groceries, so it's really nice when a lively corpse behaves. If one behaves every month, I get my groceries. It works well for everyone."

Once and only once, two corpses had felt sorry for me, and I'd gotten to have a nice steak to go with enough food to get by plus an entire pack of cigarettes.

Damn it, I could use a smoke, and I didn't care if it landed me in my grave early. If someone brought me to my work for interment, I'd go out with a bang and work hard to break every damned rule on my way out. With the way my thoughts kept going, I had a ticket to hell, and damn it all, I meant to earn it.

"That's it?"

I understood the skepticism in the old man's voice. Director Hammel knew everybody in town, and the smart ones gave my boss a wide berth for good reason.

Old Man McGregor, while considered the town's almost-lovable nuisance, wasn't stupid.

"That's it," I confirmed, although I did nod towards the placard informing guests of the funeral home's rules.

"I can do what I want as long as nobody screams?"

I pointed at the rules. "Those still apply."

Old Man McGregor turned in the chair and read, "No screaming, no murdering, no mutilation, no possessions, no kidnapping, no resurrections, and no cursing of any type. Please remain quiet and polite."

"If you obey all those rules, I'm paid a bonus in the form of a grocery store gift card tomorrow morning."

"What's in it for me?"

And there it was, the usual request for a bribe. If he wanted to be bribed, I could give him an ultimatum the dead wisely feared. "I won't call the priest or tell Director Hammel you got out of your coffin. I'll clean up before the viewing, and should you decide to do something that doesn't break the rules, I'll play dumb."

Sometimes, giving the dead a chance to stretch their legs and play harmless pranks before they returned to the ground helped them accept their final rest. If he didn't go down and stay down by tomorrow morning, the priest would handle the details with no one being the wiser his sermon was more than showing respects for the dearly not-quite departed.

"That ain't hard for you, youngin'. We all know you never did finish your schoolin' like a good girl. Why not, anyway? In my day, why, we would've given an arm and a leg for the chances you've thrown away."

I considered taking my phone and beating the corpse to his final rest. "I could just call for the priest."

"No, no. That's all right. I never did get along with that jackass anyway. Indulge an old dead man, Anwen m'dear. Why quit? You've nowhere to go now. Your old man kicked you out over it, didn't he? I've heard things you know. You made your momma cry."

I picked up the phone, cradled it between my shoulder and ear, and cracked my knuckles in a show of preparation. Disgust and fury grew as a cold seed deep within my chest. "So I did, Mr. McGregor." She'd cried because I hadn't given her any fucking money to chase after her vices. She'd never given a shit about my schooling; to her, women existed to provide men with children, and all education did was get in the way of the procreation. She'd done her duty having me, and that was as far as it went with her. "I'm going to give you three choices. I recommend you choose wisely, or the priest will be over here in ten minutes to ruin your fun."

"Three? Wasn't it two before?"

Asshole old man. With enough work, could a spine be ripped out through a nostril? "Now it's three. Are you going to cooperate and hear your choices, or am I just going to give the priest a call?"

"I'm listening."

"Choice one: you return quietly to your coffin and play dead until your funeral. Choice two: I call the priest so he can deal with you. Choice three: I tell you why I quit school, and when I'm done, you return to your coffin."

"And?"

"And what?" I returned the phone to its

cradle. "That's it. You return to your coffin. The end. Do whatever you want, but I'm not going to have some old dead coot judging me because he's an ignorant ass."

"You'll lose your groceries if you let me do what I want."

"You're the town's troublemaker. I'm an idiot for even entertaining the idea I might get a bonus tomorrow with you involved. Why get my hopes up?"

"I'll take option three, please."

Since when the hell did Old Man Mc-Gregor take mercy on any of his targets, especially when there was fun to be had? Well, if he wanted the truth, I'd give it to him—and maybe the old coot would go bother my parents for a while before heading to his grave where he belonged. "Dear old dad took my college fund and wasted it on hookers and blow in Vegas. My mother cried because I told her the truth, but she wanted me to think she hadn't taken her half. She also wanted me to give her money. She'd used her half to get high while Dad was busy banging every prostitute in Nevada. Since I couldn't afford college, why bother finishing the rest of high school? I dropped. No point in a diploma I can't do jack shit with, and since my oh-so-loving parents returned to Vegas to finish blowing whatever the fuck else money they stole, I needed to get a job and work or live on the streets. Happy, Mr. McGregor? There is your story about the town's shamed dropout." I rose from my seat, snatched my work keys from my desk, and headed for the door. "I'll be back in ten minutes. Do me the favor of returning to your coffin so I can get this place cleaned up before your family arrives."

"No, Anwen. That story didn't make me happy at all," the corpse whispered.

"That makes two of us. If crashing your own funeral makes you happy, be my guest—just try to keep the screaming to a tolerable minimum, please."

Like always, I'd get my honey rocks—and my groceries—another time.

I NEEDED A SMOKE, but one of Director Hammel's employment criteria involved abstaining from puffing away at lung cancer in a box. He viewed the smell as unprofessional, and the only stinking bodies he allowed in his funeral home were the corpses. As I could afford the occasional cigarette but couldn't afford pixie dust, not when the low grades sold for twenty dollars a pop when added to some shit coffee, I usually kept my flirtation with lung cancer to the weekends. It was one thing to light up in the comforts of my backyard, as I could wash my clothes, never smoked inside, and took every reasonable precaution possible to hide my addiction. It was another to do so where I could be caught in the act.

Director Hammel likely suspected I cheated on his stupid rules, but he hadn't complained about my habit, and until he did, I saw no point in making any changes.

I had one damned cigarette left in my pack at home and no money to get a new one.

Maybe Old Man McGregor and I could switch places; we'd both be better off.

Walking around the funeral home's pristine gardens helped clear my head, and ten minutes later, I returned to my office. The unpleasant funk of embalming fluid lingered, evidence I hadn't hallucinated Old Man McGregor's post-mortem visit. I armed myself with paper towels, spray cleaners, and air freshener before waging a bitter, futile war against the funeral home's lingering miasma of decay and death.

Lemon smelled so much better than rot. As far as the restless dead went, Old Man McGregor hadn't left me with too much of a mess to clean. He'd stayed mostly intact, limiting his oozing to a spot here and there. It took me twenty minutes to erase the evidence he'd gotten out of his coffin and taken a walk.

Five minutes later, Direct Hammel and his merry band of somberly dressed assistants arrived. Why did Direct Hammel need four men to stand around? Most viewings, even the big ones where the whole town showed up, only needed two attendants. The rest of the time, I could handle the work without any help at all.

While the viewings sometimes had upwards of the town's full three hundred people, I couldn't think of a single funeral with more than twenty attendees since I'd started working at the place. The old stayed, the young left, and with a world full of magic to discover, who wanted to stay in Sunset, Alabama? If my college fund hadn't been bled dry on drugs and hookers, I would've been on the first bus out along with the other six seniors in my class.

"Any problems?" the director asked, sniffing the air.

I bet he smelled the lemon and wanted to know why I'd been cleaning. "No problems," I replied. Any other day, Old Man McGregor rising and coming out of his coffin for a chat would've counted as a problem, but I was too worn and tired to care. Like with all things, problems were relative. If the restless dead hiding in his coffin decided to cause a problem, I'd back up and watch the fireworks. "I finished my other work for the morning, so I cleaned to make certain everything was ready for the viewing, sir."

"Good job. Our clients will arrive soon. We'll handle the rest from here. Mr. McGregor's family is rather conservative, so if you could handle inventorying and cleaning the preparation and refrigeration rooms, that would be useful. Otherwise, go home."

I didn't need a diploma to read the writing on the wall. If I went home, I wouldn't be invited back to work, which meant someone hadn't done their job cleaning the basement.

The funeral home went through inspections once a month to keep its license, and we were due to have a government worker poking around the place. Plastering a smile on my face, I nodded. "I'll be downstairs if you need me, sir."

"Good. Call the main line if there are any problems."

Once again, I read the writing on the wall: if I had any problems during the viewing, I would be in need of a new job.

I struggled to maintain a neutral, professional expression. To keep guests from wandering into the restricted parts of the funeral home, Director Hammel locked the stairwell door and turned off the lift. I'd spend the next six hours in the basement. After the surge of restless dead and corpse possessions, the funeral home boasted reinforced lower level walls and doors, fashioned of a mix of concrete and steel to keep the bodies contained should they decide to get up and take a walk.

Fortunately, excluding Old Man McGregor, we only had two bodies in storage, and John Doe had been in our freezer since before I'd been born. If he decided to get up, they'd hear my screams in the next state. While the rules kept changing, one thing stayed the same: the older the corpse, the stronger the undead it became. I hadn't seen Mr. Doe, but I sometimes heard Director Hammel talk about him in hushed, fearful tones.

Nothing scared Director Hammel except our John Doe.

The other body we had didn't worry anyone; the vampire wasn't going anywhere until someone reattached his limbs and revived him with a lot of blood. I wasn't sure why we kept the vampire on ice, but someone from the CDC came once a month, along with the funeral home inspector, to make sure he remained as alive as an undead got. I'd gotten to take a look at the vampire, as Director Hammel wanted to make certain I knew to avoid the sleepers in the freezer.

All in all, I didn't care about either corpse. Unless I put my throat to the vampire's mouth, he couldn't hurt me. As for John Doe, I wasn't sure what I thought about him.

While I wanted to curse over my foul luck, I kept smiling, grabbed my purse and coat, and descended into the basement. I made it all of two steps before the lock clicked behind me.

"Asshole," I muttered, shaking my head and reaching for switches. I flipped three of the five, bathing the stairwell and landing below in a yellowed light. The stench of embalming fluid burned my nose, and I turned on the ventilation fans so I wouldn't suffocate before the end of the viewing.

When I found out who had left the basement a reeking hell hole, there'd be a third
body in the freezer. In prison, I could study
and pretend I had a future, and I'd do so on
the government's dime until they kicked me
out and made me finish my term doing community service. Curling my lip in a snarl, I
stomped down the steps and aimed for the
disposal bin meant for the latex gloves. I
caught it with my foot and launched the
damned thing through the open doorway.

It crashed onto the metal table bolted to
the preparation room floor.

"What's the fucking point of having a
three-inch thick containment door if it's
open all the time? I'm surrounded by braindead idiots."

"Yes, you are," a husky, deep voice replied.
"I was wondering who they'd sacrifice to me
first. I knew the scarecrow would hide, but I
thought he'd betray the whiner first. How
disappointing."

A flash of red in the corner of my eye
warned me something came, but before I
could do more than flinch, a muscular
forearm slammed against my throat while a
tall, black, and crimson clad body pinned me
to the stairwell wall. A hand covered my
mouth.

I sucked in a breath, wheezing from the
pressure against my throat.

"I don't like when people scream. Remain
quiet, and you might live longer."

Unless the vampire had reattached his arms and legs, added at least six inches, and had stolen a black and red outfit better suiting the Victorian era, John Doe had gotten tired of his eternal rest, gotten up, and explored the basement. Unless someone up-stairs heard me, an impossibility through the locked door above, I was up a creek without a paddle or a boat.

Oh, well. Shit happened. As screaming or protesting, or even struggling, would do me no good, I settled for a nod.

Then again, if a prolonged life turned into a losing proposition, I'd scream myself hoarse to speed up the inevitable.

"Very good. What's your name, little lady?" My captor eased the pressure on my throat and lowered his hand from my mouth.

Well, then. If he wanted to be cordial, I could work with that. "I'm Anwen."

"Of which clan? You smell of the Isles." He paused, as though lost in thought. "I don't know what they call the Isles in this era. No matter. I've not had a clanswoman in many years. Clanswomen are always entertaining."

"I don't have a clan. I'm a Nash," I admit-ted. "My father's American, and my mother's mother is a Brit. I'm a mutt, so I'm probably not interesting or entertaining. Sorry."

"How curious. Right now, most begin beg-ging for their lives. Why don't you? I mean, I do enjoy skipping that rather tedious phase of our introduction. I've found my accommodations rather offensive, though that's no fault of yours."

I rolled my eyes at that. Seriously? What sort of weirdo asked questions like his? I suspected he redefined old, and the brief glimpses I'd caught of him implied he would be easy on the eyes. I had assumed he'd count as some sort of nasty undead predator if he got up, but he felt much warmer than any corpse I'd dealt with. "Do you want the pretty answer or the truth?"

John Doe shifted his hold on me, pulling me against him rather than keeping me trapped to the wall. Warm breath tickled my cheek. "Tell me both, but start with the truth."

"Okay. Right now, you'd probably be doing me a favor, and if you decide to draw it out, I plan on screaming so you kill me faster."

"And your pretty answer?"

"It turns out that is also my pretty answer." While he no longer strangled me, he kept me pinned against him, which beat the wall but made me question my sanity. Were all men warm? Thanks to Sunset's dwindled population and severe shortage of decent single guys, I hadn't met any men I'd wanted to cuddle up with.

Apparently, bad boys appealed to me. I needed to help my mother swallow her own damned teeth for having influenced me. Bad boy appeal must have been the reason why my mother had married my father, and that relationship consistently proved to be a train wreck destined for hell.

"How interesting."

"What sort of undead are you? You're rather warm. The other stiffs definitely aren't warm."

John Doe laughed long and loud. "My dear lady, whoever said I was dead? I assure you, I'm as alive as you. I'm no undead, although I've noticed you're keeping one in your freezer. How uncouth."

"He's not *my* undead. I'm just the receptionist who is often relegated to serve as the maid. Heaven forbid the chauvinistic male pigs upstairs be helped by a mere girl. Look, if you're not going to kill and eat me, can I get to work? If this sty isn't spotless by the time the viewing is done, the director will probably fire me. At that point, you may as well kill me."

"Are you a virgin, Miss Nash?"

What the hell? "Excuse me? What does my virginity have to do with anything? How about you? Are you a virgin? Your sex life has been on ice for at least fifty years, so you may as well be. I bet you're shriveled from disuse. Typical man. You throw your weight around, act like you're all high and mighty, and I bet when you think no one is looking, you waste all your money on hookers and blow since you're too cheap to go all the way."

Damn. I needed to either reward my mouth or gag myself. I couldn't tell which.

"I think you'll find me pleasantly experienced." John Doe released me, taking a single step away from me. "By all means, do your work, Miss Maid. It would be rude of me to jeopardize your livelihood when you're too entertaining to kill."

I rubbed at my throat and glared at all six feet plus of male perfection. Whoever had picked his funerary attire had done him justice, and his dark hair and bronzed skin brought out the icy blue of his eyes. "Do you have a name, or should I just call you Mr. Arrogant Asshole?"

"I'll tell you my name under one condition. Pray tell, what exactly do you mean by hookers and blow?"

I laughed myself hoarse. "Prostitutes," I gasped. "Cheap prostitutes on the street for a public—"

"Public?!"

Tears streamed down my cheeks, and I sank to the floor, unable to quell my giggles. "Maybe in your car. When you expired the first time, did cars even exist?"

"I am unfamiliar with cars, although thanks to the nature of my slumber, I have heard the term before. I assure you, Miss Nash, I only take my women willing, nor do I pay for one's company. By the time I'm finished with you, I promise you'll be begging for the honor of my company in your bed. After centuries of listening to men talk while preparing bodies, you count as a jewel among rubbish. Such fine entertainment only comes along every few hundred years or so, and I've been waiting far longer than that for a chance like this."

A chance like what? I considered his situation, which involved him listening to the world around him for countless years. I would be grumpy and irritable—and possibly arrogant as hell—if I had suffered through that, too. Fortunately for me, I'd kept quiet while down in the preparation and refrigeration rooms, so he likely had no idea I'd existed until now.

What was he up to, though? Why would he be interested in me? Whatever. I dodged death for a while, and that would be good enough for me. "Is that a threat or a promise?" I asked, unable to fully suppress my curiosity.

"It's both."

TWO

Please don't scream.

MR. ARROGANT ASSHOLE watched me work with a smug smile. I took my irritation out on my cleaning, hissing curses between clenched teeth. Someone had left the preparation room a mess, and one of the industrial-sized drums of formalin, the stabilized formaldehyde solution we used to preserve various bits of our deceased guests, had leaked. In time, the fumes might kill us both, but if I turned the ventilator fans to max power, closed the drum, and stayed away from the preparation room for a while, we'd be fine. But first, I needed to check why the preservative wasn't where it belonged.

I opened it to discover a damned good reason it had sprung a leak.

Someone had decided to store a body inside.

I broke every rule in the funeral home, screamed like I meant it, and bolted for the stairwell.

A split-second later, Mr. Arrogant Asshole hooked his arm around my waist, jerked me to him, and clapped his hand over my mouth. "Please don't scream. I find the sound so grating. What seems to be the problem, Miss Nash? Surely it's not been the first time you've seen a body." He leaned around me, wrinkling his nose as he considered the victim. With a shrug, he stepped away from the drum and dragged me with him. "Try this again, but with no screaming this time."

He eased his hand off my mouth.

Okay. I could handle the situation like an adult. It wouldn't take much to remember screaming really tripped the asshole's trigger. "The bodies aren't supposed to go in there. I didn't even think one would fit. That's a pretty toxic preservative, and the fumes can get dangerous. We keep it in a somewhat stable solution, but it can still kill you in a hurry if you're not careful. The drums are supposed to be sealed, and we usually work with masks when dealing with the formaldehyde. The health inspectors get really picky about the safe handling of the bodies."

"Very well. That's a legitimate reason for your reaction. Scream as much as needed, but only this once. Or until the next time there's a legitimate reason for such a reaction, I suppose."

If I pushed hard enough, could I make two bodies fit inside the drum? "I'm done screaming, but thank you. I wouldn't want to offend your delicate sensibilities again, Mr. Arrogant Asshole."

"My name is Eoghan Olin, Miss Nash."

My brows shot up at his rather unusual name. The slight intonation distinguished it from the more American Owen, although if I hadn't been paying attention, I might not have caught the slight difference in pronunciation in the middle. If I wanted to avoid tripping over my tongue while saying his name, I'd have to take care.

Whatever. I'd deal with his name properly despite my inherent dislike of the man. Well, somewhat dislike for him. I wouldn't mind if he stuck around, thus allowing me to admire him as long as he learned to stay quiet so he wouldn't annoy me.

Who knew? I liked tall men with dark hair and blue eyes. There weren't a lot of them in Sunset, with the townsfolk mostly consisting of pale hair colors and the occasional red head, with my dark brunette another mark against me.

On second thought, I needed to get my head out of the gutter.

"Well, maybe if you had graced me with it sooner, I wouldn't have needed to assign you a name. You only have yourself to blame, Mr. Arrogant Asshole."

He smirked. "You are determined to burn brightly and hold tight to your pride, I see. Excellent. I enjoy when I deal with such a woman. I dislike tedium. I dislike a great many things, but tedium? How dreary. You may wish to adjust your current antagonistic position, as I've reason to believe that the miserable excuses for humans upstairs have no intention of allowing you to live. The misguided fools truly believe they can sacrifice you to me to appease my hunger. I think they mistake me for a vampire. Had I been an undead creature of the night, their ploy may have worked, but I am not. Still, I accept their offer of you as a sacrifice, although they are incorrect on the nature of the sacrifice I require." The bastard's smirk eased to a satisfied smile. "There are perks to being my sacrifice, of course. You'll show me the nature of the world as it is now, explain the ways it has changed, and provide the knowledge I require to understand society and thrive in it. In exchange, I will provide you with certain protections, knowledge that may lead you to wealth, direct wealth depending on the situation with my current caretakers, and a way out of this place, which will become your tomb should you let it. In the eyes of those above, you have witnessed too much. You know too much. You're a threat to them."

Clenching my teeth, I pulled free of Eoghan's hold, approached the container, and peeked inside. He hadn't been dead long as far as I could tell, although I wasn't sure. "Did you know he was in here?"

"I knew something was amiss, but I didn't know what. They discussed a sacrifice, likely

you, and that the time of renewal was nigh.
They were right on that score. The land's
lifeblood once again flows freely, so here I
am. I do find my current attire perplexing,
however."

"It's a suit. Sure, it's a bit old fashioned,
but it's just a suit."

"You presume these suits were worn the
last time I freely walked the lands, Miss Nash.
They didn't. I suppose they may have been
worn during some of my brief awakenings,
but I have never seen this sort of attire before. Suits, you say? No matter. That was
then, this is now. I've no interest in the year,
either, mind you. It means nothing to me.
What sort of men wear these suits? The im-
poverished?"

I shook my head. "The wealthy eccentric
might like a suit like that."

"That will do nicely. I will have to thank
my caretaker, assuming it's not this unfortunate fellow. Tell me. Do you know who my
caretaker is in this era?"

His guess was as good as mine, but I was
inclined to believe the unfortunate fellow in
the drum was responsible for the newly
awakened man. I pointed at the container of
formaldehyde. "He's as likely as anyone else.
I've no idea. Honestly, I thought Director
Hammel was in charge of you."

Had I known our John Doe was more
than just an odd stiff on ice, I might've taken
him out of the freezer and thawed him my-

self. Not only did he appeal to the eyes, I liked his voice despite his tendency to annoy me.

"That ignoramus buffoon couldn't take charge of a carriage let alone me. Really. There's no need to be insulting. Do you know who that fellow is?"

Considering I couldn't see his face, I'd have to drain the drum or pull him out to find out. Would the fumes kill me if I dumped the chemical onto the floor? Considering the fumes were already getting to me, I expected they would. Screwing the lid into place and letting someone in a hazmat suit deal with the body was the wisest option, so I held my breath and secured the lid. Despite being the stabilized solution, my eyes burned. Backing away, I went to the staircase to breathe in cleaner air. "Are you strong enough to move that?"

"I'm not sure I want to move it, seeing your adverse reaction to it."

"Well, despite that being a more stable form of the stuff, it's pretty damned toxic."

"Where do you want me to put it?"

I pointed at the drain. "Next to that so if it continues to leak, it leaks into the toxic waste reservoir beneath the floor. There's some magic down there that keeps the toxins below where they belongs. Don't knock it over. I'd rather not die today if avoidable."

"How toxic is pretty damned toxic?"

"All they would have had to do to kill him is hold him near the vat without protections and wait a few minutes for the fumes to do him in."

"How uncouth."

"They use it to preserve dead bodies."

"I'll be most careful with it. Do stand back. I wouldn't want my new sacrifice to prematurely expire on me. It's really rare I get to have such fun at my awakening."

If staying in a freezer for decades couldn't kill him, what could? I retreated up the stairwell, which should have had the best ventilation in the entire basement. However, someone had turned the fans off, and when I checked the switches, I discovered they were in the proper position.

Someone had turned the ventilation system off from upstairs. That led me to believe the arrogant asshole moving the drum had the right idea, and that Director Hammel meant to kill me, too.

It made sense. Nobody would miss me.

Well, shit.

I really wanted to get some honey rocks and write the whole week off. Without the gift card, I had some chocolate pudding and a few dollars to tide me over until my next pay in a few days. I would enjoy the chocolate pudding, especially as I had a new jug of milk in my fridge. Unfortunately, according to my bank account, I couldn't afford the honey rocks until I was paid, and by then, I'd do the responsible thing and make sure I had enough staples to get me through to my next check.

Living paycheck to paycheck sucked.

"I've moved it. What now, Miss Nash?"

"Good question," I muttered, returning to the preparation room. "They turned off the ventilation system."

"I don't understand what that means. Please explain."

"It means that if we spill that drum or there are more fumes, I'll die. I'll suffocate. They turned off the air flow into the basement. Unless they open the door or turn on the elevator to let me out, I'm screwed. And by screwed, I mean I will be the next corpse down here."

"Are you always so pessimistic?"

"As a matter of fact, yes. If you pull that corpse out so we can get a better look at him, I'll just die a little faster, which isn't necessarily a bad thing." I sat on the bottom step and stretched out my legs, as hugging my knees and crying wasn't a great way to go and would deplete the oxygen in the basement faster. "I hope Old Man McGregor scares the piss out of those assholes upstairs. That would serve them right. I didn't even do anything wrong this time."

"Fear makes men do reprehensible things. They fear for their lives and would spend yours to preserve theirs. They're right to fear me, but they should fear you more."

"Me? Did you hit your head climbing out

of the freezer?" There was no way anyone could possibly fear *me*. The only thing that needed to fear me was my pack of pudding the instant I got home, because I was going to whip it into shape and eat the whole damned thing in one sitting. "That's nuts. I'm unrated. I have no known magic, but I have too much magic to classify as a vanilla human. Don't ask me what that means, because I don't know. It doesn't make any sense to me, but the machine they use goes beep-beep-beep near me, which means magic, but nobody has figured out what my trick is."

"I can come up with a few interesting and plausible theories in but a few minutes. I do have the advantage of many long years listening to the inane prattle of those simpletons. I'll share my wisdom with you for a price. In that, nothing has changed. Nothing is for free. What say you? I promise an extended life and servitude to me won't be terribly heinous. I'll even put a conclusion date for your servitude should you bargain with me well enough. Most importantly, I'll uphold my end of our bargain first, ensuring you leave here alive."

Ugh. I couldn't tell if I wanted to hate the bastard or spend the last minutes of my life stripping him out of his clothes. The thought of servitude of any sort disgusted me, although I also realized I did Director Hammel's bidding, which amounted to the same thing. I regarded him, tilting my head to the side. "How do I know you're not lying to me?"

"I'd be foolish to lie to you. You're no use to me dead. I'll be generous and only require your sacrifice for a year. That will give me plenty of time to secure your company as mine for however long I please. It's a fair deal. A year of your time for a secret and your life. The alternate is one I dislike, as it would involve your death."

Death came to everyone. My first few days at the funeral home had disturbed me, but once I'd gotten a chance to look death in the eyes, I hadn't found it all that frightening. Death wasn't anything more than a doorway, one I could peek through every time one of the corpses got up and decided to have a chat with me.

"Your offer might have worked if I feared death. I don't."

"Do you care to put that to the test? There's a vampire in the other room who would appreciate a new chance at life. He wouldn't need all of your blood, just a hefty amount of it. If you speak the truth, you'll survive." Eoghan stepped to me, staring down his nose with a raised brow. "You're such an interesting woman."

"If the vampire drains me dry, doesn't that mean you lose your new sacrifice? That sounds to me like you'd just be losing, unless you want a date with the vampire."

"Hardly."

"If I die, you lose," I pointed out.

"I only lose if you die. If you're telling the truth, you won't. I think you're telling the truth, so you won't die. Not today."

The confidence in his voice annoyed me. "What the hell? If I get anywhere near that vampire after he's been put back together and warmed up, he'll definitely kill me. He'll kill anyone unfortunate enough to get too close. It won't even be his fault. At that stage of revival, he'll be incoherent and unable to even attempt to behave like a human. We hear that lecture every time an inspector comes to visit."

"It's simple. For me, that is. If you test this and live, I am right, and you'll be mine. Of course, as I have no interest in slaves, you'll retain your free will. It's absolutely no fun for either one of us if you're a docile beauty with no fire in your eyes or steel in your spine. You'd be far less interesting if you are reduced to a puppet. No, I appreciate a challenge, and I will enjoy earning your cooperation. You could just agree to a year in exchange for your life and the knowledge of why I believe they may fear you. It's a good deal for you. Waking that vampire does have its benefits, however."

"You realize after that blood sucker kills me, he'll go after you, right?"

"I'm sure he'll try. Frenzied vampires are hardly sane. They've never been sane. I'd like to know what's so special about him that they preserved him rather than give him his final death. If you truly welcome your death, the vampire will calm before he kills you. I win. If you're just another human claiming you'd prefer death over servitude, he'll try to drain you dry. I will prevent him from doing that because it will make him more dangerous."

I frowned, as for my plan to work, the vampire needed to actually kill me. "That's not fair. If the vampire kills me, and he will, you should leave me to my death, as is proper. No turning me, either—or having him turn me. If things are as you say, which sounds like utter nonsense to me, and he does release me before I die, without interference from you, you win."

"No. There is no victory for you in that wager. Either I win, or you die."

Was the man daft? I stared at him. "And?"

Eoghan's eyes narrowed, and his expression turned thoughtful. "Very well. Should you live, while you will promise to work in my benefit and favor while retaining your free will, you can ask any boon of me you wish, with a few exceptions. I will not free you from my service, nor will I kill you. I will always be honest should I be unable to grant your boon, and I will tell you why I cannot. You may verify that through any means you wish, magical or mundane. Then, in either case, you have a victory of sorts. But I will not waste your death while also putting others at risk. Frenzied vampires must be approached with care, and I want him alive, which means you cannot die. Should he take you to the brink of death, I will consider it your victory. Name what you desire should it be your victory."

No matter how I looked at it, I faced death. I'd thought about putting an end to everything before, and while I'd contemplated escaping a world that cared nothing for me, I had always clung to tenacious life. Before, death had seemed empty and meaningless.

No one, not even an arrogant asshole like Eoghan Olin, deserved imprisonment in a freezer. Perhaps there was a good reason to fear vampires, but the one locked away in the funeral home's basement deserved either life or death, not the limbo hanging between the two.

Death didn't seem so empty or meaningless when another life shone at the end of the tunnel.

I regarded the egotistical man, tilting my head to the side. "It seems obvious to me. You get to serve me for a while. I'll take a year, since that was your initial offer, and I prefer the whole free will thing, too. But mostly, I'll have you do things like wash my dishes because they're a pain in the ass. Will that suffice?"

Eoghan smiled. "I accept your terms."

"I hope that vampire isn't too dangerous for you to handle, Mr. Arrogant Asshole."

"Call me Eoghan, please. I'll even accept a sir or you can address me as Olin if you snarl it in your most disapproving tone." Eoghan stared in the direction of the refrigerator room. "As for the vampire, he's old enough to survive dismemberment, but he's young enough he can't raise himself without aid. He's no older than eighty years, I suppose. Perhaps one of the first vampires of this emergence? The first ones are always more durable than the rest, and they could survive through such abuse the first night of their un-life. Is he dangerous? Yes. All vampires are dangerous, even the newborns. Will releasing him do irreparable damage to me? He would have to be much older to be a concern to me. Will he be a threat to others? There have always been far more dangerous beings in this world, and humans are one of them. Humans have always been dangerous, reckless beings."

"Good. After he's finished draining me dry, I hope he kills those backstabbing assholes upstairs."

"You're not dead yet, Miss Nash. If you mean to do this, take some care. Don't present your wrist or throat. Offer the fleshier part of your arm below your elbow. That is easier to heal later, and it will give him a chance to find his feet after he consumes some of your blood. I am a man of my word, and I do swear I will observe you while you awaken the vampire. I will not interrupt his feeding, nor will I permit him to turn you.

But I trust your word is good, too. Should you live, you will give me your loyalty, and I will give you the single, conditional boon we discussed, where I will grant you anything I can outside of your death and freedom."

"Yes. I accept those terms."

"Then our bargain is made. What are you truly made of, Miss Nash? I suppose we shall find out soon enough, won't we?"

EOGHAN BROUGHT the vampire out of the freezer, and with an intent expression, he bandaged and stitched the man's body back together. "I will not permit ignorance to influence our wager, and I will hold you to none of it should you change your mind after what I tell you. When he feeds, it will be the worst pain you'll have ever experienced in your life. He will take you to death's door, and he will hold you there. You'll scream—or you'll try to. You won't have the strength to for long. After three or four deep drinks, your body will react and do its best to conserve your life. Screaming wastes precious oxygen. Your body will understand your death comes swiftly and without mercy."

"How is that worse than starving to death, suffocating on chemical fumes, or however else someone can die down here? That's what I get to look forward to." I pointed at the drum containing the body. "That's probably going to kill me before anything else."

"If only killing me were so simple. It's not. If you're truly unafraid of death, wake him. Later, don't complain that you suffered through the pains of hell being foolish."

Well, I couldn't argue with him. Only a fool would deliberately bring a vampire back to life. I walked across the room and retrieved a scalpel from the instrument drawer, perched on the edge of the examination table, and nicked my arm halfway between my wrist and elbow. Several drops of blood welled up and streamed over my skin. I pressed the wound to the vampire's mouth and waited.

It took a few moments, but the vampire's throat contracted when he swallowed, and steam rose from his chilled body.

"It begins," Eoghan warned. "Prepare yourself."

"I think I'm a little beyond that stage, Captain Obvious. I was prep—"

The vampire's fangs tore into my arm, and steel-strong hands snatched my wrist and elbow to hold me in place. According to movies and rumor, vampires bit and sucked. The reality was a far more agonizing thing, and a great deal more brutal.

He chewed on me, tearing at my skin to release more of my blood so it was easier for him to swallow. Some thought of pain as an ever-strengthening inferno, but lightning jolted through me, zapping to my shoulder, striking with the fury of a tempest.

My chest tightened, and my heart stuttered.

The truth of Eoghan's words stabbed to my bones. I opened my mouth, but my voice betrayed me. A gasp slipped between my lips, but my scream failed to make it beyond my throat. The first time my heart skipped several beats, I recognized the truth. If I let him, the vampire truly would bleed me dry. His teeth tore at my arm again, deeper.

A line separated the living from the dead, and I straddled it. The pain convinced me I still lived, but a cool quiet lurked just beyond my reach. If I stretched for it, I could claim it and make it my own. No longer would I drift, a victim of greed and as listless as any ghost. I knew all about ghosts, although I'd forgotten about them.

They had kept me company as a child, watching over me when I had had no one else. When I refused to believe in ghosts out of fear of my parents' wrath, they'd kept their distance, although I'd remained aware of them still. That had been a boundary, too, one that allowed me to please my parents and indulged their dislike of magic, true to their vanilla roots.

Maybe if they had snorted some pixie dust, I wouldn't have thought restoring a vampire to life by letting him chew my arm off was a good idea. No, I still would have cut my arm and woken him.

Some said there was always hope, but I couldn't see it. I could barely afford a place to sleep, I couldn't always afford food to eat, and I got the occasional pack of smokes, but in everything that actually mattered, I had nothing but dead ends.

I had a dead-end job, a dead-end education, and dead-end friendships, which all led to the same place, a dead-end life. Why couldn't I choose when I hit the dead end?

This way, I made my life and my death worth something, although I hoped the vampire would hurry up and finish his work. The rending agony in my arm dulled, but a sharper throb in my chest promised my heart would give out soon enough.

Closing my eyes, I waited. I drifted over the line between life and death, straining for the cool and calm place beyond my reach. My traitorous heart refused to stop beating.

I supposed Eoghan had been right. Either the vampire had lost interest in bleeding me dry or there was something to his claim. How could I be robbed of even death?

Life was truly a cruel, unfair mistress.

The agony ebbed to a tolerable dull throb, which matched my faltering heartbeat. Sounds filtered in one by one, but a scream captured my attention. Eoghan snarled at the noise he loathed, and the ruckus ended with a gurgle. A body thumped to the floor. Something dripped, and the harsh stench of the embalming fluids burned my nose. My lungs stung, and my chest tightened further.

Some fool had likely killed us all knocking over the formaldehyde.

Another scream broke the quiet, and Eoghan snarled a curse. "Why must they always scream? Maybe if you hadn't attempted to sacrifice an unwilling to me, maybe I wouldn't have bothered waking your vampire. You deserve your fate. Had you brought me a willing sacrifice, things would be different right now. No matter. Willing or not, she belongs to me now. It's a pity you won't learn from this mistake."

Eoghan needed to stop talking to corpses. It never accomplished anything, although I had taken up talking to the less lively residents a time or two out of boredom. After hundreds of years on ice, I couldn't really blame him for talking to anyone—or anything—that might listen to him.

Warm arms lifted me, and cold, clawed hands wrapped around my limp wrist.

"This place is tainted," a voice rasped.

"That it is. Should we find that director, rip his throat out. Drain him if you like, although he might turn your stomach," Eoghan ordered.

I took that to mean the vampire lived. Huh. I'd actually lost, although winning wasn't much different from losing, and losing had benefits if I tilted my head to the side and

squinted. I couldn't open my eyes or otherwise move, much to my disgust.

The cold hands released me, and the
world once again fell silent.

A siren, shrill and headache-inducing,
dragged me from the peace I'd found in rest,
tearing me away from the line until it became
a wall I couldn't climb. I cracked open an eye,
and Eoghan leaned over me, his lips curving
into a smile. "I won."

What an asshole. "Your loss. There are far
better prizes to be had," I whispered, unable
to find the strength for anything more than
that.

"Gordon tells me this age has a place
called a hospital, where the sick and injured
are treated. We're taking you to one. As night
has fallen, he will accompany us. The
militia—"

"Police," I corrected.

"Police," he spat in reply, and he scowled
at me. Good. He needed someone to put him
in his place. "I told them the director of this
place had meddled with magic he didn't understand, meaning to kill you to perform his
working. I find it odd this means your care is
his responsibility. You are mine now."

When everything stopped hurting, I
would have to have a long talk with the
psycho antique. "Money. He has to pay
money."

"It's a fiscal responsibility?"

"Yes." I sighed. "Why aren't I dead yet?"

"It is exactly as I told you, Miss Nash. You're not dead because you, without a seed of doubt, chose his life over yours. To a vampire, there is no better nourishment. You live, for that is one of the paradoxes of magic. Try not to think on it too much. I'm far older and have seen many ages, and not even I understand the full truth of why magic works as it does. Have no doubt, however. You do belong to me. That was our deal. Of course, I would have won regardless. A single cut of my arm would have brought your vampire to me, for mine is the sweetest of vintages for his kind. That would have secured your life."

Damn. That was one hell of a card he'd kept tucked up his sleeve. "You bastard."

"You'll find out soon enough just how right you are, for I have already found an enemy for this age, and I look forward to destroying him."

THREE

I was surrounded by assholes.

EOGHAN AND THE newly reassembled vampire sat beside my bed while a pair of nurses drooled over them. I figured their primary target was Eoghan; the vampire was a little worse for wear and wore a rather disconcerting amount of blood. I assumed some of it was mine, and I didn't want to know who the rest had come from. I had a few candidates among the funeral home staff who deserved such a fate, and Director Hammel took the top spot.

I was surrounded by assholes. Everywhere I turned, an asshole surely waited for me. As far as the assholes in my life went, Eoghan made up for his failings in the looks department. I could work with the latest jerk in my life being an attractive jerk, although I'd have to do my best to establish some boundaries while restraining my urge to drool all over him like the nurses.

The two women took turns revealing the

wonders of their cell phones to the men, who regarded the devices with open suspicion. The vampire took the bait first, accepting the offered device. I watched with amusement as they demonstrated what a phone was and how it placed calls.

The cell rang, playing the opening theme of a television show.

Eoghan jumped in his seat while the vampire bolted across the room, dropping the phone. The nurse caught it before it could crack into the floor, and both of them giggled.

My laugh emerged as a rasp, and I wished I had money so I could give both nurses a tip for the entertainment. "You're scared of a phone."

Eoghan relaxed, and his smile made both nurses blush. A better woman would've warned them they flirted with an arrogant ass, but I needed to stay on my guard. A smile like his meant trouble.

I had enough trouble already.

Well, maybe I could use a little trouble to keep things interesting, but only a little. My life needed some nice spice, and I'd already landed myself into a huge mess. I'd need to find a lot of silver linings to get through the next year of my life.

Surrounding myself with good-looking men counted as a silver lining, right? I bet even the vampire would turn heads once he got cleaned up.

Blood was not a good look on anyone. Especially me. I did a quick check to confirm I no longer wore my own blood. I didn't.

If I had money, I would have tipped the hospital staff for that. The last thing I needed was to wear my own blood. It needed to stay in my veins where it belonged for a while. "How much blood did I lose, anyway?"

"Too much," Eoghan replied.

I rolled my eyes at that. "How much is too much?"

"Enough you required something the nurses called a transfusion. Our blood is the same type," Eoghan announced. "This pleases me."

His proclamation startled me into staring at him, my mouth hanging open. "You donated your blood?" I blurted, unable to comprehend why any arrogant asshole like him would do something like donate his blood to a stranger.

After rolling up his sleeve, he showed off a bandaid. "I offered, so they used this fascinating beeping box to perform a test. The doctor deemed my blood is safe for your use, so they took mine and gave it to you. According to him, we're rare vintages."

O-negative made us great donors, but when it came to receiving blood, we drew the short lot. When it came to transfusions, our blood type had the highest risk of accidental death. "Don't let it go to your head."

Offering a thank you would have been

more appropriate, but I figured Eoghan wouldn't know what to do even if I did manage to choke out the words.

The nurses remembered they had jobs to do, ordered the men out of the room, and went to work checking my health, questioning me to test my memory, and grilling me about Eoghan and Gordon, the vampire. Since I wasn't about to relegate myself to being Eoghan's property or call myself a sacrifice, I dubbed him as a colleague. A colleague sounded harmless enough, and it established we had some form of relationship.

The real trouble began when a pair of cops and a woman dressed in a blazer and a pencil skirt showed up with Eoghan and Gordon in tow. She belonged in the funeral home, ready to attend a service in her black and white attire.

"CDC," the woman barked, showing me her badge. According to the identification card, Cecily Barrows could eat me for lunch on the magical front without chipping one of her perfect nails. "What's your rating?"

Great. Why did everyone care about my damned rating? If I wanted people to know I didn't have a rating, I'd wear a damned sign. "I don't have one."

"I find that unlikely."

Ugh. Someone from the CDC must have used a scanner on me while I was unconscious, which meant they had a positive ping for magic. Like every other CDC agent to cross my path, I bet Cecily would fight with me for an hour about my lack of a magic rating. "I ping positive on magic scanners, but I have no known magic. I test out at ninety-percent human, and the DNA tests come back with errors on the rest. It's as annoying for me as it is for you. And yes, I've done every test for unknown magic they'd allow a teen in high school to do, and I registered negative on all of them."

The woman's haughty expression softened. "I expect I am not nearly as annoyed as you are over this. There's quite the mess at the funeral home. What can you tell me about that, Miss Nash?"

I could handle answering questions about my job a lot better than I could trying to explain away my shortcomings. "The director had a vampire and a John Doe on ice, and John Doe decided to get up." I pointed at Eoghan, who arched one of his perfect brows. "He's our John Doe, and I'm pretty sure he grew up in a time when men wore dresses."

"Loin cloths and robes, actually." He reclaimed his seat by my bed. "I find this garb oddly confining yet comfortable despite its flaws."

"And him?" Cecily gestured to Gordon.

"I think he's a vampire from the start of this emergence. I donated blood."

"We noticed. Your arm will require at least

three weeks to fully heal. Primarily, I need you to confirm you willingly donated."

"Despite the circumstances, I did willingly donate, and I would do so again in a similar position."

"Then no laws were broken," she announced.

I found that difficult to believe. "By me, you mean? And by him? Gordon wasn't in a position to contribute to my decision, as he was on ice at the time I decided to donate." At worst, I'd get a slap on the wrist for donating to a vampire without the proper health checks and permits. "I don't have a permit to donate to vampires."

Maybe I needed to get one; a single donation a month would put me in a better position, and while it had hurt like hell, I remembered my teachers telling us that the CDC had ways of making direct-vein donations somewhat tolerable to donors.

"That's correct, Miss Nash. In practical terms, you only need a permit to accept money for a donation to a vampire in need. In a situation where a vampire may become dangerous, it is classified as an act of defense of another, which is not a crime. You came to the assistance of someone in need despite the physical harm you took. At absolute most, the vampire would be liable for your medical care, but the authorities have already notified me that another is responsible for all costs of your care."

"Oh, that's good. I can't afford to pay any fines. I'm broke."

"All of your expenses are being covered," Cecily promised.

Careful to avoid moving my injured arm, I pointed at Eoghan and Gordon. "I don't know what to do with these two, but I think I'm responsible for them now."

"The CDC is looking into the matter, but Mr. Olin is the owner of a rather substantial fund. His caretaker's murder will—"

"Miss Nash will take over the majority of his responsibilities, if you please." According to Eoghan's tone, he didn't give a rat's ass if she pleased or not.

"Miss Nash is cleared to stay in the hospital for a week, after which she will be evaluated to ensure the trauma of the vampire's bite didn't awaken any new abilities. According to the scanner, this is probable."

"No." Eoghan scowled, and he flexed his hands. "You will not perform any experiments on her. I forbid it."

Well, I had to give him credit. I liked when someone other than me jumped to my general defense. Still, I rolled my eyes at his attitude. "Evaluations aren't experimentations. They'll poke me with a few scanners and try to teach me how to do some common magic tricks. It's no big deal. They've been doing this to me for years. It'll take a few hours at most for them to figure out I don't have any abilities, and if I do, we'll all be surprised."

Cecily chuckled, and she matched Eoghan's skeptical expression with one of her own. "Miss Nash will come to no harm. Miss Nash, if you could convince him the CDC is not the evil organization he believes, it would be most appreciated."

"Eoghan, behave."

Rather than the irritation I expected, the man chuckled. "Should they damage even a single hair on your head, I will dismantle them."

For fuck's sake. "Eoghan, please behave."

"I won't allow them to harm you."

"You have control issues and no under-standing of how large the CDC is. It's a global entity. You would not win. As such, you should behave."

"You're mine, and it's my privilege to pro-tect you."

Ugh. In high school, I'd heard the other girls talk about how they wanted a protective man who'd keep the nasties away. Even then, I'd thought of the idea rather odd. Why have someone protect me when I could protect myself? Then again, maybe they'd had the right idea.

Having someone around to take over some of the burdens of life seemed pretty nice when viewed from a hospital bed. Fortu-nately, I could knock the man down a few pegs with little effort on my part. "Yet you had no problem with me feeding my arm to Gordon."

"Thank you for that, by the way," the vampire said.

"You're welcome. Try not to need that sort of feeding again. That hurt like hell."

"I owe you a debt."

"See, Eoghan? Look how easy that was. He thanked me, I accepted, I offered a bit of cordial advice with my complaint, and he acknowledged a debt, although I don't believe one is owed. I did it with zero expectation of repayment. Be more like Gordon."

"To win our wager, it was a necessary evil, one I plan on repaying properly. Gordon will meet his final death should he bite you again."

"Eoghan, we do not threaten the nice vampire. Look at him. He's being a perfect gentleman. We don't threaten friendly gentlemen. That's rude. What are you? A child? Behave yourself. Anyway, Gordon won't bite me again. Right, Gordon?"

"I have been told there are donors who are willing to provide blood," the vampire replied. "I didn't ask to be as I am. I just died at the wrong time."

"The right time," Eoghan corrected with a haughty sniff. "Magic doesn't make mistakes, and you are as you are for a reason. You were chosen by the magic, and it would be a pity for you to be wasted."

Within a week, I'd go mad. "Would you please behave?"

"I am behaving. I haven't lifted a hand against anyone, not even that physician who made you whimper while repairing your arm."

Cecily sighed. "Due to blood loss, there were concerns of how you would react to painkillers. You were eased into the lightest viable dose, but there was a single stitch done that caused you pain. Your companion did not react well to this, but he did tolerably behave himself. He takes his role as your protector quite seriously. Anyway, don't worry. The CDC has programs in place to help vampires feed. There are volunteers who enjoy the tax benefits and payments of donating, and some criminals are given an option to help feed vampires in exchange for a reduced sentence."

I shuddered at the memory of Gordon's teeth tearing into my arm. "It's legalized cruel and unusual punishment, and that's kind of terrible."

Cecily's smile had a sharp edge to it. "The convicts are told precisely what to expect. Those who opt into the program might not see the light of day again otherwise. It also allows the vampires to lay certain beguilements onto those volunteers to ensure they do not repeat the same crimes that landed them into prison in the first place. It is beneficial to the vampires, it is beneficial to society, and it's ultimately beneficial to the convict, although some emerge from prison changed people."

I bet. Gordon's bite had inevitably

changed me—and gave me a healthy respect for vampires in general.

Eoghan took his time considering the woman, and after a few minutes, he crossed his arms, which revealed the harder edge of tense muscles beneath his clothes. "My thoughts on this matter haven't changed. Don't damage even a hair on her head. Even giants can fall."

"Noted," the CDC agent replied.

It worried me that the woman hesitated to correct the man about his delusions regarding his ability to take out the CDC. "You can't destroy the CDC, Eoghan."

"Why the bloody hell not?"

"It's a global organization."

"Even giants can fall. I already said that. Anyway, I appreciate a challenge. Should they wish to test their luck, I will be challenged, and I will enjoy it."

"Are you insane?" I blurted.

"No, I'm not insane. I'm merely determined to do my duty and protect you as is proper. That is part of our bargain. If this CDC must fall, so be it."

I sighed and wondered how I could convince such a headstrong, displaced idiot about how modern society worked.

Cecily cleared her throat, catching my attention. "It won't be an issue, Mr. Olin. We will limit our work with her to non-invasive testing."

"Wait. You have invasive testing? Do you use locusts as part of your invasive testing?"

I bit my lip so I wouldn't laugh. "She means poke or prod at me physically, Eoghan. The CDC is not an invasive species. Also, locusts?"

"Those were one of the more invasive pests of my youth. Annoying blighters, locusts. A swarm could destroy crops in matters of hours, leaving us all to starve. Cursing someone with a plague of locusts was, in my age, quite a foul thing to do, for it was a slow and agonizing death from starvation. As long as this testing is not harmful to you, I will tolerate it."

We'd have to work on that. I expected life with Eoghan to create a great deal of trouble for me.

THE GHOSTS WERE BACK.

I would've felt a little better about the situation if they hadn't liked me. They congregated around my room, some lurking in the walls, some bold enough to manifest near my bedside. Time had reduced most to blurs and faint chills in the air.

An old woman occupied Eoghan's chair, wearing the hospital gown she'd died in. "A piece of advice, dear. Don't order the chicken."

Great. Seeing the ghosts was one thing,

but talking to them would earn me a one-way trip to the psych ward. I grunted to acknowledge her while contemplating if I could escape from the hospital. According to Eoghan, who meant serious business about keeping me safer than Fort Knox, Gordon would show up sometime after dark to act as my evening babysitter. It amazed me the CDC managed to keep Eoghan away, although I suspect they made a few implications about potentially impairing my health if he hovered while the doctors worked.

I'd seen that a few times in town. Overprotective men became easily manipulated men when it came to their women. It took subtlety and practice, but the women saddled with overprotective men had ways of taking back control. I regretted my lack of attention to their methods.

I would need every trick in the book within a week.

Making a bargain was one thing, but sticking around in the hospital to become a guinea pig for the CDC was another. I disliked the idea of becoming a gopher for an overprotective relic, but I would keep my word. However, Eoghan hadn't told me I couldn't leave the hospital. Best of all, I had new, clean clothes, and my purse was in easy reach. To aid in my escape efforts, the nurse had removed the IV's catheter already. I got out of bed, grabbed my clothes, and ignored the ghosts watching me change.

Damned ghosts.

"The old one isn't going to be happy if you leave. He asked us to stand watch while he's gone," the old woman announced. "You'll anger him."

My brows shot up at the implication Eoghan could also talk to ghosts. While various forms of undead were generally accepted in society, people had trouble believing in ghosts. Zombies? People could buy into the idea a corpse might get up and cause a fuss before burial. Vampires made their presence known and integrated into society. Mummies liked guarding things, and the devil's heir tended to wake mummies up every time she visited a museum.

It amazed me museums let her in the door at the rate she caused trouble in the exhibits. Then again, the mummies did tend to guard the museums they occupied, making them highly desired.

But ghosts? Nope. For some unfathomable reason, people dug in their heels over the idea of ghosts being real.

Magic tended to explain away the incorporeal undead. The bumps in the night with no known source? They blamed kids discovering practitioner tricks for the first time. The cold chills in the air? Once again, practitioners took the blame.

Practitioners got blamed for a lot of things they didn't do, although people were right to worry about those who mastered magic they hadn't been born with. Sometimes, I thought about studying practitioner magic, despite its reputation.

It beat staying a nobody forever, and practitioners weren't classified as vanilla humans.

The ghost watched me and waited.

As she'd probably haunt me if I didn't answer her, I replied, "If he wanted me to stay here, he would have told me to stay here. As he hadn't told me that, I think I'll go home and enjoy my bed."

"While this is true, it isn't wise." The ghost pointed at my wrapped arm, which hurt whenever I moved, but it would heal in time. I'd head to the doctor's office near home to have it checked, get a prescription for an antibiotic I couldn't afford to fill, and pretend like I had my shit together while I searched for a new job—or checked to see if Eoghan could actually afford minimum wage for whatever he needed me for.

I could work with minimum wage. I'd just have to eat salty noodles for the rest of my life.

"Why not? Experiencing new things is good. I've never escaped from a hospital before. What's not wise about this?"

"You have no money in that purse of yours, nor do you have your keys. He swiped them after conferring with the vampire. Deterrents to keep you from leaving, I believe."

I peeked into my purse to discover the antique had robbed me. Unfortunately for the antique, I had a spare key at the house I rented, and who needed an empty wallet anyway? It wasn't like I could buy anything with money I didn't have. The lack of identification would annoy me after a long sleep, but I figured Eoghan would be able to figure out where I lived with some help from Gordon or the CDC. "Mr. Arrogant Asshole needs to be knocked down a few pegs. First, I have a spare key. It is hidden somewhere safe and sound where I can readily retrieve it. Second, I think they're serving chicken tomorrow, so you can tell the arrogant asshole this is an act of self-preservation."

The old woman cackled. "There's nothing wrong with running so a handsome man will chase you. He looks like he'd just love to catch you and have you for dinner."

Great. I'd found a pervy ghost granny. "He's not that handsome."

"It's a good thing we're in a hospital, dearie. You are in dire need of an eye exam. I might be dead, but I'm not blind."

"He's older than you are."

"He's very well preserved, then. I wonder how he pulled that off? He looks about your age. You two are cute together."

Ugh. Not only had I gotten the pervy ghost granny, she had matchmaking tendencies. "Black magic, obviously. And we are not cute together. He's a swan, and I won't call any duck ugly, so I'm going to go with being an earthworm in comparison. I'm probably just a cheap meal before he goes and finds someone better suited for his aesthetics."

"You should allow him to make some adjustments to your self-esteem. He's probably great in bed thanks to all that experience he surely has."

"He's probably diseased."

"Neutralizer can fix that."

I considered her point, nodding my agreement with her assessment. Neutralizer could fix a lot of things, including most sexually transmitted diseases. A few doses of neutralizer and some tender loving care would make Eoghan safe to take to my bed. At the very least, he could decorate my home. "He's still the equivalent of a swan to my earthworm. I'll pass." Obviously, I hated myself, as only an idiot would pass at a chance to take a hot man to bed. Jumping out the window might save me, but then again, the truth would better serve me as a deterrent. "He'd hate me, as the experienced men typically dislike the added complexity of virgins."

There. I could go to my grave fully humiliated. I'd also go to my grave wondering just how experienced Eoghan was. He probably got women to undress just from smiling and inviting them to come home with him.

I needed to hurry up, get over my issues with men, evict myself from the pool of virgins, and get the hell out of Sunset while I was at it.

"Any man who can't take proper care of a

virgin doesn't deserve a good woman in the first place. He's a doter. The doters are the best unless you like it rough, then you need to teach them to handle you like they mean it. He looks versatile."

Heaven help me, I'd found the world's most perviest granny. "You want him?"

"Oh, no. No, no. These old bones of mine would intimidate that stallion. I'll save him for you. After all, I wouldn't want to ruin him for all other women."

Holy hell. The granny must have had one active sex life before she'd kicked the bucket. "That's disturbing." And irritating. I lived in a one-horse town, it'd take me at least four hours to walk home, and I'd spend the entire damned hike thinking about some deceased granny rejecting a ride with Eoghan because she worried she'd tire him out.

Damn it. I wanted my job back along with the illusion of stability. In reality, without my next paycheck, I'd be getting the wrong kind of slow screw. Without money, I wouldn't be paying my rent.

If I couldn't pay the rent, I foresaw myself falling prey to the antique's scheming or trying my luck as a homeless woman living on the streets. I couldn't guess what Eoghan wanted with me, so I assumed I'd be facing life as a homeless woman in search of viable work. While death would have simplified matters, I needed to play with the cards I'd been dealt. Regretting my decision to wager with Eoghan changed nothing.

No matter how I viewed it, screwed only scratched the surface of my issues. I sighed and considered my choices, which were few and far between.

"You could go hunt your pretty man and have him tuck you in," the pervy granny suggested. "He's probably at the hotel across the street, and I'd bet he'd like it if you crawled into bed with him. While naked. He looked hungry."

The truth always worked best when faced with a pervy ghost granny on a matchmaking mission. "The last thing I need right now is a man."

"Well, you're stuck with that one, honey. He means business."

That I could believe. "What's the easiest way out of this joint?"

"At this time of night? Good luck. You can wander the floor, but they monitor the stairwells and elevators at night. You can get out if you say you're in need of a smoke, though. They've got a section for the cranky who aren't authorized to have pixie dust. They'd have much higher satisfaction rates if they just gave all the inmates pixie dust."

She considered the patients to be inmates? Then again, the hospital had a rather confining atmosphere, and as a ghost, she'd be sticking around for a lot longer than she likely wanted. "Well, that sucks."

"They'll let you out more in the morning."

"That sucks a little less, but it still sucks."

"It would be easiest on you if you waited patiently until morning."

Well, I had asked for what was easiest, and staying put was the path of least resistance—it just prevented my escape. Then again, escaping would send Eoghan an important message:

I would not be an easy conquest.

FOUR

> They need to leave so I can
> thoroughly scold you.

A PLAINTIVE WHINE that I needed a smoke got me outside. The hospital boasted a well-traveled path to where those lighting up bitched and moaned about the cruelty of being forced to have their cigarettes outside while the pixie dust junkies got their hits inside.

A hit of pixie dust would make everything better, but I hadn't qualified for it. I expected the money had something to do with it. The hospital-grade dust cost a lot more than the standard crap served in licensed coffee shops, and I couldn't afford the standard crap.

They likely figured they were sparing me from the sticker shock when the bill came in. Truth be told, I would appreciate that later. Director Hammel would ultimately be responsible for paying the bill, assuming he was found so he could be charged for his crimes. But until then, the bill belonged to me.

Hooray.

"If they would offer us hits of dust, we wouldn't be freezing our asses off out here," an older man complained between puffs, dragging his IV stand along with him while he paced. As the youngest, and the only one without an IV stand, I drew a lot of unwanted attention. "What are you in for, sweetheart?"

If he called me sweetheart again, I'd be in for a charge of assault when I took his IV stand and shoved it up his ass. I showed off the bandage covering my stitches instead. "A vampire got a hold of me."

Everyone stared, and despite having already bummed a cigarette, several offered me another. I accepted one, and I found myself the happy owner of an entire pack and a lighter to go with it. "Thanks."

"After that sort of attack, they should have you on a drip of dust," my elderly benefactor announced. "I've been bitten before. It is not a good time."

"Well, I wouldn't say no to some dust right now, but these will help in the meantime." I saluted him with my new pack. "What's stopping any of you from just walking off, anyway?"

"Nothing," everyone chorused.

Hmm. I'd have to tell Eoghan that the granny with a perverted side had done her best to convince me to stay, sometime after I went home and sulked over my new circumstances. After having my arm chewed up, I deserved to indulge in a sulk. "Do you know what happens when someone does decide to wander off?"

They nodded, and the eldest of the lot, who already had one foot in the grave and insisted on flipping the devil off before kicking the bucket, replied, "You get the bill for the care you were given. They don't care unless you show up back here in worse shape, then they'll fine you five hundred for being stupid. It's called the second admittance fee, but really, it's a fine for being an idiot."

I bet the old geezer had a reputation of running away and had amassed a huge debt in second admittance fees. "Nice. What's the best way out of here?"

They pointed down the trail, which meandered through the dark woods.

"That's not scary at all," I muttered. "Where does that go?"

"It'll take you right to the bus stop."

The bus stop wouldn't do me any good, not without any cash or a pass, but it would take me to the road, which would eventually lead me home. I wouldn't like the walk. The walk might finish me off. In good news, I'd stashed some pudding in my otherwise empty pantry, and unless some bastard had taken my keys and stolen the fresh milk from the fridge, I had enough to make it and have milk to drink with it. Some chocolate would help. Chocolate always helped.

"Thanks for the help and the smokes. Have yourselves a good night."

As promised, the trail led to the bus stop and the road, and I headed for the question-able comfort of home.

NO AMOUNT of chocolate pudding could sal-vage a morning involving my dead-beat par-ents. Had I not expected Eoghan to show up, I wouldn't have answered the door at all, es-pecially not while dressed in my pajamas and eating right out of the mixing bowl.

Damn it, damn it, damn it. Why couldn't I have been blessed with some form of fire magic? I would've torched the bastards and been done with them if only I had the right spark of magic. "What now?" I demanded, de-bating slamming the door in their faces.

"We need money," my mother announced, and her tone implied she expected me to give it to her without a fuss.

Had they lost their minds? Me? Give *them* money? "What makes you think I have any money to give you?"

Then, because my life needed some extra spice to go with the bitter brew of parental visitation, a limo pulled up the street, and a rather annoyed Eoghan emerged wearing a modern black suit. The only way he'd look better would be naked in my bed immediately if not sooner.

Damn it all. Modern times worked won-ders on the man, and I was the one thirsty and hungry for a chance with him. The pervy granny had it all wrong. Who cared if he was hungry? With him in that suit, I'd have to work hard to keep my hands off him.

Fortunately for me, nobody had said I couldn't look.

To add to my problems, Gordon stepped out of the limo, hissed at the sunlight, and headed my way.

I could keep Eoghan outside to yank on his chain, but I wouldn't risk the vampire. I got out of his way and gestured for him to enter my home. "The curtains are drawn in the living room, and there's a basement if that's not dark enough for you. The basement's bare, though, but I can bring something down for you if you need."

"Thank you, Lady Anwen. The living room should be fine." The vampire dipped into a bow before strolling inside, and he relaxed the moment he stepped out of the sunlight.

My parents sputtered.

"As I was saying, I don't know what makes you think I have money, but there's no way in fucking hell I'm paying for your drugs or hookers. I have enough trouble paying my rent."

Eoghan's huff fringed on snort territory, and if looks could kill, my entire family would've fallen over dead, myself included. As I wasn't going to let some pre-emergence antique frighten me, I looked him in the eyes and ate more of my pudding before asking, "And what's your problem?"

He reached out and rubbed his thumb against the corner of my mouth, stared me in the eyes, and licked my chocolate off his skin.

How unfair.

"You ran away," he replied after his rather indecent and suggestive pause.

Okay. I had no idea what I was supposed to do beyond invite him to go to my room and get naked, but I couldn't let him just come to my house and steal my damned chocolate off my mouth. "You need to go away until I deal with my parents."

That might buy me enough time to cool off and convince my hormones to take a hike and a chill pill.

"I think not. They need to leave so I can thoroughly scold you."

My peace of mind went on vacation and took my common sense with it, as I enjoyed the thought of him scolding me while dressed to my liking. "I ran off because I don't need even more medical bills."

"Detox?" my mother asked.

"Fuck you and go away. Eoghan, in. The assholes, leave. I'm not giving you a cent. You took my damned college funds to pay for your shit habits. I have chocolate pudding, and you're out of your fucking mind if you think I am going to share any with you."

Eoghan opened his mouth, and I shoved a

spoonful of pudding onto his tongue to keep him quiet. "In, Eoghan."

The bastard took my spoon with him. Whatever. I had fingers, and I wasn't afraid to use them. I didn't need to impress anyone, especially my parents. They could kiss my ass.

"We need money," my mother said.

"And I need a high school diploma, a college degree, and a new job. Get in line. Just because you two decided to have sex with each other doesn't mean you get to leech off me. Go find some other idiot to leech from." I stepped into my house and slammed the door before locking it. They cursed at me, and I flipped my middle finger at the peep hole.

"How interesting," Eoghan said.

"Don't start." I turned to him, snatched my spoon, and marched for my barren kitchen. "If I ignore them, they'll eventually go away."

They might knock their knuckles bloody on my door first, but they'd eventually go away. It might take calling the cops, but they'd *eventually* go away.

"I'm paying your medical bills. I've already made arrangements. That insolent fool will pay restitutions, and the excess belongs to you. I have been told I will be compensated for all fees I've paid to restore your health." Eoghan sat at my table like he owned the place, which wasn't far from the truth. "This house. Do you like it?"

I loved it, I hated it'd never be mine, and I meant to enjoy my last few weeks in it. "I do.

I can only afford the rent because the couple who used to live here moved, and they figured I could pay their mortgage, which I can. Barely. This is too small of a town for there to be real apartments."

"Then I will handle the payments as part of your compensation for being my aide. I am told that's the term I should use for you. Or personal assistant. They claim secretary would also be appropriate. Sacrifice, apparently, is an inappropriate term, as I am not murdering you or giving you to some jealous divine. I find their dislike of the term amusing."

I giggled at the thought of Cecily or another CDC representative calling Eoghan out on his term of choice. It also made me feel a little better about the situation, too.

Aide or personal assistant sounded a lot better than sacrifice to me. Those roles also paid a lot better, too. "I see you have the CDC dancing to your tune. How did you pull that off?"

"Gordon offered knowledge of the start of this emergence, and I, too, am offering historic knowledge of past emergences I was awake for. I have not been awake for all of them, but I have been awake during the strongest of them, which is what they want to study. A lot of those who were awake during those emergences do not like discussing them. Those were dark times."

Great. The CDC would cater to their

every wish to get as much information out of them as possible. No matter what I did, I was screwed. As long as Eoghan wanted my company, the CDC would cooperate with him. Worse, I couldn't just kick them out. They'd been displaced enough.

We lived in a much different world than when even Gordon had been put on ice.

Eoghan watched me and waited.

"I've won staring contests against corpses, so don't you think that's going to work on me." Granted, the corpses I'd won staring contests against had gotten up out of their caskets, which made it easier to win compared against the regular bodies in residence at the morgue.

"Why would you do such a thing?"

"They didn't want to get back into their caskets where they belonged. Every few weeks, one of the stiffs would decide to get up and take a walk. For a funeral home, it was a pretty lively place. Damn it all, I really needed that damned job."

"You have a better job now."

I rolled my eyes at that. "Until I get my first pay and check out my benefits, I'm sticking to my story about needing that damned job. I just can't get rid of the dead guys though, can I? Why can't a live guy be interested in me for a change?"

"I'm quite alive, I assure you."

"You've been on ice for probably a thousand years. I don't think you count as a live guy."

"Immortality has its perks. However, I am definitely alive."

"Mortality has its perks, too. Escaping through death is one of them."

"No, it's not. Frankly spoken, I forbid it."

I laughed at Eoghan and his ego. "You're something else. You can't stop death. There are limited immortals who can avoid it. Hey, Gordon? How are you holding up in there?"

"I'm quite fine, thank you. This is a pleasant home, although the unpleasant company at your door is tempting. I could have a morning snack and stop them from bothering your neighbors."

I bet my parents did tempt the vampire. "I won't tell if you don't."

"They'd taste terrible, and I don't know if I'd be able to purify myself of their taint afterwards."

Wow. I didn't like my parents, but the viciousness of Gordon's rejection startled me.

Eoghan chuckled. "We'll try not to offend your sense of taste too much. However much they deserve it, we should be courteous guests, which means we can't rid the world of Anwen's parents. Now, should they bring harm to her, you should consider putting their blood to better use before I deal with their bodies."

Men. Then again, as far as most men in my life went, Eoghan and Gordon were somewhat tolerable. I gave it a few days before the town's single women sniffed out potential marriage material and wealth. Every time a new man came around, the story stayed the same.

She with the best looks and manners won herself a husband and a ticket out of town, leaving everyone else to gossip about her once she was gone. I avoided the men and the gossips, which gave me an even worse reputation.

I finished off my pudding, sighed, and dumped the mixing bowl into the sink. "Unfortunately, killing them is illegal."

"Only if we do not adhere to specific guidelines," Eoghan replied with a smug smile. "The CDC courteously explained the rules of legalized murder, the allowed methods, and how a vampire might hunt the night for guilty souls who need to be killed for the safety of others. This era has many guilty souls ripe for the plundering. I must admit I do like how death is typically a private matter now. I do not enjoy public spectacles and drawn-out executions. I've witnessed many torturous deaths in my life. Humans can be the cruelest of creatures."

That I could readily believe. "We're still cruel. We're just cruel in different ways now. That said, I think I can live without witnessing a crucifixion. Half a year ago, we had a car accident victim in. We had to stitch him back together because of his family's religious beliefs. We tried to warn them against an open-casket viewing, but they demanded proof. That was not a good day. There was screaming."

"The screaming is so annoying. Most scream when they die young. The old understand the rules of life and time, although the ones who go out in great pain will scream. That's fair enough." Eoghan wrinkled his nose, and he scowled. "I would not mind the screams of the ones haunting your doorstep."

I listened. Sure enough, my parents yelled at my door, and their various vices added a hoarse edge to their cursing. "If we ignore them long enough, they'll go away. They're not stupid enough to break my door or windows. I'll call the cops on them, and they hate spending their hooker or drug money on repairs. They probably have some money but want to spend mine first."

Shrugging, I cleaned the bowl and spoon before putting them away. "It is what it is. You seem to have a decent grasp of modern times so far. What do you need me for? It looks like I'm out of a job, and I like eating."

"As I said, you'll assist me with whatever I need to adapt to this era. The CDC is dealing with the matter of my murdered caretaker, who was the last of a long, proud lineage. Vengeance will be acquired, and that director will find justice to be painful at best."

"He'll probably scream," I warned the scream-disliking annoyance.

"I can accept his screams. I might even enjoy them."

I gave it a week before Eoghan changed his mind about brutal public executions. "Should I be concerned?"

"Only if you care about his long-term survival. He won't last for more than a few minutes in my hands, despite my inclination to crucify him in a rather gruesome manner."

"Please don't crucify Director Hammel."

"He deserves such a fate." Eoghan sighed. "How else should he die?"

"Don't kill him. Force him into life-long community service instead. He'd hate having to work for the sake of others without being able to charge them an arm and a leg for it. He price-gouged the families of the dead because he could."

"How despicable of him. He would have been compensated well for the storage of my body. I become quite cranky when I have to rebuild my mortal form. It takes months, sometimes years. The dead do not appreciate when I'm grouchy."

"You might say he has a rather grave sense of humor fresh from his dirt nap," Gordon contributed from the other room.

"I do not know why I like you, vampire."

"You like me because I make an excellent guardian of your lady, and I proved her worth."

Eoghan grunted.

"Sorry to interrupt your posturing, but

I'm no lady. I attend to corpses for a living, and I keep records when I'm not making sure the bodies are in their caskets where they belong. For all I know, Old Man McGregor's out and about causing someone problems."

"Ah. The restless dead that was in the upstairs parlor?" Relaxing, Eoghan smiled and leaned back in his seat. "He's quite an interesting gentleman. He didn't scream despite being helped to his grave."

My eyes widened. "Are you saying someone killed that old man?"

"That is precisely what I'm saying."

Well, shit. Murders were few and far between in Sunset, but they did happen—but I couldn't see anyone having a real reason to kill Old Man McGregor despite some of his more annoying tendencies. "Is that why he was restless?"

"Oh, no. He's restless because there's a node here, and it awakens all manner of things, myself included. I can't tell you where it is precisely, but I can sense its power. It's a strong one, too—and as neutral as death itself."

"Death is neutral?"

"Of course. Death welcomes all into its embrace. All are the same when life leaves the body, and all face death one day. Well, mostly."

"Mostly?" Well, mostly made sense considering there were a few immortals who stuck around, including the devil.

"Mostly. There are a few souls who never truly die."

"Do I want to know?" On second thought, I didn't want to know, but it was too late to take back my foolish question.

"Probably not yet."

"Yet? I mean, the devil is supposedly one of the immortals that can't be killed, but I don't know if I want to know about his problems." I recognized a bad omen when I heard one, and yet it implied Eoghan meant to tell me in detail at some point in the future.

"Yet. I'd rather not overwhelm you with old magic right now. The world was a much different place the last time I fully awakened."

"You thrive on being secretive, don't you?"

"It is a joy in life. Human curiosity is so entertaining."

Ah-ha! "Does that mean you're not human?"

"I started life as a human, but magic changed me long ago."

"Bummer. Now you're a freak."

My unwanted albeit sexy houseguest scowled. "Hardly."

"What are you then, if you're not a human or a freak?"

"If you want to know, you'll need to investigate me yourself."

Hmm. Hello, temptation. I could do a lot of personal investigation in my bed. I had no experience, but I wouldn't mind learning how to seduce answers out of him.

Damn it. I couldn't afford to indulge in lustful thoughts involving him. I'd go crazy that way. Crazier, even. Maybe I could send him over to the pervy ghost granny at the hospital.

Oh, right. The pervy ghost granny. "This is going to sound a little weird, but there was a dead granny at the hospital, and she really did try to keep me there, but after hearing about how she'd tire you out in bed, I needed to go home before I got checked into the psych ward."

Eoghan stared at me as though I'd lost my mind. "You saw her? Yes, I did ask her to watch over you."

"She was doing that. I'm just not the best at doing what I'm told. And, also, you couldn't have been serious about me investigating you."

He snickered, and I wasn't sure which part of my statement he found amusing. "I want you to investigate me and learn my secrets."

Why did I always have to deal with the crazy ones? If I played his game, I'd lose, but I'd lose happy and hopefully in my bed since he didn't have one of his own yet. If I pretended to play his game, he might leave me alone. Then again, even if I pretended to play his game, I'd play it anyway, as curiosity would inevitably take hold. Why wasn't he human? If he wasn't a freak, how could he be human but not human? How could he be not quite human yet not a freak?

The world had a lot of freaks, and I liked most of them.

"All right, Eoghan. What do I get should I discover your secret?"

The arrogant asshole smirked at me. "Good behavior is always rewarded."

Given a week, he would drive me completely insane. Worse, I might like the ride. "Are you going to be terribly upset if I go back to bed? I think I've reached my capacity for insanity for one day."

"Absolutely not. You need to rest. Will you be able to sleep with those annoying people grousing at your door?"

"I'm certainly going to try."

"Well, if they disturb you, I'll make them regret their choice to haunt your door."

As I couldn't judge how serious he was, I did my asshole parents a favor and didn't tell Eoghan they already disturbed me. I sought the sanctuary of my bedroom, leaving my house guests to fend for themselves.

Tomorrow, I'd try to play a proper hostess.

FIVE

Satan would offer his residents air
conditioning first.

MY BEDROOM, one of two located on the
small second floor of my house, offered little
protection from my asshole parents. Their
bitching and moaning annoyed my neighbors, who called the cops. Leaving Eoghan
and Gordon to fend for themselves and deal
with the police counted as rude, but I passed
out the instant my parents shut up.

I woke to a gentle touch on my shoulder,
and I burrowed beneath my blanket. "I don't
want to get up."

My arm hurt, and getting up meant I'd
have to deal with my dismal lack of
painkillers in the house, yet another luxury I
couldn't afford. Eoghan could afford it, if I
got over my pride and asked him to get some
for me.

Satan would offer his residents air conditioning first.

"You need dinner. It is ready," Eoghan announced.

Wait. Dinner? Where had dinner come from? What was dinner? How had it arrived? Who had made it? Had Eoghan discovered the wonders of delivery? Had delivery existed in his era? I'd cleaned out my pantry during my pudding bender. Then, as I doubted the antique had seen a stove in his life, I blurted, "You can cook?"

"I required some base education regarding your oven, but it proved to be an adequate replacement for what I am accustomed to. It is a very convenient tool, and I think I may enjoy the offerings of this era. Gordon helped with the shopping after it got dark. More accurately, he did the shopping while I kept an eye on you and made certain those humans didn't return and bother you. I made him a list. Well, not precisely. He made the list for me, as I do not write any languages he can read."

"Yet you speak English."

"I can speak any language I hear thanks to my magic. Your English is not my native tongue. It didn't even exist when I first lived."

Right. Eoghan more than classified as an ancient artifact. How ancient? I wasn't sure I wanted to know. "How convenient."

"At times, learning a new written language will be vexing for both of us, I'm sure. I suspect you don't use the same runes I know. Language tends to evolve over time. The last time I awoke for any lengthy duration, few wrote anything at all."

"Almost everybody can read and write now."

"How bothersome. Another thing I must learn to do, I see."

I translated that to mean I would be teaching him the basics of life in America. "Maybe you'll be a quick study."

Old dogs could learn new tricks, right? I could only hope.

I'd be doing a lot of hoping and wishing in the upcoming days.

"You sound quite skeptical."

"Well, you've got to be pushing at least three thousand years old. Or older. I should sell you to a museum. I'd get a fortune for you." I got out of bed, wincing at the throb in my arm. "I won't sell you to a museum if you use some of that annoying magic of yours to provide painkillers."

"I don't need magic for that. After you left the hospital, the nurses contacted the CDC to notify them you had wandered off, and one of the representatives got the appropriate remedies to make certain you don't have to return to that place you so dislike."

"I don't dislike hospitals. I just don't like paying the bill for medical care. A bill I couldn't afford yesterday," I muttered.

"It is a bill you are not paying because I am paying it. You need to take these remedies with your dinner, and I have been told they will help your arm heal and make it hurt less."

Painkillers made my world go round, and

the thought of having a dose motivated me enough I got out of bed. If he wanted me to change, he'd have to wait until after I took a long soak in my tub. "What's for dinner?"

"Chicken stew. The doctors thought it would be good for you, and I have made many a stew in my lifetime. Gordon showed me the quicker alternatives, and I find them less than appealing, so I will only use them when I do not have the time to properly prepare food for you. Tonight's offering is not as good as what you will enjoy in the future."

Okay. Eoghan redefined what it meant to be handsome when wearing a suit, he had money, and he could cook. The instant word got out he was in town, every single woman would be knocking down my door to get to him. I'd have to get out the baseball bat to hold them at bay. "What's wrong with you?"

He smirked. "Nothing, I assure you. I'm perfect with a few minor exceptions, including my ignorance on how to write modern languages. I will resolve these short-comings soon enough. You'll find I am a dedicated scholar when it comes to rectifying ignorance."

"Well, you have a lot to learn, but if you're good at cooking, you might be worth keeping around." I yawned and headed downstairs to discover the vampire tending to a pot on the stove. "Do vampires need to eat?"

"We don't need to, but we can, although in very limited quantities. A bite or two here and there is something we can digest, but blood provides everything we require." Gordon took a bowl from my cupboard, filled it with stew, and set it on the table along with a spoon. "Eat, then you can explain these wretched bottles we haven't been able to open."

I laughed. Child-safety caps could defeat even modern adults, but I enjoyed the mental image of the two men fighting to open the caps. "Show me the bottles, and I'll teach you how to open them. I'll take the pills while eating, and I'll translate how prescriptions work for you. It's a little complicated."

Gordon went into the living room and returned a moment later with a white paper bag. "There are many pages of instruction inside."

"Warnings, mostly, to prevent them from being sued if a side-effect turns nasty. There'll also be directions on how to take the medications." I dumped the bag out on the table, checked the pages, and set them across the table from me. "As there's no better time than now to start your English lessons, we're going to use that as our starting exercise."

"You are a force of pure evil," Gordon observed. "Could you have picked drier reading material?"

"Maybe if I tried. It would be a challenge." I checked the bottles, pressed down on the cap, and gave it a twist to access the pills, and I fished out the appropriate number of each.

"These are child-safety caps. If you press down and twist, they'll open. They're a pain in the ass, and they're kind of pointless, as children are typically better at opening these damned things than adults are. They *do* keep little babies from getting into the bottles, however."

"That's important." Gordon picked up one of the sheets. "Amoxicillin?"

"That's an antibiotic. It'll help keep my arm from getting infected. I need to take it three times a day until they're all gone."

"And the other one?"

"Painkiller, the light-grade stuff." I went for the third bottle, which would be my best friend for a while. "And this is prescription-level pixie dust. This is the good stuff. After taking one of these, I won't give a shit if my arm hurts. Apparently, they feel Eoghan might flip his lid if I am in any discomfort at all. I now know my first line of offense when I have a condition that requires painkillers. I will make Eoghan deal with the doctors."

"Pixie dust." Eoghan wrinkled his nose. "In my time, that was frowned upon. Now, it is prescribed as a remedy?"

"It's a safe recreational drug. Just don't get the top-grade stuff. That's how you lose your free will. Otherwise, it's harmless. It just makes you happy for a while. The higher grade stuff, like this, makes you happy, oblivious, and generally inclined to do what others want. The next grade up makes you powerless to do anything other than what you're told. I'll have a great time. You? You might not. A side-effect includes a tendency to try to make everyone happy, too."

"I do not see how this is a problem."

"As long as I think you're happy all of the time, it probably won't be. If I think you're upset for any reason, I'm going to try to make you happy, and I will be obnoxious about it. I was on this once growing up, and I was a menace. I'm surprised my asshole parents didn't drown me from trying to make everything better for everybody. I don't remember much about it, which is one of the side effects of this grade of dust for me. My parents wish they could get this stuff, but the government is aware people chase highs so restrict the higher grades. You need a permit to get this grade or a prescription. Most people have theirs with coffee or some other drink."

"Yes, even in my time, the devil's dust did the same. But then, we were not aware it is otherwise harmless."

"It's been studied carefully. It's harmless. It's also used to make neutralizer."

"Neutralizer?"

"It's basically a miracle drug. It can cure a lot of ailments, it stops most viruses, it can reverse things like petrification—it's basically the most useful thing ever made. It uses pixie dust to make it, but it undergoes some process. Apparently, it doesn't take too much pixie dust to make it, and the pixies are paid good money to shed wing glitter to produce it."

"The pixies are willing?"

"Of course. They're paid for their dust. The higher the grade of dust, the better they're paid. It doesn't hurt them at all, and it actually helps them. They can get sick if they don't shed enough of their dust."

"Interesting. The last emergence, they were considered winged devils."

"Nah, Satan doesn't want pixies. They're far too nice and cheerful for his hells, or some such like that. Someone asked him once."

Eoghan's eyes widened. "Someone *asked* Satan?"

"Sure. He lives in Georgia right now. From what I've seen of him, a pretty nice guy for being, well, the devil. He's got a daughter—"

"How can he have a daughter?"

"He adopted her."

Eoghan's mouth dropped open. "That's not right!"

"What's not right about it? I mean, if you look at the legend and lore, he's not really supposed to be a family man, but everything I've seen indicates he dotes on his daughter to the point she wants to kill him. She hasn't had any luck on that front. There's an entire website dedicated to the devil's activities on Earth, and frankly, it's pretty funny most of the time. I sometimes used my work computer to follow his news."

"Are we talking about the same creature? Satan, the Lord of Hell? Lord of Lies? The Fallen?"

"Yep. That's the guy."

"And you think he's a *nice* guy?"

"Sure? I don't know him personally, but he seems to be a much better parent than mine will ever be. His wife seems like an interesting lady, too. Most of the time, she takes the form of a succubus, but there are a few pictures of her wandering around as either a hybrid lycanthrope or a shapeshifter. Nobody is really sure which. Even his angelic brothers like him."

"What is wrong with this era?" Eoghan asked, his expression and tone of pure disgust.

"Nothing." I tried the stew, discovered it to be rich and full of flavor, and ate enough I could take my medications. "In five minutes, I'm going to be very, very happy. Tomorrow, I can take you somewhere to get you set up with everything you need to join modern times. When we're back, I'll take my next dose of pixie dust and resume being very happy. The world changed while you were napping. Change isn't necessarily bad. It's just change. So, the devil seems to be a pretty nice guy for someone who rules over the many hells. I guess for that faith, somebody has to do it. And anyway, for most, isn't evil just a matter of perspective?"

"How can evil be a matter of perspective?"

"A mouse certainly thinks a cat is evil, but the barn's owner loves the cat because it gets rid of the mouse, who eats their grain and may poison their food. It's a matter of perspective. And really, the only time I think we need to worry is when everyone agrees something is evil—and that's *really* evil."

"Wouldn't that be the devil himself?" Eoghan asked. "He is the fallen one, after all."

"Angels fall. Maybe he was the first, but he wasn't the last. Some new angel ultimately takes the old one's place. The CDC has a whole section on their website dedicated to the various pantheons. Christianity is a fairly big deal here, so they have a lot about the Christian pantheon. Personally, I'm more of the agnostic bent."

"Agnostic?"

"I'm unwilling to say I believe in any one specific thing but I am willing to believe there are higher powers out there, including the devil. Well, I'm less agnostic and more 'I don't care what you believe in but don't ask me to believe in it, too.' There are a lot of religions out there, and I don't feel like adhering to any one of them. I think they're all dangerous, and I'd rather not pick any side in that divine brawl. I'm not an atheist, though."

"Atheist?"

"Atheism is the active disbelief in religion."

"Oh. Heathens."

I rolled my eyes. "Heathens are people

who believe in something you don't. That's not atheism."

"I see modern times have become complicated." Eoghan sighed. "To be expected, I suppose. Tell me. What do you think about dogs?"

I perked up at his question. "Dogs? I fucking *love* dogs. They're cute, they're loyal, when they're trained they do as they're told, and they make good companions. I like lycanthropes, too—even the ones that aren't wolves or canines. They get what it means to be loyal. Sunset has exactly zero lycanthropes, because Sunset is populated by a bunch of backwater racists." I pointed at myself. "I am typically compared to a slightly overcooked loaf of bread, which is a barely tolerable shade as far as this shit town is concerned."

"Lycanthropes? You like the diseased?"

Oy. There was Eoghan's fatal flaw. Well, maybe I could beat it out of him with some work. It was worth a try. "Sure. As far as diseases go, I'll take one that allows me to shapeshift into a dog. Or a cat. Or whatever else lycanthropes can become. Loyalty is sexy, and the virus demands it. Loyalty is very sexy. If men could be half as loyal as the diseased who can shapeshift into dogs, they'd be a lot more useful to me."

"Gordon? Has the world gone mad since I was last awake?"

"No," the vampire replied with a smile.

"The world has become more tolerant and accepting of differences. This isn't a bad thing, but it does make the world a strange place. When the emergence began, many thought as you do. Lycanthropy is a disease. It's been at least eighty years since I was killed for the second time. Even then, people were beginning to accept they might become infected. It's hard to hate the diseased when it's your sister, brother, father, or mother. Small towns tend to maintain their loathing of those who aren't pure. That CDC agent said Lady Anwen is registered as a pure vanilla human. Her DNA is predominantly human, she has no magic despite making scanners ping, and this makes her a prime specimen of what it is to be human nowadays. In a larger city, she would be showcased for her pedigree."

"Her pedigree?" Eoghan asked, and his tone took on a dark edge.

I giggled. "You get offended over that, but you don't get offended over actually offensive things."

"And that would be the pixie dust kicking in," Gordon said, smiling and shaking his head. "Well, Eoghan. You were concerned about her. She's going to be the happiest of women for a while, but have fun bringing her down from the clouds. The dust is particularly potent, and she wasn't kidding about how it makes people behave. The nicer the person, the more desperate they are to make others happy, too. Just smile a lot, and that should keep her people pleasing ways at bay. I'll look into that other matter we discussed while you keep an eye on her."

"I'll take care of her. Stay safe while handling your business."

"I'll call you if there's an issue."

Eoghan sighed. "Must you? Those things are disturbing."

"Anwen, he has a phone in his pocket. Make him answer it should I call him."

"Okay! I can do that."

Gordon chuckled. "Finish your stew, and if you're still hungry after, make yourself another bowl."

"Oh. I'm always hungry."

"Not anymore," Eoghan muttered beneath his breath.

As telling him the realities of uncertain income wouldn't help anything, I focused on my dinner instead, grateful for what I had and determined to not worry about what tomorrow would bring for a little while.

TOMORROW BROUGHT an angel and an incubus to my door, and there wasn't enough pixie dust on the planet to deal with a headless divine engaging in an argument with a gorgeous sex demon wearing a suit. Suits were a problem. When hot men wore suits, my common sense dribbled out of my ears.

For several minutes, I enjoyed the view, doing a mental comparison of the demon and Eoghan.

It bothered the hell out of me I couldn't figure out which one took the top prize for sexiest male on the block. As far as I could tell, the angel and demon were arguing over a woman, they'd forgotten they'd knocked on my door and bothered me, and had captured the attention of my neighbors.

Like me, Mrs. Smithy took her time admiring the incubus. As far as the older married women in town went, she was one of the nicer ones, probably because she saw the shit my parents pulled every few weeks. While I disliked her pity, it beat the constant barrage of disapproval the older women across town tended to fling in my direction.

My parents would have given the town gossip fodder for a month. An angel and an incubus would keep people speculating for a year. Add in Eoghan, and I'd be the talk of the town for the rest of my life.

I waited in my doorway with Eoghan standing nearby, his body tense. He wore a new suit, and I wondered how the CDC had gotten them for him under such short notice, especially in a place like Sunset. Nobody outside of church or the funeral home wore suits at all, and everybody went over to one of the larger towns nearby to buy clothes.

"Excuse me?" I asked, already regretting I hadn't taken my morning medications yet.

The incubus shook his wings, smacked the angel with his tail, and smiled at me.

Eoghan scowled.

"I'm not going to seduce her," the incubus announced. "She's not my type."

Wow. I'd been rejected a lot over the years, but never by a sex demon who lived to despoil virgins. I considered going back inside, getting my pixie dust, and downing the entire damned bottle.

The angel smacked the incubus with its wing hard enough to knock him off my front steps. "He would absolutely love to deflower you, Miss Nash. That's what they do the instant they are not carefully supervised. I assure you, this one is being supervised. He was attempting to prevent a rather bitter dispute with your companion, who would not be pleased over such seductions."

For a headless being lacking any obvious sexuality, the angel sounded remarkably male.

"Now that I've started my morning with being rejected by an incubus, how can I help you?"

"The CDC requested angelic verification about the events leading up to you choosing to wake a slumbering vampire."

"Gordon, there's an angel and a demon here asking about you," I hollered into the house.

"Can you ask them to come back tonight? I'm getting ready to sleep."

I still found it amusing the vampire loved the couch despite being invited to take over my bedroom for the day. I had no idea what I was going to do with Eoghan, but I'd cross that bridge when I came to it. As far as I knew, he was sleeping on the couch when Gordon wasn't.

Ugh. I was jealous over my damned couch, which was getting more action from men than I had in my entire lifetime.

"Can you please come back tonight? The slumbering vampire wishes to slumber."

"The vampire is here?"

"His name is Gordon, and he's currently catching a nap on my couch. I have good curtains in the living room, so he's safe enough from the burning daystar."

"I had not been told the vampire—"

"Gordon," I corrected.

"Gordon was staying with you."

"Is there a reason he shouldn't be staying with me? He's a vampire, not Satan, Lucifer, or whatever you angels call the devil."

"Any one of those names is an appropriate form of address, although I would caution you about invoking his name. He gets curious and sometimes decides to show up when his name is invoked."

"Really? I can just say his name and he might appear? Do I need to click my heels together? Should I dress nicely first? How does one go about potentially summoning Christianity's biggest bad guy?"

"I would not precisely call him the biggest bad guy," the angel replied. "He is more like the jail warden, although he has, by his very nature, sinned. Other pantheons tend to disapprove of our particular family feud, as they do not rate Lucifer's sins as worth the punishment he paid for it. Of course, Lucifer does not view his punishment as much of a punishment, either. He is merely grouchy most days of the week. I would be, too, if I had to deal with so many sinners whining over their punishments. Worse, he has to deal with the sinners of the other pantheons, too. Hades quit, and Anubis and the other Egyptian divines are on vacation right now."

"Hades quit?" I blurted. "The others are on vacation?"

"Why have multiple divines doing the same job? Lucifer does the job well enough, and Hades has picked up some new roles, as have the other divines of death from varying faiths. In truth, not even Lucifer is truly needed. The universe itself ensures the souls can be sorted if there is no one else available for the job. The universe prefers to stay out of mortal affairs, though. The Egyptians will show up and do some of the heavy lifting if Lucifer needs some time off from dealing with the sinners."

If the angel kept talking, I would develop a headache not even pixie dust could cure. "Is there a reason I need to know this?"

"Yes," the angel answered.

"No," Eoghan announced the instant the angel quieted.

Okay. That got my attention and piqued my curiosity. "Why yes? And Eoghan, I'll ask you why no in a moment."

Eoghan huffed. "Angels are meddling beasts."

I regarded the angel, trying to decide how he classified as a beast. "Angels are more like headless humans with wings rather than beasts. Sure, they're a little creepy, but that's hardly a reason to call him a beast."

"A little creepy is more generous than most," the angel said, his tone amused. "He did not mean beast as in animal, Miss Anwen, but rather in the sense he views me as a monster and a threat. He is not wrong. Lucifer is the one who is typically called the beast, but one might view angels as monsters as well. We have power, and we do not necessarily use our power for the sake of specific humans. Your companion understands the universal laws better than most, and he is aware of what my presence means in its entirety. You'll find him a most annoying mongrel, although harmless enough to you."

I snickered, peeking at the incubus, who stretched out on my grass without a care in the world. "Your friend seems to be tired."

"He is lazy, rather annoying, and determined to vex me as often as possible. You are fortunate he will not challenge your companion for your company. He tends to stick around, worse than any mosquito I have had the misfortune of meeting. It is annoying having to swat those wretched things out of existence. They are not wise enough to leave me alone."

"What do you need to know about what happened at the funeral home?"

"Primarily, I need to verify you were willing to restore the vampire to his unlife."

"I was willing. I was aware of the risks when I did it, and Eoghan made a recommendation to make it as safe for me as possible. I would do it again."

"Thank you for your honesty. And your companion?"

"What about him? I didn't help him get up. He got up all on his own. He startled me, but that was all. He also spouted some nonsense about sacrifices."

"In his first era, someone would be chosen to accompany him. It was called a sacrifice because it typically meant that someone would be separated from their family and friends. It was also considered a great honor to be chosen."

Eoghan grunted.

"His era was weird."

The angel laughed. "That is very true. It was as weird as this one, although the era of his birth was a much more violent and unpleasant place in many ways. He will need to adapt to the relative peace of modern society."

"I have noticed he doesn't like screaming."

The angel remained quiet for a while. "Yes, I suppose he wouldn't. What do you call yourself now?"

"Eoghan," he replied. "Eoghan Olin."

"You must have awoken for a brief time during the age of the Celts to have picked up that name. It is fitting you would show up here and choose someone like her."

"I definitely dislike when she screams," Eoghan muttered.

The incubus snickered. "You'll have to work on that. You want to make your woman scream. It's the best."

The angel shook his wings, hopped off the steps, and kicked the incubus. "I do not know why I put up with you."

"You love me. You'd be sad and lonely without me. I keep your life interesting."

The angel heaved a sigh. "Do not antagonize Mr. Olin. We are not here to antagonize. We are here to verify the truth, which I have."

"Do you need to verify the part about the murder and the attempted murder?" I asked.

"The CDC spoke to Mr. Olin about such matters."

"You are too tired for such questionings," Eoghan said.

Okay. I could work with that. "I need to take my medications and get to my errands so I can have my pixie dust tonight. Is there anything else you need from me?"

"Yes, as a matter of fact, there is." The

angel returned to my front steps, held out his hand, and a briefcase appeared in a flash of bright light. "I was asked to deliver this, as it has vital information on Mr. Olin's estates, financial investments, and so on. Inside, you'll find critical paperwork, a laptop, and how to access the files you'll need to modernize your new companion and help him handle his affairs."

I took the briefcase and swallowed my sigh. "I'm not being paid nearly well enough to deal with this."

"You will find the CDC's proposal for your hiring contract, benefits, and so on inside as well. Mr. Olin had made the request for a fair hiring arrangement for modern times with some additions. You will find you are being paid quite well for the work. He was very concerned over your fair treatment."

The hells would start freezing over if things continued to go my way for once in my life. I'd have to send a card to the devil asking him for his forgiveness for running up his electric bill. "Some additions?"

"He requested your salary be marked up, as humans do not change that much over the years, and the averages are rarely what the staff are worth, and he would not like to take advantage of you in that fashion. Sacrifice truly is a poor term for the work of a high-grade executive secretary, Mr. Olin."

The angel's implication Eoghan might take advantage of me in other ways caught my attention and did a good job of holding it. Rather than ask, I narrowed my eyes and considered the headless being.

"Executive what?" Eoghan asked.

The angel sighed.

I couldn't understand how a headless being spoke or sighed, so I moved on to my next problem: Eoghan. "I don't think executive secretaries existed when men wore dresses and loin cloths, Mr. Angel."

"Dimitri," the angel replied. "The annoyance on your lawn is Theo. I expect we'll be in touch again, as my residence while on the mortal coil is a rather short distance away by mundane methods of travel. Fortunately, we can both teleport, which makes this easier."

"Wait, you live here?"

Dimitri pointed behind him. "It would take you approximately two hours to drive if you went that way."

I could only think of one somewhat major city about two hours away from Sunset in the general direction the angel had pointed. "You live in Huntsville?"

"Not precisely, but close enough."

"Do you have a phone number I can reach you at in case I have any questions?"

"My business card is in the briefcase, along with contact information for our wife."

Wait. What? "Our wife? As in you two are sharing a wife?"

"Yes, our wife. I am a part of a triad with

Theo. Our wife enjoys vexing us at every opportunity."

Some women had all the luck. She had an angel *and* a sex demon? "So his taste in women is restricted to only your wife?"

"Precisely."

Well, that made me feel a little better about being rejected by a sex demon. "Do you think your wife would mind me asking for tips? I'm fairly hopeless."

"I think you'll find your problems easy to resolve, although you will find yourself besieged with gentlemanly ways. You will find it quite vexing."

"Besieged with gentlemanly ways?"

Theo leered at me. "Your companion is as old-fashioned as they come. Good luck with that. You're going to need all the luck you can get."

I wondered if that meant I wouldn't be able to lure the hot antique to bed without a fight.

"That is precisely what he means, I'm afraid," the angel replied. "Humans. You are your own worst enemy. Should you find yourself overly vexed, do give our wife a call. I'm sure she'd love to share the tricks of her trade with you while doing her best to embarrass us."

"Can angels even be embarrassed?"

"Absolutely," Dimitri replied. "And our wife has turned embarrassing me into an art. You'll find her to be a most excellent friend, so try not to be too shy about putting her number to use. Also, you'll want to get yourself a proper cell phone, Miss Anwen. You'll need it. If my wife gets her hands on you, you'll be a changed woman within a week, and it'll be great fun for her. I live to make certain my wife enjoys her life, so do give her a call."

Without another word, the pair disappeared, and the sex demon left behind the faintest hint of brimstone in the air. I sniffed, puzzled over the stench.

"Interesting. That was a devil," Eoghan murmured, and he stepped out of my house to investigate where Theo had been rolling about on my grass. "But why would an angel cohort with a devil?"

"I thought incubi were sex demons," I admitted. "Anyway, they're part of a triad. That means they live with a human, and they're probably going to have a child or already have one. They teach about triads in school, as nobody knows when an angel will show up and fall in love with a woman. Well, usually women. There's a case or two of a pairing taking interest in a man, but it's pretty uncommon."

Ugh. Great. My interest in academics was showing through—an interest I couldn't even pursue thanks to my dead-beat parents.

"Demon, devils... there is no difference."

"Actually, there are differences between the two. It's basic enough it's taught in school.

Devils are born directly under the influence of Satan in one of his various hells or converted into one. Demons are born on the mortal coil, particularly Earth. They have different ranges of powers, but I didn't pay too much attention. I never expected to meet either a devil or a demon."

"I see I have much to learn. Let us begin with the issue of your cell phone. What is wrong with yours?"

"Beyond the fact I don't have one because I can't afford one?"

"Ah. I see. You can afford one now. Are you up for making a venture to a store? I can call a driver. I was shown how, and Miss Cecily taught me how to access the money available to me. She became quite amicable following our general negotiations."

"Well, let me see what's in this briefcase before I decide what I can and can't afford. According to my finances yesterday, I couldn't afford jack shit."

"Today, you can," Eoghan replied, and before I could argue with him, he disappeared into my house, leaving me to follow.

SIX

In good news, there would be honey
rocks in my future.

THE LAPTOP COULD RUN laps around the
computer I'd used at the funeral home, and I
couldn't help but wonder if it was wasted on
me. It begged to be put to better use, including playing some high-end game I'd
never even considered buying for myself.
Whomever had installed its software had
gone on a shopping spree, and it included the
kitchen sink. I hoped nobody needed me to
understand how to use most of the programs;
my job had required little more than word
processing and spreadsheets, which I used
with tolerable skill.

Eoghan observed, and while his scrutiny
unsettled me, he kept quiet, even when I
struggled to access the accounts I was supposed to manage on his behalf. To help
manage Eoghan's money, I had a complete set
of cards in my name linked to his accounts,
along with a note that the CDC wished me

the best of luck teaching him how to use an ATM.

The machines startled him, and he didn't trust most forms of technology.

Fortunately, the instructions on how to manage his accounts helped, which came with a promise of the CDC providing a tutor should I need one. I gave it a few days before I called and begged for help. The nightmare waiting for me would test my patience.

Eoghan had millions upon millions of dollars in his name in his bank accounts alone. According to the account nicknames, he received payouts from stock dividends, profits from property rentals, and real estate. The general earnings account would vex me, as there was no indication what counted as general earnings—or why it had twenty million dollars in liquid funds.

"You're ridiculously wealthy," I announced. His wealth would make trying to take him to bed even more of a challenge. Wealthy men tended to suspect poor women, and it didn't matter if I had wanted to take him out of his clothes before finding out he could pay my salary for the rest of my life and not miss a penny of it.

In good news, there would be honey rocks in my future. There would be a lot of honey rocks in my future. I'd make a point of having a honey rock once a month, and I planned on whispering sweet nothings to it before devouring its sweet, sweet flesh.

"I was wealthy during my last awakening as well, but I find your use of ridiculous to be amusing. Please elaborate," the antique replied.

I pointed at the general earnings account, which represented approximately ten percent of his liquid assets. "The amount in this account would leave me comfortable for life, I would never have to work another day in my life, and I'd leave someone a nice inheritance when I kicked the bucket."

"You would become bored if you never worked."

I nodded, as I doubted he could ever understand what it was like to never be able to miss a day of work even if ill. A missed day meant I wouldn't be eating for a few days, and starving sucked. I'd done it a few too many times since dropping out of high school. "I likely would, yes. And you?"

"I find ways to keep engaged and busy during my awakenings."

"I figured. Your caretakers needed something to get them started to accumulate this much wealth on your behalf."

"They had good incentive. I look forward to that director's demise for his part in killing them."

"But you didn't know them."

"I don't need to know them. While it has long since been repaid, I once owed their ancestor a debt. I remember such things. Director Hammel will not appreciate his fate."

Eoghan wouldn't hear me complain about that. "I just don't understand how you can be so wealthy."

"When I first lost my humanity, I chased wealth to give me mundane purpose. I exist for a reason, and I understand that. Mine is a role that I cannot escape, which is something I accepted long ago. But then, I did not and could not. As such, I chased wealth. I owed a debt, and I used my pursuit of wealth to repay that debt. We forged an alliance after, and so here we are. The circle completes. Their line is lost, and a new line begins with you. The circumstances are reversed, although a wager is not quite the same sort of debt I owed."

"But it is still a debt. It's my turn to try to fill these shoes?"

"They have generations of experience and drive, passed down from father to son, mother to daughter—and even aunts and uncles to nieces and nephews. It saddens me a family so old no longer walks upon this Earth, but few can avoid death's neutral embrace. You'll have time to learn, and if you need help, I will find capable people to help you."

Guilt over my self-centered tendencies reared its head. I'd just lost a shit job, albeit one of the only jobs in the town I could get. He'd lost everything important, things no amount of money could buy. "It must be hard for you."

"How so?"

"Everyone you've ever known is gone."

Eoghan nodded. "This is true. They have all gone, but death is not the final conclusion of a life's journey. I have lived long enough to see old friends be reborn, and I rejoice when I cross their path a second time. The soul remembers. Have you ever met someone you feel like you've known forever?"

I shook my head. "I'm weird that way. I never have."

"Then yours may be a new soul, one that can find the true joy of first discoveries. I have met many souls for a second time. That's something. The friends I once had are gone, but their soul continues on, and that makes things easier. I never know who I'll meet again down the road."

"But how do you know?"

"Magic, of course. For most, when they meet me again, it is a feeling they've met me somewhere else before. For me, it is a sense of recognition, and with some thought, I can usually remember who they'd once been."

"Deja vu!"

Eoghan's brow furrowed. "That is not your English, is it? It sounds wrong somehow."

"It's French."

"Ah. How odd. It's as if it's a part of your language yet it's also not."

"English is the language that takes other languages into dark alleys and mugs them for their loose grammar."

"Pardon?"

"English butchers other languages in dark alleys, taking their words and grammar and claiming them for itself. As a result, us English speakers can't even figure out how our own language works because it insists on breaking all of the rules. The only consistent rule in English is that every rule has an exception. Then, to make matters worse, it keeps changing. Every damned time I think I get something right, someone goes and decides we should do it a different way. English is a rebellious language."

"You speak a rebellious language?"

"Yes. Yes, I do. It's a vicious, terrible language. It's completely wild and untamed, and if left unsupervised, I'm certain it will start a revolt for the hell of it."

Eoghan chuckled. "I am up for a challenge. I believe you'll find me to be an excellent student. I have learned many languages over the years. Your English will not defeat me, no matter how rebellious it is."

While I couldn't fix all of Eoghan's problems, I could do something to make life a little easier on him—and it would give me an excuse to keep a close eye on him. "If I have to teach you English, you should teach me your first language."

"Nobody speaks it anymore."

I viewed that as a challenge, one I couldn't refuse without some attempt to learn it. "Except you," I countered. "Then I can speak to

you in your own language. It's not a dead language if there are those who can still speak it.
If you can teach me, then you can teach others, too. We'd bring an entire language back
to life!"

As far as hare-brained ideas went, I liked
mine. It would take up a lot of time, it
wouldn't cost me anything, and I'd be kept
busy. It would give me a purpose, one that
didn't involve worrying about what had happened at the funeral home.

I still hadn't checked the employment offer, which waited inside the briefcase. It, far
more than Eoghan's shocking wealth, scared
me. Once I looked, there'd be no turning
back. I'd keep my word and deal with it, no
matter how little I was paid, although it'd be
almost impossible to pay me less than what
I'd gotten at the funeral home. If I got any
sort of decent health care plan, I'd be ahead of
the game, as my insurance bill murdered my
account each and every month.

"You're one of them, aren't you?"

His question startled me from my
thoughts. "Excuse me?"

"You're an academic type. The type who
learns for the sake of learning. Your eyes got
quite the gleam in them at the thought of
learning my language."

I thought about that, realizing the antique
had been profiling me as much as I'd been
profiling him. "I guess so. I liked school when
I could worry less about the idiots I went to

school with and more about learning stuff. It's probably more about wanting what I can't have."

"If learning is what you want, then it is what you will have, although I hope you are willing to wait some time for me to handle this matter with Director Hammel. I would rather teach you in a time of peace than a time of turmoil. And money will not be an issue should you wish to attend an institution. Does this emergence have only religious institutions of learning? It varies between the emergences, and I no longer bother trying to guess how humans will behave."

"They're not religious in nature normally now. And as for Director Hammel, that seems like a wise idea, especially since he tried to kill me."

"He made assumptions, entirely wrong ones. While he was wise to offer you as a sacrifice, he didn't realize the word was meant in a different fashion. I expect he killed my caretaker believing in the wrong definition of that word. I regret that. He will regret his choice more."

I wondered if his guilt would follow him the rest of his long life. "Director Hammel is an idiot."

"Yes, he is. He won't live long enough to learn from his mistakes, but I want to find out all of his motivations. He wanted either Gordon or I awake, and I want to know why.

That means finding him and asking a few questions."

"That sounds vaguely threatening," I admitted.

"There are many ways to get answers out of a body, and I know them all. If his mouth won't speak the truth to me, I have other methods I can use, ones that he cannot lie his way through. I just hate the screams."

My eyes widened. "You mean to torture him?"

"Oh, no. I mean to slice him open and read the truth on his entrails and heart. That's far more satisfying than torture, and his screams won't last long that way. The moment of death is when all of a human's truths are brought to light. It is a rather brutal method, but it works. My magic allows me to read many truths at the moment of death. You can consider that a clue if you'd like."

I'd heard of necromancy before, although few toyed with such magics, as it could have dire consequences. "Are you a necromancer?"

I wasn't sure if I wanted to take someone who used the dead as a puppet to bed with me, and it would put a bit of a damper on our non-existent relationship.

"No, I'm nothing so foul as that lot. Well, I don't know if your necromancers are like the ones I knew. The ones I knew were foul at best. It makes sense why you might think I am one, however. The necromancers I'm familiar with can read the truth in that method, but they're far more limited than I am. They can only ask one question of the body. I can learn the entire truth. But I am not a necromancer and have no interest in controlling the dead or falsely bringing them back to life."

Huh. "There were necromancers back then, too? I'll admit, I don't really know much about them except they work some type of death magic."

"Of course. There were many forms of magic that dealt with the dead and dying back then. Humans had not yet come to terms with their lifespan. When I first lived, most were lucky to live to see forty. A few lived many long years, but they were few and far between—or touched by the gods who were still forming."

"The divines weren't just there?"

"No, of course not. Most of the divines, with limited exception, are creations."

Hello, information. "Created by whom, exactly?"

"People, of course. The power of belief in an era of magic is a magnificent thing, Anwen. Be careful what you wish for. You may get it."

I returned to attempting to make sense of Eoghan's finances and new life, and I wondered.

IT TOOK me several hours to confirm what I'd

guessed when I'd first gotten a hold of Eoghan's finances. The man had turned the wealth of the past into an empire for himself, one he could enjoy without lifting a finger. The previous caretaker, a thirty-six year old named Jones, had left a meticulous list of all contacts in charge of Eoghan's accounts, contact information, and account instructions, which I'd use as the basis for preserving the antique's prosperity.

The account managers split ten percent of the profits, I would take ten percent of the profits for dealing with the managers and the details of Eoghan's daily life, and Eoghan got the rest, distributed to his various accounts depending on where the funds had come from.

From banking to general investing to even patent licensing, Eoghan's empire had a little of everything.

It might take me an entire lifetime to make sense of it all.

Lucky antique bastard. No wonder he'd come out of the freezer as an arrogant asshole. He had expected to step into a world of luxury straight from his lengthy nap.

With no other excuse to delay, I dug out the employment terms the CDC had drawn up for Eoghan, wondering what sort of fresh hell waited for me—and what sort of pay I'd receive. In truth, the ten percent I'd skim just from managing the people managing his money would last me an entire lifetime after

one or two years, assuming they didn't screw
the pooch on whatever they did to earn him
money.

According to the front sheet, I would get
full health insurance, my entire premiums
paid for by him and offered through the
CDC, which would give me the best of the
best. No doctor's office refused CDC coverage, and I'd be able to get any treatments necessary to keep me alive—and I'd never pay for
any of it.

With the CDC, complete coverage meant
just that.

I considered setting up a shrine to every
damned divine I could think of to thank them
for my change of fortunes.

"Did you sell your soul to get this insurance plan?" I demanded, smacking my hand
onto the paper. I couldn't comprehend my
actual base salary, which was more than
seven times what I'd been paid at the funeral
home before bonuses. I'd gone from the
lowest of the low to competing with the
wealthiest in town. One part of me wanted to
jump Eoghan right then and there, although I
blamed his suit for that general reaction.

Even without the year-end bonus and the
ten percent from his account growth and new
ventures, I could buy honey rocks whenever I
wanted, and I wouldn't worry if they'd be the
reason I starved before my next paycheck.

Mhmm. Honey rocks. A pair of them, just
for me. I added a trip to the grocery store to

my list of things I needed to do. I'd even get four honey rocks, and I'd give one to Eoghan and share the other with Gordon, which would give me two honey rocks plus one with a few bite marks taken out of it.

I'd even one up the honey rocks and get a few kiwis, too.

Somehow, I kept from licking my lips.

Eoghan grunted. "No, I merely informed them I couldn't give them the knowledge they wanted if I needed to spend my time worrying about your health. This was their solution to that problem. I commented you were willing to threaten your health because of financial concerns, and I found that to be reprehensible at best. I also mentioned that you are the kind to willingly cut open your wrist for the sake of a captive vampire, so I recommended Gordon be cared for as well, and that I would pay for his health plan as needed. I've been told it's harder for a solo vampire to make a good living in this era. I find it interesting vampires tend to have large family groups, much like how wolves live and hunt in packs. Now that I have had time to think about it, I find it very gratifying this era belongs to the lycanthropes, though."

Eoghan liked lycanthropes? He hadn't before. "Huh. There's a lot of prejudices against lycanthropes, although I like them. There's a lot to be said about the benefits of the infection. It doesn't hurt I really like dogs." I referred to the file of agreements on the laptop.

"You're only paying a hundred a month for full coverage for us *and* for Gordon. You're getting away with highway robbery."

"I have been told the hundred a month will cover administrative fees, as any incidents and care require CDC employees to make certain everything goes smoothly. Your hospital trip, for example, required several hours of someone handling the paperwork. I thought this was fair, although I am unclear still on how much these handlers are paid. Money does not work the same way now as it did when I was last awake. Coin did exist, but the poor bartered more often than not—and most were poor."

"But you weren't."

"I discovered the value of silver, gold, and some other precious things early, and I founded my wealth on those. I learned to trade where these things were rare, and that began my empire. My caretakers continued my empire. The last time I awoke, I still had much of these things left."

I searched the computer for gemstones and precious metals, and several files came up, which supported his claim. According to one of the documents, he owned numerous mines—and the caretaker had meticulously detailed workers' rights to make them as safe as possible.

It amazed me that Eoghan's ethics had survived centuries without his presence reinforcing his wishes.

Damn. I could get away with calling him arrogant, but the asshole part of my favored nickname for him lost a lot of steam when I considered the foundations of his wealth and how he liked to operate.

Argh. How could I make use of my favorite barb if the arrogant asshole refused to be an asshole? How unfair. Worse, it made me want to take him to bed even more than before.

His bad boy appeal partnered with seeming like a good person in general did terrible things for my peace of mind. I needed a cold shower, but focusing on work would do in the meantime. "It does seem like you own a lot of mines and things like that. It's going to take a lot of time to figure all of this out."

"And I still need to acquire a proper phone for you. Have you taken your remedies?"

I'd taken everything but the pixie dust, as I hadn't wanted to be impaired while trying to figure out the rest of my life. "I'm good there, but I'll bring the bottles in case we're out longer than I expect. I'll take the pixie dust with dinner so I can sleep tonight."

"Excellent. Tell me. Do you drive?"

"Do I? No. Can I? Yes. That's the one thing my dipshit parents hadn't screwed up. I'm licensed. I just can't afford a car." It took forty minutes to walk to work, and luckily for me, the town's bus had a stop near the house and another near the funeral home for the rainy days.

"You can afford a car now. More accurately, I can afford a car, which I will purchase for you. Cars are much more comfortable than wagons, chariots, or even carriages. I will use my card to purchase a nice one, although you will have to help me judge what a nice one is. Now, if you want to know what a good horse is, I can help you with that. But your cars have an unfortunate lack of horses."

When he found out engines were rated by their horsepower, I bet he'd have a fit. "We'll have to head over to a different town for that. There are no car dealerships here. Well, none that you want a vehicle from. The town's mechanic fixes up the junkers so they can last a little longer, but they're pieces of shit."

"I do not wish to handle any shit."

I giggled. "Neither do I. Will Gordon be fine on his own?"

"Vampires rest lightly, and any foolish enough to enter your home will find themselves in an unfortunate position. I have been told a donor or two will come by tonight to offer him sustenance. He'll be thirsty by then, so I believe your home will be safe enough."

"I was less concerned about the house and more concerned about him, but that will work. Did the CDC say how I'd be paid?"

"You have been put into a payroll system they manage, and they have access to one of the accounts to draw your wages from. They are also handling the tax issues. Taxes," he spat. "There's no escape from those wretched things, not even after a thousand years."

"Then I guess I'll call a cab. I'm sure you can afford it."

Given two weeks and my first pay, I'd be able to afford it, too.

Whomever said money couldn't buy happiness needed their head examined, because it'd been a long damned time since anything had made me quite as happy as knowing I could afford dinner.

Then again, after stealing a few peeks at Eoghan in his suit, I could think of a few things that'd make me pretty damned happy, and getting him out of his shirt for a look topped my list. After I took him car and phone shopping, I needed to get my head examined.

I'd just blame Gordon. The blood loss had gotten to me. Then again, small-town life and no men up for grabs had gotten to me, too.

Until the town's single women figured out Eoghan was around, I'd enjoy the scenery. Then I'd contemplate murder because no matter how much things changed, they stayed the same, especially in a place like Sunset.

THE INSTANT EOGHAN spotted the black Chevy Silverado, he stilled, his eyes widened, and I understood the war had been lost. Men loved a big, powerful truck, and the Silverado delivered. My driveway would barely fit the workhorse, and Eoghan would become the talk of the town, as everyone around wanted the biggest, baddest Chevy money could buy.

Even me. No, especially me. Every time I rode in a big truck, the sense of invulnerability and power went straight to my head along with a healthy dose of security.

The men would be after him and his truck more than the women would be after him and his money. On the way home, I'd buy extra popcorn, as I couldn't buy such entertainment anywhere. I'd enjoy the show, as Sunset had an unfair population of handsome men, and they'd congregate on my lawn.

Forget the milkshakes, the truck would bring the men to my yard. Best of all, with the help of an angel and an incubus, I'd figured out Eoghan really was the jealous kind, so my truck would result in a peacock display from the antique.

For once in my life, things were looking good.

While Eoghan drooled, I hunted for a salesman, pointing at the Silverado. "We want that one. How long until I can pick it up and drive it home?"

"It's already ready. The original buyer backed out right after we got it onto the lot and ready for them. He was going to pay upon delivery, but it didn't work out. It's not quite fully loaded, but it'll do just about anything you want except pull a fifth wheel. If you need to pull a fifth wheel on it, we'll need a day to set it up."

That worked for me. "We don't need a fifth wheel. Any miles on it?"

"Two, which came from a test drive around the block and on and off the truck."

Huh. Good luck rained down on me, and I took a moment to thank whichever benevolent divine had decided to be nice to me for a change. I might even give up my agnostic ways for a few minutes as a gesture of gratitude for my changed fortunes. "Can I drive it off the lot today if we're paying cash?"

"If you're paying cash, I can give you a discount while I'm at it. You'll have to run on dealer tags until tomorrow, though; the DMV is already closed. You'll need to provide insurance information for the vehicle. Assuming you have everything in order, we can process the sale of the truck within an hour. The manager is available to sign off on it."

Ugh. Insurance. Fortunately, any insurance company worth its salt would cover me over the phone, although I didn't look forward to explaining why I was getting a truck when I was the assistant of a rich man. Then again, it beat getting a truck while I was working over at the funeral home.

"Just give me the paperwork, and I'll take care of that tomorrow and return the dealership tags as soon as its official plates are on. I want to be out of here as soon as possible. I want the best warranty you've got on it, and if it hasn't been rust-proofed, I need to know how long it'll take to apply it."

"It's rust-proofed and has an extra layer of protective coating on the paint. The initial owner was planning to make it earn its keep, but the money didn't work out. A pity, because it's a good truck."

I glanced at Eoghan, who prowled around my new truck. If a man looked at me like he looked at the vehicle, I'd be set for life.

Oh, well.

Lucky truck.

"Can you ask one of the salesmen to wax eloquent over the truck while I fill out the paperwork?" I'd be able to put Eoghan's debit card to the test, but I'd have to call someone at the CDC to unlock the account to pay for the vehicle. Someone would laugh at me before I finished, that much I knew. "Preferably someone who can convince him that the truck is the best thing ever to walk into his life."

"I think we can manage that, although it looks like he's doing a good job of convincing himself that truck is all he ever wanted."

"Just wait until the salesman figures out he has no idea how trucks work," I muttered. "It's my truck, I'll just be driving him around."

"Lucky man."

No, lucky truck. Rather than argue with him, I smiled. Smiling tended to put people at ease, and sure enough, he led me into the building to begin the gauntlet of paperwork required to make the vehicle mine.

The CDC call took all of five minutes, the payment for over eighty thousand cleared without a hitch, and the CDC hooked me up with an insurance company who wouldn't take me for my soul.

Fifty-three minutes after arriving, I became the proud owner of a truck, and the entire time, Eoghan stayed with his new baby, examining every inch of it. According to the scuffs on his suit, he'd even crawled under it for a look at the undercarriage. The salesman watched with open amusement, especially when the antique stroked the glossy black paint.

"Goodness, Eoghan. Are you petting it?"

"There are a lot of horses under the hood of this truck, and I've been told it'll roar like a lion when you rev the engine."

Yep, the truck had gotten to him. I unlocked the truck, opened the door, and used the step to climb inside. I put the keys in the ignition and started the engine. Sure enough, the truck rumbled, growled, and did a pretty good impression of a roar. "It looks like there's truth in advertising."

"They just let you get into the truck?"

"Yes, because I bought the truck using your money while you were admiring it. These nice gentlemen are going to remove the stickers and make sure we have our dealership tags, and then we'll do the rest of our

chores. You don't get to drive it, but you can
listen to the horses whine and the lion growl
and roar while I drive you around. Fortunately for you, this monster of a truck will fit
in my driveway. You're going to be the talk of
the town as soon as anyone finds out you got
this baby. It is customary to name such a nice
vehicle, but since I'm the driver, I get to
name it."

Technically, the truck was mine, but it
seemed wrong to deny the man his baby.
Having a new love of his life would make his
integration into the modern world easier.

I could come to an agreement with the
truck. She could have him outside of the
house. I could have him inside of the house.
We could share without serious issues.

"That seems fair." Eoghan circled the
truck, opened the passenger door, and got
inside. He buckled in as he'd been taught,
and when he closed the door, the panel with
buttons drew his attention. "What do
these do?"

"They control the locks and windows." I
reached over and pressed the button to lock
the doors, and they clicked. Then I showed
him how the windows worked before
drawing his attention to his personal air conditioning dials. "These can change the tem-
perature to whatever you like."

"This truck is magical," he whispered.

Yep, I owned one lucky truck. "She's a nice
truck. I'm naming her Lady Luck." I patted

the dashboard. "One day, I will even teach you how to drive her."

"Is it difficult to learn how to drive?"

"Not really, but you need to learn how to read English first."

"Consider me a very motivated student, please."

Damn. Given a few minutes, I really would be jealous of my damned truck. "I'll have to repay you for the truck, though. I bought her with your money, but she's in my name."

"Consider her a gift, then. I can't drive her, and when I learn to drive, I will buy myself one just like her. Perhaps in a different color, so it is easy to tell which beauty belongs to who."

It had taken me less than an hour to create a monster, and I expected there would be cars, trucks, and other vehicles littering the lawn and parked on the street within a week. I understood how obsessed men with money operated. When they decided they wanted something, they bought it.

Common sense need not apply.

"That's a very expensive gift, Eoghan."

"And I'm an arrogant asshole who will make you earn it through monotonous tasks, if that makes you feel better about now having a truck in your name you bought with my money."

Damn. At his current rate, Mr. Arrogant Asshole would work his way under my skin by the end of the week and make me like it. "I can agree to that."

It took a few minutes for them to remove the stickers, and once they waved for me to go, I put the truck into gear and eased it out of the parking lot. It handled a lot better than my parents' rust bucket, and I pondered what excuses I could make to drive it around. I had no idea how far a full tank of gas would take me, but I wanted to find out.

"Excellent. We must now address your phone situation."

"The mall." I rarely got to go to the mall, and it would be an adventure in teaching Eoghan about the modern world. "The mall has some rules."

"What sort of rules?"

"We do not make fun of, attack, or annoy the gorgons, the centaurs, the pixies, or any non-humans that may be present. We also do not stare at them as though they are critters in the zoo. Lycanthropes are common elsewhere but fairly rare here. As long as you don't sleep with them or get into a fight with one, they're mostly harmless."

"I cannot contract lycanthropy."

Right. Eoghan looked human but wasn't one. "Well, I can. I'm just a human, so I'd rather not end up mated to some lycanthrope because you picked a fight with him."

"Pardon?"

"If a woman gets infected with a male lycanthrope's virus, the virus typically attempts to form a bond between them. It can become a fight between multiple lycanthropes over a woman, but if the woman sticks around for too long, she gets to keep the lycanthrope permanently. So, don't pick any fights with lycanthropes."

"I find this to be unacceptable."

"Lycanthropes are monitored fairly closely to prevent it from happening accidentally. And when the woman wants it to happen, it's legal as long as she consented to it. There's usually a waiver."

"Ah. I see. And your opinion on lycanthropes?"

"If I meet the right furry gentleman, I see no reason to be concerned about a virus that guarantees his loyalty, lengthens my general lifespan, and otherwise benefits me in all ways except a hotter temper and a tendency to sprout fur."

"Interesting. You are open about this? In my day, most were not."

"In your day, lycanthropes were viewed as an abomination."

"You would be correct. The CDC agents told me there are more than wolves now, too. In my day, they were only wolves."

"Well, yeah. Turns out the virus can turn you into just about any mammal. There are even a few avian lycanthropes. Don't ask me what. I just read about them. To date, there are no cold-blooded lycanthropes. Nobody knows why."

"Interesting. And they teach this to everybody?"

"For the most part, I assume? I learned about it in high school before I started working at the funeral home. Sunset is more superstitious than most places, so I think it's more about keeping us scared of the big, bad, and scary monsters of the world. In my case, I found them interesting." Driving with a shredded arm hurt, but I kept both hands on the wheel until I got a better feel for how Lady Luck handled. "How about you?"

"I never minded lycanthropes all that much, but most were wise to fear them. They are excellent predators. They always have been."

"They always will be. I mean, they become huge wolves or other animals, and the hybrids can bend metal—or rip someone they don't like to shreds."

"Hybrids? What are those?"

"When a lycanthrope can become a mix of man and their beast."

"Ah! Wolf-men. They're lycanthropes? They were always rare. I've never met one."

"They're just lycanthropes. They have really strong viruses or something like that. You could ask someone in the CDC for more information. It's public information. Hybrids are prized."

"They are? Why?"

"Hell if I know. That's what we were taught." When I reached the first stop light, I tapped on the truck's navigation panel, input the mall's name, and giggled when it offered to guide me to my destination. Then, because I could, I selected a female voice for Lady Luck.

"Turn right at the next set of lights," Lady Luck ordered.

Eoghan's eyes widened. "She talks!"

"It's a computer. I put the address for the mall into the navigation panel, and she's going to give me directions on how to get there." I obeyed Lady Luck, turning right at the next set of lights.

"Continue for three miles. Your destination will be on your right," Lady Luck instructed.

"She seems like a competent guide."

"She is until she develops a severe case of stupid. I'll show you some videos on the internet of the navigation systems losing their minds. There was one incident where a system tried to instruct drivers to drive off a bridge. Most were smart enough to avoid obeying."

"Most implies not all were."

"It didn't end well for the driver. The system was fixed for that stretch of road, but you shouldn't blindly trust the navigation systems."

"I will keep this in mind."

If the navigation system blew his mind, the mall would finish him off, and I intended to enjoy every minute of it.

SEVEN

I'm in a mood tonight, so call me
Lucy.

THE PARKING LOT gods mocked me, and I had
to make three circuits around the mall before
I found a space capable of handling my new
truck and Eoghan's ego. His ego might spill
over, possibly contaminate the tiny cars I
parked between, and drive me insane, but I'd
cope somehow.

When he wasn't trying to drive me crazy, I
liked his company. I could only assume I'd already lost my mind. That I was proving to be
my mother's daughter annoyed the hell out of
me, but I would do my best to enjoy the advantage while I still had it. I expected life
would backhand me soon enough.

"Does everyone have a car?" Eoghan
asked, sliding out of the truck and eyeing the
junker parked next to us. "This one is a rather
sad vehicle compared to the ones I saw where
we acquired Lady Luck."

"Lady Luck is new. That car is probably
close to twenty years old. That's the kind of

car the mechanic in Sunset sells. Trust me on this one. You don't want a car like that. The owner probably can't afford something newer, so they dump a lot of money down the drain keeping that one running. That's the problem with being poor. You can't afford something newer, but you can't afford to fix what you have, so you run it into the ground and then scrape together enough to get something else you can run into the ground. I couldn't afford anything at all, so I walked or took the bus."

"The bus?"

"Think of it as a very large car that can move a lot of people at one time. People who don't own a car ride them to stops to get where they need to go. I would take the bus to work on rainy days but walk the rest of the time." I hopped out of the truck, grunted when I landed harder than I expected, and grimaced at the throb in my arm.

Some mistakes I wouldn't repeat, and the next time I got out of my truck, I'd be a hell of a lot more careful.

"This is more complicated than I anticipated."

"Just wait until you see how we do our taxes."

"It is not a flat rate per person?"

"Nope. It's based on how much you've earned in the year, and it's complicated as hell to figure out. You have a tax accountant, so you won't have to do too much, but it's not going to be fun for me, who'll have to make sure everything is prepared for the accountant." I didn't look forward to figuring out what I needed to give the accountant. I had enough trouble with my own taxes, which was simple enough.

Being dirt poor and only having one job helped with that.

I locked the truck, gave her a fond pat, and gestured towards the mall's glass entry. "There are a lot of stores inside."

"Like a bazaar?"

Fortunately, I'd paid attention in history class and understood what a bazaar was despite never having seen one. "Somewhat, but the stores are contained and separated rather than a bunch of stalls crammed together. You'll see soon enough," I promised.

In the time it took us to cross the parking lot, dodging cars coming in and out of the mall, Eoghan got a close look at several lycanthropes, a quartet of gorgon women wearing veils, and an entire flock of pixies, who shed pink, sparkly dust everywhere they went.

Security would have a field day with the pixies, who were supposed to keep their dust to themselves, although it didn't take long for me to clue in they weren't packing much of a punch in the magic department. At most, it took the edge off, which put them at E or D grade.

"They're dusting the ground?" Eoghan asked after the winged menaces disappeared into the mall, leaving a glimmering trail in their wake. "Are they supposed to be doing that?"

"Nope." I lifted my hand, which had a pink shine to it after exposure to the dust. "They're low-grade pixies, so at most you'll feel a little better about life for a while before it wears off. No big deal. They might get scolded by security, but that's it, unless the security guards are having a bad night. If they call the cops, I guess it'd be a misdemeanor."

"Misdemeanor?"

"Low-ranked crime."

"I see. And how are these crimes punished?"

"Community service, usually. The government doesn't like jailing people because people started using jails as a way to get free board and meals, so they'd commit crimes to be imprisoned. It beat starving on the streets. Now the community service still comes bundled with lunch, and if homeless, they're sheltered. It's cheaper that way—and benefits the community."

"So thieves don't have their hand cut off?"

"No."

"Pity, that. It usually helped keep people from stealing."

"I understand what it's like to starve, and when you're starving, pilfering beats death. I just can't blame someone for stealing food to survive."

Eoghan made a thoughtful noise in his throat. "Have you stolen food?"

Being honest only hurt my pride, so I shrugged and replied, "No, but I've thought about it."

"That is something you will not have to worry about anymore."

"After we get a new phone for me, I plan on hitting a grocery store."

"Your refrigerator has been fully stocked. Gordon took care of that last night."

"But did he stock my refrigerator with honey rocks?"

"With what?"

"They're a type of melon, and I swore the next time I got extra money, I was buying them for myself." I marched to the doors, ignored the pink shine covering everything, and pushed my way inside. "If you think the mall is bad, wait until you see the grocery store."

"Should I be concerned?"

"Only if you get in the way of me buying my damned honey rocks."

"I'm concerned that you want to eat rocks."

"Melons, Eoghan! They're a melon."

"But what are melons?"

I stopped, turned, and faced him, my mouth dropping open. He'd never had a melon before? I would blitz through the mall, acquire what I needed in record time, and rectify the situation. "We are going grocery shopping when we are done here, and we will go to every fucking store in the city until I find honey rocks."

He smiled. "If that makes you happy."

"Fixing that travesty will make me happy," I muttered. I spun and pointed. "To the cell phone store!"

"We should also go to a proper computer store. I have been told a laptop is a good system for travel, but you deserve a desktop. We may also need to acquire you a desk while we are in the store."

Ugh. More shopping. With only a few hours before closing, we'd have to hurry—and then I'd have to settle with late-night grocers for melons. "You're going to need stuff, too."

"I have been told that."

With Lady Luck on my side, I could buy everything and haul it home without issue, and Eoghan could do the lifting so I wouldn't have to worry about hurting my arm. "All right. Phone first, and I'll look at tablets while I'm there. Tablets can be useful, and I've never been able to afford one."

"Then get a tablet. I'm certain I can afford it."

"You could afford to buy one of everything in this mall and not miss a cent."

"That seems wasteful."

"It would be."

"Let's not do that. I will insist you purchase the best phone you can. I have been told there are brand wars when it comes to these things, and that I should encourage you to buy the brand you lust for the most, and get the best one of that brand."

I needed to thank the CDC for giving him good advice. "I can do that."

I knew which brand I wanted, as I sometimes blew time shopping for things I couldn't afford during the down times at work. It would take me less than ten minutes to pick out my desktop, too. If I went for gold, I'd get a television, a gaming console, and a player so I could get all the movies I missed being unable to afford to go to the theater.

With my arm out of commission, I could blow through a lot of hours watching television.

As expected, the mall at night was a zoo, and an entire pack of lycanthropes in their wolf form took over the center food court along with a bunch of centaurs of varying species. Eoghan sucked in a breath, and his eyes widened. "Centaurs? What are those others with them?"

"Also centaurs." I nodded to the lion centaur who was lounging beside one of the wolves and taking a nap. "Centaurs indicate any quadruped species that blends animals and humans without the lycanthropy virus."

"Quadruped?"

"Four legs. Shapeshifters include anyone

who can transform from a human to an animal without the lycanthropy virus."

"This is like lycanthropy, then? It doesn't matter what they actually are, but because horses were the first, the whole species takes their name?"

"Yes. It simplifies things. How are we supposed to name every centaur species? There's a lot of them." After a quick count, I spotted seven different species of centaur loitering in the food court. "The food courts in the malls are favored gathering points." After pointing across the food court to one of the other wings, I picked my way through the crowd, careful to avoid stepping on any rogue tails. "If you want to see all the weird people of the world, you eat at the food court. Within an hour, you'll see a pretty good variety."

"This isn't a pretty good variety?"

I considered the gathering and shrugged. "This is just scratching the surface, I think."

"How curious. And sorcerers?"

"Sorcerers?"

"Users of arcane arts."

I frowned, stepping around a few more centaurs of the feline bent. "You're going to have to help me here. How do they do their magic?"

"Through spell books and spoken incantations and rituals."

"Those would probably be practitioners. You can't tell who those are from a glance. You'd have to see their driver's license. I'm not one, but anyone can learn to be one for the most part. Desperate vanillas will become practitioners to protect themselves if they're worried. I've thought about it, then I could justify that damned ping on the scanners."

"They are not evil in this era?"

"No. Why would they be? A lot of people pick up a few practitioner tricks. It's convenient when you can draw a rune on a piece of paper and have it glow in the dark, for example. There are rules about what sorts of tricks people should do. They're on the CDC's website. That doesn't stop people from experimenting with magic they shouldn't, but practitioners are practitioners. They have their purpose, I guess."

"Priests?"

"That I can't help you with. I generally avoid religion. An angel appearing on my doorstep is as close to religion as I get, and let's just say I'd rather skip that again. I'm pretty sure I'd rather deal with the devil after having an angel show up, but I might give his wife a call. She has to be an interesting woman."

A faint pop behind me and a faint hint of brimstone in the air froze me in place, and every hair on my arm stood upright.

When the angel had warned me that the devil sometimes listened in on people who said his name, I hadn't thought he'd been *serious*.

Eoghan turned. "Well, I'll be." The antique

whistled. "You're not anywhere near as horrific as depicted."

"Your people had overactive imaginations," a deep voice rumbled, and the stench of brimstone strengthened. "As for you, yes, I do have a rather annoying habit of listening in on people who invoke my name, especially when one of my brothers is involved. Which one was talking about me this time?"

"Dimitri," I answered, taking a deep breath before turning around to face the devil. The devil wore an Armani, gave the incubus a run for his money in the looks department, had skin paler than mine, and sported a pair of ram horns and flaming hair. "I thought you'd at least have a tan," I admitted.

"When I want to scare people, I go for the ebon look, but right now, I'd rather mesh. I like keeping people on their toes."

I pointed at his horns and flaming hair. "You're not going to be meshing with those."

Both the flames and the horns disappeared. "How right you are. Naughty horns, showing up. I even remembered to skip the hooves this time. And the wings. Nothing turns heads quite like wings. What brings you to the mall tonight?"

The devil wanted to know about my errands? "I need a phone, maybe a computer, and I was thinking about getting a television."

Something tickled the inside of my head, and I winced at the sensation. "And you have a good truck for taking it all home with you.

Excellent." The devil rubbed his hands together. "I'm in a mood tonight, so call me Lucy. It beats what my daughter has been flinging at me all day. I could use some sensible company, and it's not often I can take a night off."

Okay. The devil wanted sensible company. I looked around, wondering where the hell he was going to find sensible company in my neck of the woods. Shrugging, I gestured in the direction of the cellular service store that actually worked in Sunset somewhat reliably. "What can we do for you, Lucy?"

"It's less you and more your companion, Anwen. The dragons beat you awake, Eoghan."

Eoghan sighed. "They're probably the reason I'm awake."

"Oh, no. My daughter is why you're awake. I'd apologize for that, but I'm not at all sorry. It was either that or the beginning of the end. Well, that's mostly why you're awake. You were right about there being a node in the area, but it's not what you think. Alas, you'll just have to figure that part out. Mostly, you're here because we missed our date with the beginning of the end."

"Already?"

"We dodged it by a breath." The devil rolled his shoulders. "We did reach the trigger this time, but we stepped back from the point of no return."

Eoghan huffed. "Marvelous. And to think

I may have slept through it. Why are you here?"

"This is an era of new experiences. I'm experiencing something new. Some think you're the devil, and until now, they've never seen us together in the same room. Now Anwen can confirm she's seen you and the devil sharing the same space, and because we both like Anwen, we won't even try to kill each other."

"You truly believe you're funny, don't you?" Eoghan sighed. "Must you be here?"

"Old prejudices die hard, Anwen. You'll have your hands full trying to unteach those bad habits of his. In many of the eras he lived, I had such a foul reputation. Unearned, even. Do I look like I eat children to you?"

"It wouldn't surprise me," I replied, leading the way to the cell store serving Sunset. "I see you two know of each other."

"We are related closer than he might like," the devil announced in an amused tone. "I considered showing up earlier, but my daughter was right in the middle of her latest rant, and she absolutely hates when I ditch on her in the middle of her rants. She's a delight, and she hates when I enjoy when she's trying to put me in my place."

"Who would like something like that?" I asked.

"Me. I do. It makes life fun."

Eoghan sighed. "You must have a purpose coming here. What is it, Lucifer?"

"Lucy, please. It annoys my daughter when I embrace one of her wretched nicknames for me, and that one turns heads while making my wife laugh."

"Fine, Lucy. What do you want?"

"Can't I be a benevolent being because I want to?"

Wrinkling his nose, Eoghan kept close to my side while glaring at the devil. "No. You're Lucifer. You're the Lord of Lies. You are not benevolent."

"I'm misunderstood more than anything else. Just because I've disobeyed and do what I want doesn't mean I'm not benevolent. I'm disobedient. Those are two different things. Just because I'm the jail warden doesn't mean I belong in the jail. I am as much of a representation of divine failings as I am the black knight. I have done many a benevolent thing in my life. I will do many more. Perception matters. Absolute sins are a much different thing from perceived sins. For example, take young Anwen here. Should she decide to sleep with every man in the mall tonight, she would be deemed a sinner by the Christian pantheon. She would be praised in others. It would not earn her a place in my hells despite it being deemed a sin. No, my hells are reserved for the absolute sins. That is the point of forgiveness, after all. My hells are reserved for those who have sinned beyond the point of forgiveness. No amount of apologizing will absolve absolute sin. It is my job to safeguard the passage of those souls until they have paid the wages for their sins and have returned to the point of forgiveness."

"I got rejected by an incubus this morning, Lucy. There is zero chance I'm going to be sleeping with every man in the mall tonight. There's also a lot of men in the mall tonight I'm not even realistically compatible with."

"You'd just have to get creative."

"No."

"A pity. We could have made it a party. You could have started with your friend here, and once you tired him out, you could try out the other studs here. You would have had a great time."

"No," I repeated, and I kept marching for the phone store. "I'm curious about why you're really here, though."

"I'm being benevolent, and I'm bored. I hate being bored."

"You're not supposed to meddle," Eoghan grumbled.

"I'm a sinner, Eoghan. Were you really expecting me to do anything other than what I want? I obey the universal laws out of necessity, but that's as far as my tendency to be obedient goes. Of course, I limit my meddling somewhat. If she hadn't invoked my name, I wouldn't have popped on over for a chat. That's just a consequence of her talking about me. Had she not talked about me, I wouldn't be here right now. I'm not even cheating this time; I've no interest in looking into the future of this matter. I just wanted to see you face to face rather than walking in each other's shadow. This is an era of new experiences, and you would do well to remember that. This era is ripest for you."

"Humanity walks through the valley of the shadow of death."

Eoghan's reply startled me into stopping. "Why do you say that?"

He shrugged, and the devil grinned.

As the antique didn't want to talk to me, I focused on the Lord of Lies, wondering if he'd give me a straight answer or offer me a pile of falsehoods and trickery. "If you want an outing, just tell Eoghan what you want from him, then you can help me pick a phone. Until this morning, I was poor, and I just know which one looks prettiest. Now he's buying me things, and I'm trying to enjoy it while I can."

"You'll be able to enjoy that for a long while, so try not to worry about it much. There will be some hiccups. It's the hiccups I'm here to address. Eoghan, it would be in your best interest to locate the node here, make it yours, and hold it close. The one who killed your caretaker has interest in it, too. By locating it and possessing it, your quarry will come right to you. I recommend you begin your search at Anwen's former place of employment. There is much for you to learn there, and there are those who would benefit walking in your shadow."

Eoghan scowled. "Why would you say that?"

"The node you want is not the one making the dead restless, but the one making the dead restless infringes on your territory."

Eoghan cursed, and the words spilling out of his mouth made no sense to me, but there was something almost musical to the language he spoke.

"That is his mother tongue, Anwen. Beautiful, isn't it?"

"Very."

"His people were long gone before even the Babylonians built their towers and sought the world's knowledge. His language was long dead before Christianity's flame first sparked to life. I existed, of course—but I did not exist then as I do now."

Eoghan sighed. "She already knows I am old."

"Yes, but this will make her question just how old. That is what you want, isn't it? For her to become curious enough to seek out your secrets?"

I bit my finger so I wouldn't grin or laugh at Eoghan's disgruntled expression. As I suspected the devil might be listening to my every thought, I considered my fledgling plan to lure the antique to my bed and try to seduce answers out of him.

"That's a good thought, Anwen, but you'll find him terribly prudish about such things. He is stubborn, and you'll find that stubbornness will become a barrier. I'm sure you'll figure out how to get to him. There are options to make such a plan work, but you'll have to get creative. You can also choose to be more aggressive about it. That will win you the result you want, although you'll deal with a great deal of shock, which will interfere with your desired result."

Great. I'd gone from barely tolerating Eoghan's advances to having to bludgeon the man if I wanted to drag him to bed? Life truly wasn't fair.

"What are you talking about?" Eoghan demanded.

"Your prudish nature."

"My nature is not prudish."

"Your nature is most definitely prudish in modern society."

Enlightenment struck, and I pointed at Eoghan. "You came from a structured patriarchal society, and you probably did things like dowries and sold your daughters for cows!"

"I do not have any daughters, but I would not sell one for a mere *cow* even if I did have one. I would not sell her for several cows, either."

"In that regard, you'll be fine, Anwen. He is a most jealous specimen."

I rolled my eyes. "He's currently in love with my truck."

"This is true. I'm sure you'll be able to handle his affections for your truck. Now, about that phone. Why don't you allow me to help you with that matter? I have a most excellent plan, and it would be prudent if no one could bother you."

"No deals," Eoghan snapped.

"There's no deal. My daughter likes telling me I'm an entity of pure evil, so I feel this disgusting compulsion to do random nice things to annoy her. This will heavily annoy her, as she will not be able to comprehend the reasoning behind this act of kindness."

"But will your plan work in my town?"

"My plan works in all towns. If there's a cellular tower, it'll work. You'll like it. It comes with unlimited data, international calling, and it can even reach me in my hells should you have a reason to give me a ring. I'll even be nice and give you my wife's number."

"Your wife's number?" I asked.

"Darlene could use some mortal friends. She gets tired of putting rowdy devils in their place."

Okay. I could deal with being friends with the devil's wife. I could deal with being friends with an angel's wife, too. "If you don't think she'll mind."

"She'll do anything for a chance for those wretchedly sweet coffees she loves, but she rarely strays far from home without an excuse. I keep trying to tell her she can go create trouble whenever she wants, but then she tells me she has to keep *me* out of trouble. She's really not all that good at keeping me out of trouble, in case you were wondering."

"I really wasn't, but I'm not surprised. In the slightest."

Laughing, the devil grinned at Eoghan. "You should just surrender now."

"No one had warned me you enjoy spewing nonsense."

The devil shrugged. "I tried, Anwen."

He had, and that amazed me. "How do we pay you for the phone plan?"

"I'll have one of my minions get in contact with you after we go to the store and pick your phone. And best of all, you can replace your phone at any cellular store. For some reason, mortals try to avoid offending my delicate sensibilities. I'm not sure why," the Lord of Lies lied.

"Right. All right, Lucy. Let's go get your random act of kindness done so you can resume annoying your daughter. It just wouldn't do to annoy you, would it?" I shook my head at the insanity of it all and led the devil and the antique into a cell phone store, hoping for the best but expecting chaos and possibly some brimstone to go with it.

EIGHT

These are strange times.

THE DEVIL LACKED in common sense, and because he didn't like my cheap purse, he bought me a Prada. I regarded the red leather in confusion. As that wasn't enough for the Lord of Lies, he insisted on dragging us both into the computer store.

I did give him credit. The store employees scrambled whenever he made a request, and it took less than thirty minutes to acquire two desktops, two laptops, several tablets, four monitors, and a ridiculous number of cables. The math made no sense to me, but I kept my mouth closed.

Had I kept better control of my thoughts, the devil might have forgotten about the television, movie player, gaming console, and games.

To complicate matters, Eoghan and the devil argued about who would be paying the bill. The cashier grinned at the mayhem, and I wanted to climb behind the register and disappear.

"You two are worse than children," I muttered, and as I lacked self-preservation skills, I snatched the devil's credit card out of his hand and gave it to the cashier. "Use this one. It's a punishment for bad behavior in a public place."

Lucy frowned, staring at his empty hand. "Are you sure you're not already friends with my wife? She used that one on me last week. She also asked if I was raised in a barn. I thought that was particularly amusing."

"Were you?"

"Heaven, a barn... close enough."

The cashier swiped the devil's credit card, printed a receipt, and held it out along with a pen. "Sign here, please."

The devil signed. "Eoghan, I recommend you keep a close eye on your woman. She will take you for everything you own and then some if you let her. She is naturally versed in the art of cutting a deal—or making demands and expecting them to be fulfilled to her likings."

I rolled my eyes at that. "Or I just got tired of your shit and solved the problem."

"Same difference. Now, if you could bring your truck around, we can get this loaded and send you home. As I have been thoroughly amused this evening, I will work a little devilish magic to keep everything in the bed of your truck where it belongs for the trip home. The grocery store down the street is open and has what you want, so do make sure you swing by there on the way."

Honey rocks. Like a dog offered a steak, I drooled. I swallowed and failed to control the impulse to lick my lips.

The devil laughed at me, and as soon as he handed over the signed receipt, he waved me away. "Off you go. I'll guard your loot and have a chat with your antique."

Eoghan scowled. "I am not an antique."

"You're one of the oldest living things on this planet. You most certainly are an antique, and you're lucky that the lady here has no issues with age gaps, because the gap between you? It's utterly ridiculous. And I thought the gap between me and my wife redefined insane. But no, you're even worse."

That implied Eoghan had existed before even the devil, and I raised a brow at that. Before either could bring me into their posturing, I escaped, marching across the mall to retrieve my truck and bring it around the building to load everything into the back, questioning everything about my changed life. By the time I made it back, Eoghan glared at the devil and the devil smirked. As the store was still standing and none of the purchases seemed damaged, I decided to ignore them, lowering the tailgate and going for one of the lighter boxes so I could at least look like I was helping get everything loaded.

Once everything was in, the devil snapped

his fingers, and ribbons of blue fire lashed everything down. "Once you're home, just give the end a tug, and it'll come out. Don't worry. It'll only sting a lot, and it'll help your arm heal a little quicker, too. *He* hates when I use holy fire for frivolous things. This is about as frivolous as it gets."

With that, the devil vanished with a pop and a faint hint of brimstone.

"I told you the mall could get weird," I announced, getting into my truck and unlocking the door so Eoghan could join me. He did, and he buckled up as he'd been taught. "I was not expecting him to show up."

Lesson learned: I would not invoke the devil's name unless I could accept him showing up at his leisure.

"The world has changed."

Poor Eoghan. "I'm sure it has. But think about it this way. I just goosed the devil for thousands of dollars in really, really cool stuff, and after we go to the grocery store, we can haul it all into the house, set up the important things, and have dinner. I fully intend on having some pixie dust before bed, too. I need to get you a bed."

"I find your couch to be quite comfortable."

"Beds are much more comfortable than couches. You can afford a bed, and I have a room upstairs you can share with Gordon. I can also turn the basement into a bedroom, too. There's nothing down there, but we'll have to clean it somewhat." I checked the map for the location of the open grocery store, tapped on it, and had Lady Luck guide me to my honey rocks. While open, the grocery store parking lot was abandoned save for two other vehicles, and I parked near the front doors so I could run in. "We probably shouldn't leave the truck unattended."

"Lucifer warned me you would be worried, and he told me no one will notice anything in the truck."

Well, then. "Come on out, then, and I'll show you the grocery store. It can be another lesson about the modern world."

With a little luck, we wouldn't run into anything else crazy, but all bets were off in a world ruled by magic. Once, it had rained frogs because a gorgon passing through town had thought it was a good idea to try her hand at practitioner magic.

"Is it not just a type of market?"

"It is a type of market, but it won't be what you're expecting." I led him inside and headed for the fresh produce section. Sure enough, the devil had spoken the truth; honey rocks waited for me along with other types of cantaloupes, honey dews, and watermelons. I grabbed a cart, and I began the tedious process of checking for the best honey rocks. I picked four, thought about all the times I'd wanted one and couldn't have them, and got four more. I might turn into a honey rock, but I would regret nothing. I refused to regret anything.

Eight honey rocks would fall to my gluttony.

"What are these?" Eoghan asked, picking up one of the honey rocks I'd considered, which would hit the perfectly ripe phase in a day or two.

"These are honey rocks. These are the melons over all melons, the reason I would do my best to have the dead cooperate when they got up. Every time I had a little extra money, I would get one. That was rare. I will dine like a queen."

Eoghan gave the melon a cautious sniff. "And this tastes good?"

"I fucking love them."

Eoghan turned and put his in the cart. "You spent a long time considering this one, so you should get it, too."

"You're right. I should definitely get it. How does this compare to what you know?"

"This is very orderly, and there is no one watching for thieves. Why are there no guards?"

I pointed at the ceiling corners where the surveillance cameras watched over the store. "Those are cameras, and a store employee is monitoring everything. It's an honor system with some digital policing. Should someone be caught stealing, the police will be called."

According to the antique's expression, he likely believed the world had gone mad, and he wasn't wrong. While still staring at the camera, he picked up another honey rock and went to place it in the cart.

"You have to check if it's good first, Eoghan."

That drew his attention from the security camera, and he mimicked how I'd sniffed the melons. "What is it supposed to smell like?"

I picked up the best of my honey rocks and handed it to him. "Like this. Also look at where the stem used to grow. See what that looks like? See how the netting around the rind is nice and thick? These are the signs of a good honey rock."

Eoghan examined the one in his hands, wrinkled his nose, and after some thought, he put it back and then sorted through the others until he found one matching my ripe one. "Like this?"

"Like that," I confirmed.

He added it to the cart with the others. "What else should we acquire?"

"Chocolate pudding."

Eoghan laughed.

WE BOUGHT HALF the grocery store thanks to Eoghan's curiosity, although I'd managed to mostly steer him to the shelf-stable sections. I'd need another refrigerator and freezer if I allowed him to get everything that caught his interest. I got my chocolate pudding, instant mashed potatoes because he couldn't believe a foil packet could contain what started out as a round potato, a bag of potatoes because potatoes made his world go round, carrots because I wasn't having potatoes without them and they weren't the right color according to him and couldn't actually be a carrot, canned foods of too many types because cans intrigued him, coffee, and tea.

Then when he sighed over the utter lack of mead to be found, I made one final pit stop to the last open liquor store in the area. Mead wasn't common, but the place had a few bottles, and I got that for him along with some ales and wines, as those were what he knew.

I expected he'd get an unpleasant surprise when he tasted them, as I doubted our current alcohols came anywhere near to what he'd drunk so many years ago.

Hopefully, he wouldn't prove to be a drunk, but I'd find out soon enough.

Gordon waited on the front step when we got back, and his mouth dropped open at my truck. "What is that?"

I hopped out of the cab and gave the hood of my baby a fond pat. "This is Lady Luck, and she's my truck. I bought her with Eoghan's money, but I'll repay him for her eventually."

"You will not," the antique replied, and he got out of my truck. "The fault is with me, as I stared longer than is polite, which she rightfully interpreted as my interest in this truck.

She growls, and she roars. I've been told there are horses under the hood. Several hundred of them. They're not literal horses, which is a pity. We have made purchases. Would you help us move them into the house, please?"

As instructed by the devil, I grabbed the end of the flaming rope lashing everything down and gave a tug. It stung, but it unraveled, bathing my hands in blue light before vanishing. I lowered the tailgate and scratched my head, wondering how we'd get everything out without breaking anything.

Gordon joined me, and he whistled. "I see you were not exaggerating."

"Almost everything is fragile," I warned.

"Then I will carry it with upmost care." The vampire grabbed the television's box, pulled it to him, and lifted it as though it weighed nothing rather than its awkward hundred pounds. He marched to the front door, and Eoghan opened it, allowing the vampire to head inside.

That simplified things. I grabbed the first bag of groceries from the cab and began ferrying everything to the kitchen while I let the men handle the electronics. Within thirty minutes, my living room had everything needed to become an entertainment lover's dream come true, I had a desktop computer on my desk in the bedroom, and I'd have enough toys to keep three adults amused for possibly all of eternity.

Huh. Who knew almost dying could bring such good fortune?

Well, mostly. I had a devil problem on my hands, an incubus who wanted me to be friends with his wife, and an antique I'd have to figure out if I wanted to keep around for life or seduce before I died of old age—a real enough risk if I believed the devil.

Strangely enough, I did.

Huh. The Lord of Lies came across as a disgustingly honest fellow.

Once everything was inside and I locked Lady Luck, I grabbed the ripest honey rock, got out my cutting board, and cut it in half to reveal its delicious flesh. I scooped out the seeds, put them in a baggie, and put them on the counter in the slim chance I could somehow make them grow in my yard. Then, as I was not a complete monster, I shared with Gordon and Eoghan, who followed me around like a pair of sad, lost puppies.

"This is a honey rock. Just a taste for you, Gordon, since I don't want to make you sick. It's not blood, so it's not good for you."

"You say that as though you mean well by me, but in reality, you say that so you have more for yourself," the vampire teased.

"You're absolutely fucking correct." I gave him a thin slice, and as I liked Eoghan but not enough to give him an entire half a honey rock, I gave him a quarter served in narrow slices. If he behaved, I would even consider cracking open a second one for him. "You're getting this much because it gives me an excuse to make more if you like it."

"Clever," Eoghan replied, accepting my offering and sitting at the table. "How does one eat this?"

I grabbed one of my slices and chomped on it, closing my eyes at its sweet juices, which dripped down my chin and all over my plate. I'd lick the plate after, as I couldn't waste even a drop of my delicious treat. I chomped to the rind, nibbled as much as the good flesh from my slice as I could, discarded the unwanted bits, and snatched my next piece. "Like that."

If they wanted more instruction, they'd have to ask after I finished stuffing myself with my precious honey rock.

"It is much like watching a starved wolf fall upon a doe with a broken leg. Quick, brutal, and efficient, partnered with a determination to prevent other scavengers from partaking of her prize." Eoghan took a bite of his, his expression thoughtful. "For all the times have changed and this era is not like my past, it seems women still love sweet things."

Damn straight I loved sweet things. Another slice fell prey to my appetite. "I have many honey rocks to eat in several days. You might be able to convince me to eat other food, but you would need to give me a damned good reason."

Gordon laughed and tried his, and the vampire ate his entire slice before setting his rind aside. "That is good, and I can see why you would buy so many. I do have to admit, when I saw you bring them in, I wondered why such an obsession with cantaloupes."

"These are honey rocks, and they transcend all other melons."

"It is clear these are your obsession. Can you get them all of the time?" Eoghan asked, and unlike me, he took his time with his share of my melon.

I devoured another slice, as the only way I could ensure its safety was to consume it immediately. "Mostly. Honey rocks are a type of musk melon, a fancier relative of the standard cantaloupe, which are usually available. These are usually called a cantaloupe despite not really being one. I like honey rocks better than cantaloupe because they're sweeter and more delicate in flavor. I'm going to try to grow some myself."

When working at the funeral home, I'd been too tired, stressed, and poor to even think about trying to turn my yard into a viable garden.

"Ah, planting is something I have skills at. I can help you."

I stared at Eoghan with wide eyes. "We're going to have to make a trip to the hardware store this weekend, as I have no supplies. But I would love to have a garden in the back."

"That is because you are wise, and having a garden means you have a supply of your own food. I remember those days well.

Starving is not something someone forgets, even with time. Or they shouldn't. It is a good motivation to never return to those days."

I nodded, grabbed another slice, and went to work getting it into my stomach where it belonged.

"Try not to make yourself sick. I, too, remember that."

"I have a difficult time imagining you starving," Gordon admitted.

"We all start from nothing, even the most powerful of beings and immortals. Even Christianity's God is a being of creation, birthed by the universe in answer to a prayer."

Christians wouldn't like hearing that bit of lore. "But don't Christians believe that he is the creator?"

"Many people who believe the same incorrect thing are still incorrect, no matter how badly they wish for it to be true. Christianity's God is a constant, but not in the way you might believe. For as long as there are people, there will be people who will believe in such an entity. The same applies to that one, too."

I snickered at Eoghan's refusal to invoke the devil's name. "No kidding. But don't the legends claim they'll be the first reborn after the end times?"

"Those two seeds, in particular, will be preserved. That is a gift of life itself. But there are others, and there will always be others.

They just take forms you may not expect. I don't know all of Earth's secrets, and truth be told, I don't want to learn them all. Right now, my aspirations involve protecting you and dealing with that director. I suspect he wants the node—or nodes, if rumor is to be believed. If there are multiple nodes here, it could be a problem. Nodes can conflict."

"What do you mean by conflict?"

Gordon winced. "Should two nodes conflict, the reaction between them can become violent. I was created due to the clashing of two nodes."

Sighing, Eoghan set aside his finished rind and picked up a new piece, taking a bite before saying, "Nodes conflict often at the beginning of an emergence. Magic surges into the world, and when it does, those sleeping nodes flare to life. Should two nodes be too close together, they go into a state of flux. This can create strong surges of magic, destruction, and general chaos. Should there be two nodes, we will need to be careful about relocating one to a safe distance. Anything can happen when nodes clash. Gordon's existence as this emergence's firstborn vampire is a prime example."

"Which is why you survived being hacked apart, Gordon?"

"I wasn't awake when I was hacked apart, much to my relief. I was staked first."

Ew. "How'd you survive being staked?"

Eoghan laughed. "Staking is an ineffective

method of killing a vampire. That's superstitious nonsense meant to make people feel safer at night when a vampire hunts. Stakes mostly amuse vampires, especially the stronger ones. It would take a great deal to kill an emergence's firstborn vampire. Every era has creatures like that. Every era I have witnessed has birthed at least a few new ones. Gordon should, like the other firstborn before him, survive from emergence to emergence, although I expect he will slumber between them much as I do. There are some who do not rest. I pity them."

I found that hard to believe. "Why do you pity them?"

"Time is not kind to those who have seen a great deal of it. Our new friend is likely as he is because he has experienced so much time. He never rests, unlike Christianity's God, who changes over time. *He* isn't a true immortal, and when *He* dies, some new mortal takes over. It's always interesting when this happens as a public event. I've witnessed it twice. Unfortunately, I'm the only one to live to tell such tales; at the moment of rebirth, *He* is visible in *His* full glory. Humans perish. As I'm not human, I didn't perish, but I left with a greater understanding than I liked of the balance in the universe, which is strongly represented by those within Christianity. I wouldn't go so far as to say their way is the right way, but it is representative of the universe, which is why the prophecies of their religion tend to hold great sway."

"This is complicated," I complained.

"Things worth knowing usually are. That leaves us with the matter of this director. He will be a risk to you. He likely believes he is a risk to me, but I know much he does not. You, however, are a much easier target. I still do not know what his true intentions were locking you in that cellar with me upon my awakening, but it was for no good purpose."

"He probably thought you were like the vampire and needed to feed when you got up. That's what we all believed," I admitted. "All we knew was that the funeral home was being paid a sum yearly to keep you on ice. The CDC invoked an operational clause to keep you there, Gordon. I never found out why our funeral home was picked."

"This is a remote place, and should I have awoken in a foul mood, there would have been fewer victims," the vampire replied. "The CDC told me why I had been kept there. It had been their recommendation to keep me in pieces as well, as that does make it difficult to rise unattended."

"Difficult or impossible?"

"Difficult. In time, I would have awoken, I suspect. And I would have awoken rather upset over the circumstances."

"My method was the safest for all involved, and it helped you have such an amicable relationship with death."

I considered the antique's words, narrowing my eyes and enjoying another slice of my honey rock. It occurred to me my arm no longer hurt, and I broke all the rules and peeled off the bandages to check on the stitches.

The stitches flickered with blue flames, but beyond a few red marks where the threads remained embedded in my skin, all evidence of Gordon's bites were gone. "Now *that* is cool." I held out my arm to Gordon. "You have super teeth and sharp, pointy claws. Can you remove those stitches? I don't need them anymore."

Gordon examined my arm, made a soft noise in his throat, and checked my kitchen drawers until he found a pair of scissors, which he used to cut the stitches and pick them out. Removing them stung, but the blue fire jumped from the material to my skin and sealed the holes with a soothing warmth. "Who did this to you?"

"If we say his name he might show up," I whispered, rubbing my arm where the vampire had bitten me. "I don't know if I can deal with him showing up again tonight. Him showing up the first time rattled my nerves enough."

"One of the fallen ones with a certain notoriety made an appearance after Anwen invoked his name at the mall. He went shopping with us, and he annoyed her so much she spent his money numerous times. It was a most amusing manipulation. I am still uncertain why he wished to show you favor, but you enjoyed yourself despite his presence, and I find he was strangely tolerable for what he is."

Gordon sucked in a breath. "How notorious are we discussing here?"

"There are none more notorious than the one we discuss."

"You met that one at the mall?"

I nodded, grabbing my next honey rock victim and chomping on it. "Poof! He just showed up. Don't say his name unless you don't mind him making an appearance. I had no idea that bit of lore was true—or why he'd care. He wants me to call his wife. Her name is Darlene."

"This era is stranger than most," Eoghan muttered, and he consoled himself with another piece of melon.

I considered my remaining slices, and as he'd had a long day, I transferred one to his plate. "But now we have a television, gaming consoles, games, enough controllers for all three of us, and computers. Maybe he just wants us to be happy."

That anyone wanted me to be happy might break me, but I'd keep my confused tears to myself, contained in the privacy and comfort of my bedroom.

"These are strange times," Eoghan muttered.

That they were.

NINE

Ain't nobody dumb enough to keep
a dog that ugly around here.

I GORGED myself into a comatose state on
four honey rocks and a bowl of leftover stew.
At Eoghan's insistence, I took all of my med-
ication, which resulted in me heading to bed
as quite possibly the happiest woman alive.

A full stomach, no pain, and a general
sense of security made all the difference in
the world for me. Tomorrow, I'd look into
getting furniture for the antique and the
vampire, and I'd make my home into their
home, too.

Having their own rooms and comfortable
things they could call their own would make
it harder for them to leave, and I found I enjoyed their company.

I went to sleep with a contented heart,
and I woke ready to take on the world. I
bounced downstairs in my pajamas to find
Gordon completely covered with the blanket
on the couch. I frowned at the gap in the curtains, which I grabbed to close to prevent the

sun from reaching the vampire. Something dark sat on my front steps, and I frowned, blinked, and did a double take.

A big, black dog with baleful eyes sat on my front steps and guarded my lawn.

Huh. Sane people would worry over having a mean-looking dog on their front step. Me? I drew the curtains, made sure no sunlight could get through, and went to my front door to introduce myself to the puppy capable of ripping my face off if he decided he didn't like me.

Well, I supposed he could be a she, but until I identified the dogs gender, he was a he, and that was that.

I cracked open the door, and the dog flicked one of its half-flopped ears in my direction. Old scars marred the animal's nose, and I pegged him as a stray. "Hey, baby."

The baby woofed at me, and he lifted a paw as though to shake with me.

Okay. I could work with that. If I contracted rabies, I'd go see someone at the CDC and get treatments. I stepped outside, crouched, and put my hand out for the puppy to shake with me. He placed his paw on my palm, and I shook with him. "Good baby. What are you doing out here? The neighbors don't like strays, so you're just going to have to come inside and become my pet."

The dog flicked an ear back, but as he otherwise didn't show any signs of aggression, I released his paw and held my hand closer to his nose so he could sniff. He did, and when that went well, I scratched behind his ears and praised him for being a good boy.

Then I opened the door to see if I could lure my new pet inside.

My new pet did not seem inclined to enter my house.

"It's nicer in the house, and I'll give you a nice bath, clean your fur, and transform you into a prince."

"What are you doing, Anwen?" Gordon asked.

"There's a puppy on the steps. I'm trying to adopt him. He looks like an older dog, and he could use a few good meals. The assholes down the street shoot strays."

"How uncouth."

"You stole that from Eoghan, didn't you?"

"It seems I have. This dog is friendly?"

"He offered his paw to shake, and he let me pet him. He could use a bath. He's a little dirty." By a little, on second look, I really meant a lot. "I've never had a dog before. I couldn't afford one, and I promised I'd never get an animal I couldn't afford. It's not fair to the dog. But I love dogs, Gordon."

"Could the dog not be someone's pet?"

I didn't like the idea of my new dog being someone's pet. "I've never seen him around town before."

"Why don't you bring him in, give him a bath, and then start looking around to see if someone from a nearby town lost their dog. That's the polite thing to do."

"But I don't want to be polite. I want a dog."

"You can get a dog after this one is returned to his owners, should he have owners."

I considered that. "Okay, I suppose that's fair. But I should take him to the vet for a checkup."

"You may not need to if you find his owner quickly."

While that was true, I scowled at the interference in my plan to have a dog. "But what if he's sick?"

Gordon got off the couch, stayed out of the direct sunlight, and eyed the dog. "He looks healthy enough to me. I'm sure he'll be fine. Do you even have anything you need to care for a dog?"

"No, but I have a truck. Using my truck, I can get everything I need to care for a dog."

"I see you were quite serious about your love of dogs."

I nodded, and I scratched the stray behind his ears. "I have a back yard. He might be happy back there."

"He might be happy digging up the melons you want to plant, too."

I frowned at that. "He can live in the house, too. I do not mind walking a dog, especially if he's mine."

"Why don't you try finding his owner first

before you decide you own him. Someone might be missing their dog."

I heaved a sigh. "Fine, I'll go check if there's a listing for a missing dog like him. But if I don't find one, I'm taking my truck, I'm buying supplies, and I'm going to lure my new dog into the house and keep him."

Gordon sighed and returned to the couch. "Whatever makes you happy, Anwen."

"Not having to look for his owner would make me happy!"

The vampire laughed. "You'll live."

"Maybe I'll live, but maybe I'll perish from a broken heart from not being able to keep such a cute dog."

"He's uglier than hell, Anwen. He looks like he got into a knife fight and barely escaped with his life. He is not precisely cute."

"But look at his ears."

"They are ears. What is special about them?"

I gestured to the dog and his scarred face and ears. "They're floppyish."

"Floppyish?"

"A little floppy but not all the way floppy. They're adorable."

"Are you sure you slept well enough last night? He is a very ugly dog."

"I slept fine. I just really like dogs." I attempted to coax the dog into the house again, and the animal ignored me, remaining on my front step and keeping a close eye on the lawn. Sighing, I debated leaving the door open so the pooch could invite himself in, but I opted against it.

Bugs would accept the invitation before the dog would, and I didn't need an insect infestation to go with my other problems. My problems had improved somewhat, however. My arm no longer counted as a problem, and I'd have to thank the devil for that somehow.

I'd probably call his wife and thank him that way. A happy wife meant a happy husband, or so 'they' said.

Closing the door, I retrieved my new laptop, booted it up, used my new phone as my internet connection, and began a tedious search for my dog's owner—if he had an owner.

Sometimes, doing the right thing sucked, but in any case, I'd do my best to make sure the dog had a good home.

AFTER SEVERAL HOURS of searching every dog rescue, shelter, and listing for missing dogs, I came to the conclusion everyone took close care of their big, black dogs that weren't labradors. In a fifty mile radius, I couldn't find a single missing dog listing matching my pup's description. When I went to check on the dog, he'd moved off my front steps to lounge on the grass.

"Gordon, I'm going to get a bag of dog food and some bowls. Even if he won't come into the house, I want to feed him. I haven't found anything yet. I'll probably run some errands while I'm out, so I'll be a few hours."

The vampire grunted at me, which I assumed meant he wouldn't remember a damned thing come nightfall, as I rarely did when somebody bothered me while I was sleeping. I wrote a note, left it on the coffee table, and grabbed my keys, new purse, and everything else I might need for an adventure into town.

It occurred to me if I headed a few miles down the road, I could go to the bookstore, get a few novels, and start a library of my own. I'd repay Eoghan for using his account with interest after I got my first check.

I stopped long enough to pet the dog before climbing into the cab of the truck and starting the engine, grinning at the rumble. Yep, maybe Lady Luck had seduced Eoghan first, but she made my greedy little heart happy, too.

After I plugged the address in for the bookstore into the navigation system, I backed the truck out of my driveway, keeping a careful eye on the dog so I wouldn't hit him if he decided to play a game of chase my truck.

He stayed put, yawning and showing off his teeth before resting his head on his paws to take a nap on the grass.

I'd have to get him some bones to chew on, too. A collar went onto my mental list, one with my address on it, which might deter the asshole neighbors from taking pot shots at the stray.

One trip to the bookstore, a pet store, and a furniture store later, and I had everything needed to turn my house into a home for three, enough material to teach Eoghan how to read English, a dog bed, bowls, treats, food, a collar, and a leash. I needed to hit another store for bookcases, but I'd do that after I got everything else home.

The dog had moved to my front step again, and one of my crankier neighbors stood at the end of my driveway, eyeing the animal with a scowl fixed in place. Given a single excuse, Jeff Henrys would get his shotgun and put an end to the stray, which meant I'd have to take steps.

Step one involved pulling up in the driveway and letting the engine growl at the old coot. "Hurt that dog, and the cops get your name," I warned, parking and climbing out without any care if I banged the bastard with the door. He wisely got out of my way. I snagged the bag with the collar, new tags, and leash. Without bothering to wait for Jeff's reply, I went to my porch, crouched in front of the dog, and slipped the bright red leather around his neck, buckling it into the place. "There you go, buddy. Now if you get lost, somebody can give me a call."

I scratched him behind his ears.

The front door opened, and while careful

to avoid the sunlight, Gordon poked his head outside. "He's been staring at the dog for the past hour, grumbling to himself. He doesn't seem like he's willing to step onto your property much."

"That's because I'm an asshole, and he knows the people who own the house, and they're bigger assholes than I am."

"That your dog, Anwen?" Jeff asked.

"He's a stray I'm adopting, so as of now, yes, he is. I've looked high and low for his owner, and there ain't anyone missing a dog like him around here."

"Ain't nobody dumb enough to keep a dog that ugly around here."

I snorted at that. "Except me, so don't you be calling my dog ugly, Henrys. I've a mind to teach him to guard the place, and I've also a mind to teach him you're bad news. And don't you think I won't be calling the cops and demanding an angel if you think you can come shoot my dog when I'm not looking."

"That's not neighborly of you."

"Neither is shooting my dog."

He narrowed his eyes. "I reckon you're right on that. You try to keep that dog where he belongs, then."

"Or just give me a call if he shows up. He's got a lot of learning to do, and I'd rather there be no misunderstandings. I'll make the whole damned town answer to an angel if somebody hurts him."

I supposed my open aggression on the

matter startled him almost as much as it startled me. I'd spent the last few years of my life keeping my head down to avoid being the talk of the town.

"Fair enough. You've got men around. Who are they?"

"One is my new boss, who is new to town and needs a place for a while. The other is a vampire I'm keeping an eye on for the CDC. I get better pay and company this way."

Jeff relaxed, and he grunted. "Mind if I come say hi to your mutt?"

To be safe rather than sorry, I clipped the leash to my pup's collar. "Come on up. This is Gordon. He's the vampire. If you're looking for some cash and pass the tests, the CDC might want a few extra donors. Eoghan, my new boss, is out right now, but I'm sure you'll see him around."

Chances for extra cash came few and far between, and the old man's eyes lit up. "I'm fitter than a fiddle, you know."

Yeah, I knew. He was also a rat bastard and liked to cause trouble anywhere he could for the fun of it. "You sure are."

He came up on the porch, and the dog flicked an ear back but otherwise behaved. "You sure you want to keep this mutt, Anwen? He's got mean eyes."

"He's nice to me, and I don't really much care if he's mean to people who shouldn't be at my house. Sounds like he'll make a good guard dog once I teach him where the property lines are and train him to stay where he belongs."

"Fair." Jeff crouched, and because he was as stupid as he was annoying, he held his hand out to the dog. The dog turned his head and refused to sniff his fingers. "I reckon he don't like me much."

"Well, you were probably standing over there debating if you wanted to shoot him while he was on my porch. Dogs aren't stupid."

"Right. I won't cause any trouble, and I'll spread the word to leave your mutt alone. Just try to keep him to your yard where he belongs."

"I'll do that."

"Those men will be sticking around?"

"For a while. My boss is looking into business opportunities in this area." While not necessarily the truth, it wasn't a lie, either. Business opportunities meant new jobs, and nobody wanted to annoy someone who might bring new jobs into the area.

"What about those winged folk who came around?"

"They were asking questions about the funeral home."

"Ah. McGregor. Right pity about him."

The dog turned his ears back, and I didn't need angelic abilities to recognize the bastard lied. "Just don't let him hear you saying anything like that. As far as I know, they haven't gotten him to go back to his grave where he belongs yet, not with everything going on."

Jeff grimaced at that. "That just ain't right, Anwen."

"Respect the dead, and you won't have to worry about it, now will you? And if you hear anything suspicious, you do the right thing and tell the cops about it."

"Suspicious?"

Sometimes, staring at the local idiots and waiting got the results I wanted, and it didn't take long for Jeff to clue in what I meant.

"Look, just because most of us didn't like the old bastard..."

I kept staring.

"Now, you look here, missy."

"I have an angel's phone number, Jeff. And should I find there's been suspicious things goin' on round here that cost that poor old man his life, I'll call. I don't really give a damn if you didn't like him. I don't like you much right now for looking at my dog the way you did, and you don't see me going out of my way to get you off my lawn, now do you? I don't care if people didn't like him. If you've heard something suspicious, maybe you should let somebody know, because that just ain't right."

"His wife got tired of him, and she bought a bottle of the stuff he likes best and put it out of reach, and he liked his liquor enough he took the bait and paid for it. Maybe if he hadn't been such a drunk, he'd be alive right now."

Poor Old Man McGregor. "That wasn't too hard, now was it? Everyone in town know about this?"

"Exceptin' a few, we know."

"Do the right thing, Jeff. And that don't mean toss McGregor under a bus because nobody liked him all that much. Sure, he was an annoying old man, but he was nicer than most around here."

"Pardon?"

"You heard me. From where I've been sitting, he's been nicer to me than most of the rest of you combined, so don't make me go do the right thing when you all should have been better. And I don't need a high school diploma to have a sense of decency. And maybe if you all had a sense of decency, well, maybe I'd have a high school diploma right now, but that's how towns like this are. You all are good at pretending, though, I'll give you that."

"Pretending?"

"Looking the other way when my folks come around and try to take me for even more money I don't have, screaming at my door, and making themselves the talk of the town as usual."

"Looks like those men helped you grow a spine," Jeff replied with a raised brow.

"No, sir. She had the spine all along. She's just stopped caring what you'll think about her because she valued her previous job. She's under no such restrictions now." Gordon smiled, and he showed off his pointed incisors. "Should you see Director Hammel around, do give the police a call. He's got a great deal of explaining to do."

"What's he done now, anyway?"

"Killed a good man and ushered others to their graves as well." The vampire crouched in the doorway and rested his hand on the stray's back. "Don't trust that one. He's a snake in a man's clothing."

"Not a wolf?" Jeff asked.

"I'd trust a wolf long before I trusted Director Hammel, and I recommend you adopt the same beliefs." Gordon rose and retreated into the house. "Have you finished your errands for today, Anwen?"

"Not quite. I have one more outing to do, but then I'll be done."

Jeff checked his watch. "Then you best be going, Anwen. Stores close soon."

Our stores did, but I'd have to drive thirty minutes out to get the bookcases I wanted. "Thanks."

To make it clear I wouldn't be scared off by an old man with an attitude, I unclipped the dog's leash and began ferrying my new pet supplies into the house. I put a bowl of food and water on the top step for him along with the bed, which barely fit beneath the tiny porch's overhang. I'd have to step over the bed to get into the house, but some prices were worth paying.

The stray wasted no time eating his lunch, and satisfied with my good deed of the day, I left on my last errand.

TEN

The world was a weird place.

SOMETIME AFTER BUYING bookcases and loading my truck with my new prizes, I learned the hard way that solid objects and my head didn't mix. Had I been given a choice in the matter, I would have just gone home. The company sucked, my stomach churned, and I put some serious thought into throwing up on Director Hammel's shoes. He hated even the slightest scuff on his perfect, polished shoes.

Asshole.

The basement, or whatever other concrete, unfurnished hellhole he'd brought me to, was in dire need of some renovations, a dusting, and mold removal. Worse, it reeked, and I didn't want to know what I was smelling.

I doubted a shower would remove the creepy-crawly sensation on my skin. A long soak in bleach might help.

"You could have called," I complained.

"And lead the police directly to me? Non-sense. I was generous and had an associate tip off the police about your disappearance. Un-fortunately, the kidnapper, some fool I hired, has already reached his expiration date, which will lead anyone checking into your disappearance to a chain of dead ends." The asshole nudged me with his pristine shoe. "You have created a great deal of trouble for me. While I was tempted to kill you outright, you have information I can use—and you'll be useful for the next stage of my operation."

"I have information you can use?" While sitting up hurt and made my stomach churn more, I swallowed to keep the nausea con-trolled. When I threw up, it'd be on my terms, damn it—and on his perfect shoes. "You want to know about the vampire? I guess you al-ready knew about the body, since you prob-ably put him there."

"That was an unfortunate mistake, as I've since determined. I assumed the sacrifice needed to be sacrificed to wake the sleeper in my care."

"Yeah, that didn't work too well for you."

"I need to know everything about him. Should you cooperate, I will allow you to live and dump you somewhere remote once my work is done. By the time you find your way back to civilization, I'll be long gone, and I won't care what you tell them."

"You had someone hit me in the back of the head and dragged me off so you could ask me a few questions about the arrogant asshole?"

"Do you refer to the sleeper or the vampire?"

"The sleeper, unless you had someone else in the basement other than that poor bastard you'd murdered in the formaldehyde drum. Did you really have to stuff him in there? He's an arrogant asshole. All bark and no bite, but the CDC gave me to him as a gift so he could figure out modern times." I'd give Director Hammel just enough information he thought I was telling him the truth in order to preserve my life, and I'd sprinkle as many lies in as possible to make certain he fucked up and ruined whatever plan he meant to implement.

I was tired of people stepping on me.

Director Hammel hadn't tied me up, a foolish oversight on his part. I rubbed the back of my head, which hurt enough my eyes watered. If I played weak and sickly, perhaps he'd keep me untied, which would elevate my chances of escape. Magic would have been useful, and I cursed myself for my failure to learn basic practitioner tricks. I could have drawn the runes in blood if needed. "Why did you stuff that poor man in the drum, anyway?"

My bastard of an ex-boss regarded me through narrowed eyes, and after a few moments of thought, he shrugged. "My plans changed when the sleeper didn't awaken as planned. I needed to erase the evidence, and

82

you were the cheapest life I had available at the time. I would have implicated the sacrifice in a theft of the equipment in the basement, and you would have been an unfortunate tragedy when the drum spilled. As he'd initially died from formaldehyde poisoning and preservation had begun immediately, it would have been easier to mask his actual time of death. Storing him in the drum was a matter of convenience."

Well, I gave Director Hammel some credit; assuming he hadn't waited too long between killing the poor man and sending me into the basement, the plan might've fooled an inexperienced forensics investigator. I doubted it would have tricked an experienced one—or anyone suspecting foul play.

Considering the CDC understood exactly how we operated, I found it implausible that any experienced investigator would have bought the ploy as the reality of the situation.

Industrial sized drums of formaldehyde didn't just tip over even in an accident. They weighed too much. The amount of force required to knock one over should give any experienced investigator pause.

The plan might fool the ignorant who'd never worked in a funeral home before, and it might've fooled me, as I had no idea what formaldehyde truly did to a person after death, if the chemical would slow or completely halt putrefaction and the immediate biological process that occurred following death, or if magic could be used to isolate the actual time of death despite the use of the preservative. Even then, I would've found the whole thing to be suspicious, especially considering the drum's weight. "I see."

"Did the sleeper give you his name?"

I disliked I'd have to tell the bastard anything, but if I played at cooperating, I might not be the next poor bastard dumped into a drum of formaldehyde. "Yes, I know his name. It's Eoghan Olin. According to him, he wakes up sometime during each emergence, and he gets really cranky when anyone screams. His initial reaction is to silence whomever is screaming. I've been told I'm fortunate he didn't silence me permanently." That bit fell into the lie category, but it sounded authentic enough to my ears. "I don't know how old he is, but he's been awake at least three emergences. The CDC is interested in him for research purposes, but beyond that, I have no real idea how far their interest goes. I was hired to teach him the ropes about modern society until he decides he gets bored and goes back to sleep, I guess."

"What is the likelihood he will return to his slumber? Do you think he could be reawakened should he slumber?" Something about the director's voice changed that caught my attention. "Has he mentioned anything about the dead to you?"

I grimaced at his questions, and I hoped he interpreted that as my general dislike of my situation. "Right now? He's probably investigating every grocery store in the state. He finds them fascinating, and he has a tendency to want to explore everything." Well, for at least the first five minutes, after which he would go find something else to investigate. "He does exactly what he wants, how he wants. It's annoying."

With a little luck, he'd believe my grimace was tied to a deep-set dislike of Eoghan, the biggest lie I'd told yet.

Apparently, either my ex-boss believed I was the type to resent someone like Eoghan, or I lied better than I thought, but Director Hammel considered my words, and after a long moment, he nodded. "How easy is it to break into your house at the moment?"

The change of subject startled me. "My house?"

"If that is where he is staying, that is the easiest place to capture him."

Ah. Right. Of course. If the director didn't mind killing people and using them as alibis to cover his activities, breaking into my home wouldn't bother him at all. "The neighbors get mad and they all have guns, the dog's an angel but will wake the neighborhood, and there's a vampire who doesn't have any need to sleep during the day around." I had no idea if the stray was angelic, noisy, or aggressive, but maybe my lies would protect him. I had a good lock on my door thanks to my asshole parents, and it was made of nice painted steel.

The windows would put up a decent fight unless they broke them, too. "It's a pretty safe house."

"Which neighbors would I have to worry about the most?"

I rolled my eyes. "All of them. Jeff Henrys lives across the street, and he don't take kindly to that sort of thing."

Even Director Hammel had the sense to be cautious when it came to the old coot and his gun collection. "So taking him at your house is likely not a wise idea."

"No, it really wouldn't be, and I haven't been around him long enough to figure out his habits."

"What habits does he have? Is he an early riser? What does he eat? Has he shown you any of his magic?"

Well, I could figure out what he'd do the instant he got word I'd been kidnapped; he'd set about paying Director Hammel a visit, and it would be a bloodbath, one Gordon would likely participate in. I'd help with the bloodbath part of things if opportunity allowed. I took a look around the moldy basement, lit by an old oil lamp. A crumbling stone staircase led up to a landing overhead. "Where are we, anyway?"

"This is the central mausoleum in the cemetery. I moved the previous resident so I could make better use of the building. This is the deepest wing. It's interesting, isn't it? It was built right after the beginning of this emergence, when the owners of these plots worried the dead would rise. Some dead did rise—but not in the way anyone anticipated. We expected something like a zombie."

Director Hammel didn't seem old enough to have been around when the emergence happened. "You were around during the emergence?"

"I look younger than I am. A consequence of magic. But yes, I was. I was young, though. I made it my goal to own this cemetery and the funeral home so I would have access to all of the vaults and their secrets. This is the important mausoleum, though. More importantly, the residents are important."

"Except you moved them," I muttered.

He laughed at me. "I moved them up a floor. They'll be fine. I'll put them back after my work here is done. You were always overly concerned about the departed. They're dead. They don't care what happens to their body. Now, about this Eoghan Olin. Tell me about his habits."

In retrospect, I supposed I had cared a lot about the departed, more so than the other staff at the funeral home. While the departed who got up vexed me, they deserved our best. I'd have to think about that sad reality later, turning my attention to Eoghan. Which of his behaviors counted as a habit and which were his attempts to adapt to modern society? "He gets up early in the morning, and he typically dislikes being out after dark." The dislike of being out after dark part fell into the blatant lie category, but I'd yet see him sleep in longer than I did—or sleep at all. "He was relieved when we got back after a late outing."

"What was the nature of the outing?"

Great. I couldn't just up and say the devil had popped in for a round at the mall. Even if I spoke the truth, the director wouldn't believe me. "We went to the grocery store and the mall to pick out some necessities for him. His clothes weren't precisely modern, but he's prissy, so it needed to be suits. Everything has to be the best with him."

"How can someone like him afford things like that?"

There was no way I'd reveal those secrets to Director Hammel. "I guess he has an inheritance or something—or the CDC is so thirsty for knowledge they're footing the bills. I was given a bank card to use in his name and teach him how to use, and that's all I care about."

"I guess someone like you would know how to manage money quite well. You've always done a superb job any time I've put you in control of finances at the funeral home. In a way, I regret I had not better used you before it came to this."

"You said you'd let me go after you got the information."

"Not precisely, but yes, I will keep my word. Once I am finished with my business here, I will relocate you to somewhere more appropriate and leave you alive and for someone to find. I will even keep to the spirit of the agreement and make it so you have no trouble recovering from your time with me. That is more than you deserve, and it is the best offer you're going to get. I recommend that you continue cooperating."

"I am. Cooperating, that is."

"You are. You were always smarter than your resume suggests. A pity, that. You never told me why you lack a diploma."

Well, maybe the truth would convince the asshole to let me out alive—and make him more inclined to believe my lies. "My parents cleared out my college fund on vices, and I had to work to eat. I couldn't finish school because I couldn't make enough to pay the rent and eat. They keep trying to get more money out of me. I don't know why, though. I don't have any money to give them."

The director's expression soured. "I had thought there was something untoward with your family life, but I had not believed it to be that serious. Should things go to plan, you will find your fortunes changed. I had thought you might be doing some sort of vice because of your parents' addiction, not that they had bankrupted you with their vices."

"I smoked a cigarette every now and then," I confessed. "But I didn't drink or anything like that."

"A forgivable enough vice for all I made harsh rules, especially considering those circumstances. I have learned my lesson. Next time, I will ask. I would not have been quite so strict with you about any smoking had I been aware of your familial situation."

Listening to him, had I not known better —had I not witnessed death at his hands—I might have been tricked by his compassion. His words were worse than any of the lies the devil may have told me.

If the devil had lied to me at all, which I doubted.

The world was a weird place.

"It wasn't work appropriate," I said when the director waited in expectant silent.

"You are quite professional for your age," he conceded. "It is still a pity that they ruined you."

I fought my urge to sigh. "I've done my best."

"That you have. What do you think this Eoghan values most over all?"

The question puzzled me, and I frowned. "I don't know him well enough to answer that. His reputation is important to him, and he seems to take his debts seriously. He was very concerned about his caretaker's death."

"Do you think he will seek revenge?"

"I don't know," I lied. "He didn't seem in a hurry to seek vengeance at least. He was busy trying to learn more about modern times. He seemed irritated at first, but then he turned his attention to other matters."

"Would you say he's distracted?"

"I'd sure say so."

"Was he the one who healed your arm? You don't have even a scar, and I'm aware the vampire tore you up to the point of death."

I regarded my arm, which showed no sign of Gordon's fangs having torn through my skin and gouged deep into the muscle. "The hospital did the work, and I guess the CDC helped cover the cost."

"There would be no way your insurance would cover anything beyond the basics."

Cheap bastard. As there wasn't much I could say without getting on his bad side, I nodded.

"How old is this Eoghan?"

I shrugged. "I have no idea. He didn't say, and he didn't like talking about much in front of me. I'm just there to answer questions about how the world works. He talks to the CDC about stuff like that. I'm a secretary now, basically."

"Which is good work for you. The CDC tends to take care of the displaced, so even when I've finished my work, you'll be transferred into a suitable position. You might even be hired by them permanently. That would work well for you. You'd be able to leave Sunset."

I stilled at that, as he knew I'd dreamed of leaving the small town along with everyone else in my high school class. "I had wanted to go to New York," I confessed.

"The city suits you, although I found the

truck you were driving interesting. Who owns it?"

"Technically, I do, but Eoghan bought it so I can drive him around. Learning to drive is on his list, and he has a lot of demands. I just used the card the CDC gave me after they approved the purchase. I guess they wanted him to have the feeling of independence. He really likes that truck, so I hope you didn't do anything to it."

"The truck was untouched."

Well, that was something.

I tried to relax, but my head hurt and my unease grew. "I don't know if I've told you anything of use."

"I can work with what you've given me. In a few hours, I will bring you out of here long enough to attend to your business. There's a trailer cemetery staff use for the evening rounds, and we'll only need to cut through one section of graves to get there. Don't bother trying to escape. This place was built to keep the dead from leaving their graves. The living have no chance, not without the magic you lack. Just keep doing as you're told, and you'll see this through to the end."

Director Hammel took the lamp with him and locked me in the dark.

ELEVEN

A gallon of ice cream could fix
anything.

THE ABSOLUTE DARKNESS freaked me out almost as much as my awareness I was trapped in a mausoleum in the heart of a town where the dead had a habit of getting up when left unattended. Then again, the dead had never done anything to hurt me, not even Gordon; I'd gone into that with some idea of what to expect, although I had underestimated how painful his bite would be. The dead often made decent company, like poor Old Man McGregor.

I hoped the townsfolk did the right thing. Then again, if they didn't, I would.

Maybe he annoyed most people he crossed paths with, but he deserved better.

I expected the local police would brush off my report, as the old man had caused the coppers more than a few issues over the years. That bothered me, but there wasn't anything I could do about it. I believed Eoghan's claims about Old Man McGregor.

He'd lived stubborn, and I saw no reason death would change him.

I shivered, and I wondered if the place had any ventilation, or if Director Hammel left me to face asphyxiation in the dark. All in all, my situation could be worse.

There could have been undead in the musty space with me, or there could have been an open drum of formaldehyde. Direct Hammel could have stuck around, too.

With nothing else to do, I wondered what Director Hammel wanted and why he thought Eoghan could help him—or more accurately, why Director Hammel thought Eoghan's awakening might aid his cause. How could someone waking up from a long slumber help him? Magic could do just about anything. Magic struggled when it came to renewing someone's organs, but muscles could be reknit, bones could be healed, and life could be preserved with the right talent and training. Magic's limitations intrigued me.

Only death conquered all, and it did so with no regard to right, wrong, or those left behind. Death welcomed everyone.

No, death welcomed almost everyone. Eoghan dodged death's embrace, and his tendency to sleep through the ages began to make a sickening amount of sense. Who wanted to watch the years go by without end?

Could Eoghan be one of the immortals incapable of receiving death's blessing?

Most feared death. I feared the pain of dying, but death itself opened as many doors as it closed. What waited for me in my next life? If Eoghan's belief I carried a new soul within me proved to be the truth, I gave myself decent odds of having a better life should I get a second chance.

Assuming I escaped with my life, I'd have to do some research on the nature of souls.

Time dragged, and by the time Director Hammel returned to the mausoleum, I longed for my bed, a honey rock, some time with a new book, and maybe a quart of ice cream. No, I'd go for an entire gallon. A gallon of ice cream could fix anything.

It'd been a long time since I'd had ice cream. Damn. I should've gotten some chocolate to go with my honey rocks when I'd gone on a grocery store bender.

"Come on, then," he ordered. "We don't have all night."

My time on the floor hadn't done my back, knees, or head any favors, and I lurched to my feet with a grimace. I limped the first few steps before straightening and correcting my stride. The stairs led to a miniature catacombs with rows upon rows of burial niches, most of which were opened and the bones lying at rest exposed to the open air. Decayed linens clung to the skeletons, and I gave it a few years before the mold and mildew clinging to everything would erode the dead to nothing.

Several steel caskets, newer but low-end models, rested along one of the walls. "Those are the people who were laid to rest below?"

"Not precisely."

How many people had died due to Director Hammel's scheming? "More like that man you killed in the funeral home?"

"That's closer. Their deaths were necessary. They will receive a proper burial in time. I'll show you the important bodies. They're this way."

One of the shadowy niches proved to be a hallway leading deeper into the catacombs, and even older burials waited. My eyes widened. "How old are these burials?"

I peeked into one of the niches to discover the skeleton clutched a sword and shield, much like the ones Romans were depicted as using.

"I would say some date back as far as the Western Roman Empire. I don't know how the bodies got here, but when this mausoleum was built, it was built around these catacombs, which are mostly original. I was given strict instructions on how the bodies and the catacombs were to be cared for."

I gaped at the body, wondering how someone could have gotten from the Roman Empire to Sunset, Alabama. "Was the Western Roman Empire AD or BC?"

"It represents almost a hundred years around 400 AD."

The shield showed no sign of its age, neither did the sword. A glint of red caught my eye, and I leaned closer. A ruby ring rested around the corpse's skeletal finger. "Who was he?"

"Nobody important. This way."

The answer shouldn't have surprised me, but it did.

The dead mattered. Working at the funeral home had reinforced my belief that they mattered. Some went to the next life with no one on the mortal coil to care about their loss.

The corpse's sword tempted me. I didn't really need to know how to use it to stab the bastard, did I? How hard was it to grab the hilt and run him through with it? I'd helped with the bodies often enough to understand it took a lot of force to pierce through flesh and bone.

I was willing to put in the effort to do the job right. My education on human anatomy had gotten extensive expansion since working at the funeral home.

It took me a few moments to gather the will to step from the skeleton and its sword.

Hundreds of bodies lined the walls of the catacomb, many of them Roman, and some seemed somehow older. One body caught my attention, its position reversed, and its head resting near the opening of its niche. Unlike the others, it clutched stone weapons. "What's this body?"

"Ah. That's an interesting one. He's from

the Stone Age, probably the start of it. Anatomically, he's not quite human, and we think he's likely the previous evolutionary stage of humanity. I don't know what they'd call his species, but he's not *homo sapiens.*"

"Is he a Neanderthal?"

"No." Director Hammel came close and gestured to the skeleton's skull. "See where the sphenoid should be?"

In modern humans, a small piece of bone alongside the head served as a connection point between the frontal, parietal, and temporal sections of the skull. I leaned close to examine the spot. Rather than the small bone I expected, the frontal bone jutted down and formed an odd plate that spanned over the parietal and temporal bones. When covered with skin, I suspected it would create an odd ridge near the ear. "There's no sphenoid at all."

"Right. The interior of the skull also shows a different structure. At some point in the evolutionary chain, part of the frontal section of the bone detached to form what we know as the sphenoid. There are other differences in the skeleton as well. They had an extra toe, their toes were longer and possessed an extra joint, as did their thumbs."

I checked the skeleton's thumb. Sure enough, it had an extra joint and was twice as long as I expected from a human one. "That's amazing. And nobody knows this is here?"

"That's correct. It's part of the contract for

the grounds. I see no need to keep this place secret once my work here is done. I'll have what I need. These skeletons were sacred to the prior caretakers. There are only a few bodies in here worth such care. But as they interest you, I will show you something truly interesting before I show you the important bodies."

Director Hammel had one of the missing pieces of humanity's puzzle, and he didn't think it was interesting?

His idiocy astounded me.

Still, cooperation would keep me alive longer, and I flirted with the idea of growing a mean streak to rival anyone else in town. "Okay."

"This way."

At a four-way junction in the catacombs, he led me down a narrow corridor devoid of burials. Instead, carvings depicting ancient mythology from all around the world decorated the walls. I stopped at an image portraying the devil and the heavens' congregation of angels, and a chill swept through me.

There was something dangerous about the mural, as though a few etchings of a chisel might bring the whole thing to life and bring ruin to any who might stare upon it.

"It's just a blank wall. I know it's weird, but I guess they never got to finishing that section of the catacombs."

Wait. What? I touched the devil's image,

the face recognizable as the being I knew to be Satan with a few alterations. His eyes and jawline were somehow softer. His body resembled some Olympian god's rather than the more slender visage he'd presented at the mall.

The wings showed him in full angelic glory, and he lacked horns.

I examined the rest of the wall and pointed at a portrayal of Medusa. "What is this?"

"The truth of all things, through the eyes of the catacomb's makers."

I sucked in a breath.

Angels existed in the mortal coil because their true visages would erase mortal humans from existence. I'd heard rumors the devil himself could also erase mortals should any look upon his true self. The unsettled feeling intensified, and I returned back to the image of the devil. I lifted my hand and rested my fingers on his perfect face.

While Director Hammel saw nothing, I felt every groove of the carving beneath my fingertips.

The other angels, like their devilish brother, resembled Olympian gods in their perfection, but they bore human faces.

They could have been any old Joe on the street.

I tore myself away from the curiosity and followed after Director Hammel.

Why had I seen the carvings where he saw nothing?

The corridor opened to a small chamber, and the skeletal figure standing in the center stole my breath.

We stood in the presence of an angel's earthly remains, and unlike the being I'd met on my front step, the one before me still possessed its head. I took a step closer.

Director Hammel chuckled. "It's real. I admit I was curious, so I've touched it. I figure everyone has. It's real bone, and there's a sense of magic about it. I haven't studied it much, as I've no use for a long-dead angel, but I thought you might enjoy seeing it. Angels can die. And they don't always decay to ash. No. This one is still here, standing and waiting for what, I am not sure."

My curiosity drove me into stepping to the winged skeleton. Feathers could last hundreds of years in the right conditions—even longer in some circumstances. The angel's feathers were all but gone, but a single one clung to the bones, and its color bothered me, as though someone had rubbed soot into it. "There's a feather."

"Go ahead and touch it. I have. It's stuck. And if it comes loose, it's just a feather. A dead angel can harm no one."

The unsettled feeling in my chest remained, as though we had strayed onto sacred ground and run the risk of defiling the entire catacombs—if they weren't already defiled.

I wanted to wipe the filth from the feather. "Do you have a handkerchief?"

Director Hammel pulled one out of his pocket and offered it to me.

I strolled to him, accepted the white cloth, and circled the angel, gently clasping the base of the shaft where it connected to the old bone so I could wipe the feather itself. To my amazement, the soot wiped off, and within a few minutes, I'd removed the filth, leaving it a bright white.

After a few moments, it glowed with a pale light.

The angel stood taller than me, but I stood on my toes and wiped the dust and grime of the ages off the skull, noting that like the ancient skeleton, the angel lacked a sphenoid, instead having the larger frontal bone serving both functions. Unlike the ancient skeleton, there was no overlapping ridge.

I doubted anyone would have noticed the difference in the skulls without an x-ray or examining the exposed bone.

"I can give you ten minutes, but that is all. Be quick. If you're behaved enough, I'll lock you in this section of the catacomb and leave a light with you. You can care for the dead to your heart's content that way. But yes, I understand. There's something about that angel, isn't there?"

Director Hammel likely viewed indulging

me as a kindness, assuming a happy captive would do less to try to escape. Caring for the dead should have been an honor in his eyes, not a tedious necessity.

I breathed in, and I cast my resentment of his attitude away. Ten minutes wouldn't be enough to fully clean the angel's bones, but I could do a light pass before he forced me to leave. While I classified as agnostic, meeting the devil had done a good job of reinforcing that while I didn't hold faith in Christianity, there were those who did and always would.

I wondered if anyone had said a prayer for the angel, if it had a name, or if it waited for its rebirth.

"How long has the angel been here?"

"He's the oldest thing here, I suspect, and he was dead long before the first human stood on two legs. That's what the modern records imply. The original record is written in a language I can't read."

"There's a written record?"

"There is. I'll show it to you when you're done there."

I took care with the angel, and when I checked the handkerchief, I found no evidence of the grime I wiped from the bones.

More magic.

After giving every bone a brisk rub, I stepped back, nodding my satisfaction.

The bones gleamed in the lantern's light, and even when we backed away, the feather continued to illuminate the chamber.

"Who would have thought something as simple as dusting off an old feather would bring a little light to the darkness?" Director Hammel laughed. "Every time I come down here, I discover something new. What else will you unveil for me? I can easily bar the way into the catacombs so you can stay here and do more of my work for me."

What a dick. Rather than spew curses at the man, I followed him down the corridor, hesitating at the carving of the Christian pantheon.

Much like the angel's cleaned feather, it gleamed.

Nope, that wasn't spooky. Not at all.

I lost count of the number of intersections we crossed through before we entered another small chamber without burials. Rather than the skeleton of an angel, a dark stone pedestal held a book bound in dark leather. Raising a brow, I approached the book, which lacked any decoration or a title. "This is it?"

"It's durable. You won't damage it opening it. I've flipped through the entire thing."

I waved the handkerchief and took the time to wipe down the cover before picking the book up and cleaning the back and spine. Tucking it under my arm, I dusted off its pedestal before returning the volume to its rightful place. With more care than I bet Director Hammel gave to anything, I eased the cover open.

Runic pictures rather than words decorated the first page, reminding me of a mix of Mesoamerican and Egyptian. The pristine sheets rustled when I turned them. "Vellum?"

"I'm not sure what it's made of."

Interesting. I returned to the first two pages. If I considered modern conventions, the first would be the book's title, and the next few pages would be the chapter listings, which took up four complete pages. "How many chambers are there in here?"

"A hundred and fifty-four."

I counted entries on the opening pages. Sure enough, there were a hundred and fifty-four entries after the potential title page. "It's probably a registry of the residents of the catacombs." I flipped through, and each page had a few runes and images and a few lines to accompany them. "Maybe their name and a description of who they were?"

"Interesting. But why would it be so deep within the catacombs? I would have thought they'd store such a thing near the entry."

I bit my tongue, as I wanted to remind him we kept our registries of our deceased guests under lock and key away from public view. Instead, I shrugged. Leaving such a treasure in the catacombs annoyed me—especially when I knew someone who might at least know the language the text was written in. "Mind if I hold onto this?"

"If it makes you happy and keeps you from causing me trouble."

I hoped the dead didn't take offense to me

lifting something of theirs from their resting place. If they did, I'd put it back without asking Eoghan about the contents of the book. If it was in a language he knew, it would be invaluable to him.

If it wasn't, I'd ask the devil to satisfy my curiosity.

"What's important to you in here?"

"This way," Director Hammel ordered.

I expected another hike, but he guided me through a few short hallways to a set of three steps leading up to a larger room. Instead of the niches for burials, three sarcophagi waited inside, their covers broken and littering the floor. Inside waited linen-wrapped skeletons.

"Who are they?"

Director Hammel stepped around the broken pieces of stone and he gestured to the central figure. "These are the mortal remains of gods, and I mean to claim the power from their bones upon their resurrection."

Okay. Everything made more sense. I dealt with a madman, and I regretted I hadn't fallen prey to my impulse to loot an ancient skeleton for a sword and dispatch the idiot then and there. If the skeleton got up, seeking vengeance for its disturbed rest, I'd just blame the bastard and hope for forgiveness.

Then again, while I no longer had my phone, I had a secret.

I wondered if the devil liked me enough to pay me another visit. Deliberately provoking Lucy might count as idiotic, but if I couldn't rescue myself, I'd go for the big guns and use him as a method of rescuing myself.

"How do you think Eoghan can help you with these gods?"

"I need the power that awakened him. He's just evidence the power is here somewhere."

"Would it help if I knew someone I could ask?" I could call Darlene, introduce myself, and talk to the devil that way. Maybe I didn't have a high school diploma, but I could rub a few of my brain cells together and get a charge.

"How could you possibly know someone you could ask?"

"Through the CDC," I lied.

Oh, I could ask the angel's wife. That would work even better.

"No."

Oh, well. I'd just have to invoke the devil's name and see what sort of hell I could unleash on Earth. What was a little hell down in a catacomb with the body of an angel and three gods?

I needed to take my rather grave sense of humor and introduce it to the business end of a shovel. Life would be easier without death hanging over my head all the time.

"What gods were they?"

"I don't know their names. I only know they are divines, and their bones still sing of their divinity, just like the angel still registers as an angel to the scanners."

Oh boy. Right. He had a scanner capable of identifying something's nature. "Why do you want their power?"

"I miss my wife."

In a way, my heart broke for the man. I'd still been in school when his wife had passed away. She'd stayed dead, and she rested in the cemetery above. "I'm so sorry."

"Me, too. With the power of three divines, I can bring her back. Maybe I can even use that angel."

Nothing could bring back the dead, not really. Once gone, a soul was gone, heading for its next life or some new adventure beyond the gates of death. That was the one thing everyone agreed on. Vampires were undead, but the soul in the body wasn't the body's original soul; that had moved on, perhaps to another vampire, perhaps somewhere else. I wasn't sure about what happened with the other forms of undead, but death didn't give up its prizes.

I believed in that.

So did Eoghan.

"Now that you understand, I will take you up to the cemetery for a breath of fresh air and a chance to use the facilities and eat, but then you will return here and keep the dead company until my work here is done. Don't worry. No one will find you here."

Like hell they wouldn't, but I'd wait before I used the card up my sleeve.

If I wanted to summon the devil himself, I'd need to either be lucky or use the right insults—and get the hell out of the way while making Director Hammel take the fall for my sacrilege. And if he left me alone with skeletons and their weapons, well, was it really my fault if I did some tomb robbing to stop the bastard?

His wife deserved to rest in peace, as did the gods and angel interred within the catacomb's hallowed halls.

TWELVE

Why would you put Jesus in a
bucket?

GHOSTLY FOG ROSE from the cemetery and
enshrouded the tombstones, casting a pale
yellow and green light over the ground.

Nope, that wasn't spooky, either. Not
at all.

I contemplated screaming, and I'd do my
best to wake the devil himself in Georgia
when I did it. I drew in a deep breath to do
just that when the smoky fog swirled, and a
dark shape prowled towards us. The scream
stuck in my throat.

Orange eyes burned in the darkness.

"This way," Director Hammel ordered,
and he gestured towards the nearby building
that served as the main utility building for the
cemetery.

Did he not see the fog, the lights, or the
big, black shape coming closer? My mouth
dropped open, I spluttered, and at an utter
loss, I followed, keeping an eye on the beast
lurking within the fog.

I'd heard legends of the black dog of death, something that spanned several cultures and mythologies. If I recalled correctly, the Maya had one in the form of Xolotl. I'd found that tidbit of history class interesting.

The Maya had a lot of interesting gods— nasty gods, gods capable of raining destruction on the Earth. The British had one, too. Their black dog of death had been born out of superstition. Did Anubis count as a black dog of death?

"As a matter of fact, yes," the devil announced from behind me.

I screamed, and Director Hammel spun around.

The devil placed a flaming blue hand on my shoulder. "Shh. You know he doesn't like the screaming."

"Jesus Christ in a bucket!"

"Why would you put Jesus in a bucket?" Lucy asked, his tone a mixture of amused and curious. "You've taught your companion bad habits, and he made demands of me, and I found this so entertaining I decided to comply—and to prevent the foolish from doing foolish things. Might I borrow that for a moment?"

That?

The devil lifted his hand from my shoulder and gestured to the book I carried.

I offered the book to the devil.

"What are you doing?" Director Hammel demanded.

"Giving the devil the book, because only a fucking moron pisses off the devil," I replied.

Unlike at the mall, the devil appeared with his skin darker than the night, and the blue fire cloaked his entire body. I couldn't tell if he wore clothes beneath the flames. He traced his clawed fingers over the black leather before opening it and gently turning each page. He spoke, and the ground beneath my feet trembled at the sound of his voice.

The dark shape emerged from the fog, and I realized it was the same dog that had taken to guarding my front step. Behind him, Gordon stalked through the cemetery.

Well, that would make my night interesting—and spare me from having to return to the catacombs for long.

The devil spoke, and the ground trembled again.

"Stop that," Director Hammel ordered.

"I'm only giving you what you wanted," the devil replied, and when he smiled, a chill stabbed through me. He spoke again, and I realized he invoked names from the book.

He spoke a fourth time, and a blue glow erupted from the entrance to the catacombs and bathed the cemetery in pure light.

I could scream, hold my breath until I fainted, run, or crawl under the dog and wait for the storm to finish blowing through.

"You don't want to do any of those things, my dear," the devil said, and he patted my shoulder again. "Just stay there and don't worry your pretty little head over a thing. You've served your purpose this night, and the wheels of fate will continue to turn no matter what you do for now."

"I did what?"

The devil gestured towards the catacomb's entrance, and the glow intensified.

The skeletal angel emerged from its tomb, and the sole feather left burned brighter than the sun and transformed night to day. I turned my head and squinted, raising my hand to shield my eyes. A second spot of sun-bright light coalesced near the angel's shoulders, and a new feather uncoiled from bone. Another joined it, and the angel spread its pure white wings. Beginning with its feet, skin stretched over bone and filled out with muscle and blood.

"We have a vampiric guest this night," the devil said, his tone gentle. "Dim your light, my brother, and mind your face. We are on the mortal coil."

The angel's jaw opened in a skeletal grin before a shimmering shroud encapsulated it and the skull vanished, leaving the angel as I expected, a headless being of the purest light.

My dog trotted to me, sat on my feet, and growled at Director Hammel.

"Are you all right, Anwen?" Gordon asked, and he approached although he kept a wary eye on the manifesting angel.

"I got a bump on the back of my head and a headache to go with it, but I'm all right."

Flesh knit over the angel's bone, and it stretched its hands and gave its wings a shake. "Why have I been woken from my slumber? Lucifer? Is this your doing? It does not feel as though the end of all things has begun yet. This is not my time."

"Eh, I got bored, and you know how I get when I get bored."

"Heaven help us all," the angel muttered, and I determined it was probably a he. "Could you not have waited a few more years before bothering me with your nonsense?"

I couldn't tell if the angel liked the devil or not.

"He loves me," the devil answered with a laugh. "He's just grumpy when he first gets out of bed. It is my pleasure to be the first to introduce Azrael to this era. All facets of death have been restored to this world."

"Restored?" Azrael demanded.

"All facets of death now exist, and they're all awake. Some naughty devils sought to circumvent death and almost began the End of Days. The start of their scheming planted the final seed of death for this world. While my daughter stopped that nonsense before it reached an unfortunate conclusion, all of the conditions for the true end are now in place. All is as the universe intended from the beginning. Don't tell my daughter I said this, but I'm quite proud of her."

The angel's chuckle carried a sharp edge

to it, and the hairs on my arms rose. "Coerced a daughter out of *Him*, did you?"

"I tricked her into accepting being adopted into the family, and I received the blessing of her worldly father. All conditions were met. She still gets so delightfully upset over it at times. She loves having a family, but being my heir is so troublesome. For her. She's a personification, and you'll find her to be a delight. One day, I expect her worldly father will make his introductions, and she'll find she has more parents and family than she can readily handle. I'll love it. She won't. She's a sphinx, but she's a rather terrible one. Her curses are quite potent, but she needs help from her beloved to inflict them. A good enough thing, else we'd have a cursed mortal coil, for she is as short of temper as she is long of leg."

"You disgust me," Azrael muttered. "And the rest of our brothers?"

"They're here and there. I'm sure they'll come over to say hello in a few days, after you're a little less murderous. You know you get pretty murderous first thing in the morning."

I must have hit my head harder than I thought—or I'd taken a trip straight to hell in a hand basket.

"What is it with you mortals, my hells, and hand baskets? You wouldn't even fit in one. If you want to take a trip to hell, I can take you, but I'm afraid you'll just have to accept teleportation, as I'm far too lazy to do it in any of the other ways, with or without a hand basket."

I considered returning to the catacombs, as things seemed a lot saner in the catacombs.

The devil patted my shoulder. "You'll be okay."

"You woke me with a purpose. What would you have me do?"

The devil gestured to Director Hammel, and he snapped his fingers. Black, smoking tendrils surrounded the man, who screamed before he was gagged. "There. Stay put for a while, you pathetic mortal. This will give us a moment to discuss this. Azrael, that mortal seeks to break the universal laws. You're the only facet of death who can give him a taste of what will happen should those laws be broken and still satisfy the magic blooming because of his actions. Teach this mortal the error of his beliefs. An hour should do. That will make room for the rest of this to fall into place without turning this town into a gateway to my hells. I do hate unauthorized gateways to my hells. I don't want to deal with a new gateway right now. I've a wife to get home to, and if I'm really good, she'll put on her fur coat and purr for me."

"You are even more insufferable than you were when you first fell." Azrael heaved a sigh. "You know how I hate having to work right after I've awoken."

"I know, I know. Just don't kill him. The

time for that has not yet come. See how far he can run in an hour, though. It will be entertaining. While you do that, I will set the rest of this into motion." The devil smirked at me. "Isn't this fun, Anwen?"

"No."

He handed me the book. "Do put that back where it belongs, please. Some things are best left buried—and cared for properly. You were always disgustingly considerate even in the worst of circumstances."

"But what is this?"

The devil laughed. "It's the Book of Life, of course."

My eyes widened. "The one mentioned in the Bible?"

"You're delightfully well-educated for a heathen."

"I'm agnostic."

"Agnostic, heathen—same difference. I love heathens. You change everything because you don't believe in the set courses the various religions set for the world. You follow a truly neutral path."

"I wanted to show the book to Eoghan. I wanted to know if it was in his language."

"I suppose it wouldn't hurt if it explored the mortal coil for a while."

I pointed at the entrance. "But it was in there the whole time."

"That's not part of the mortal coil. It is a gateway to the land of the dead. The Book of Life is a registry of all those who have passed on from this world to the next, and it contains the names of all who have died, who will die, and those who are dead. Few names escape record. Each room of those catacombs is representative of a different era of this world."

Crap. "I could have been looking at my own death, then? Just flipping through the pages?"

"No. It doesn't work that way."

Well, that was something. "Should I just put it back now?"

"No. It can wait. Now, it's time for you to bear witness to why the universal laws are as they are. Azrael?"

"Release the mortal, and I shall begin. The book, please."

I held out the Book of Life to the angel, who took it and flung it into the air. The covers fell open, the pages spread, and when they finally settled, the writing on the pages glowed in the same gold and green light that had suffused the cemetery.

The devil snapped his fingers, and the bindings around Director Hammel released.

"What are you doing?" the director demanded, his voice shrill.

There was something malevolent about the angel's laughter. "I am giving you what you wished, mortal. Bear witness to the fruit of awakening sleeping gods and standing in the presence of death. Behold."

Like the devil, the angel read from the

book, and every name shook the ground. Something shivered beneath my feet, and I realized I stood upon a grave.

The soil shifted under my feet, and I bolted for the questionable safety of the catacomb's entrance.

The dead rose from the niches within, and the skeletons strode towards the entrance. Unlike the movies I'd seen, they moved with grace and dignity, marching with their grave goods clutched in their bony hands.

"I would make way for them, Anwen," the devil said. He pointed to an unmarked grave. "No one rests there, and it should be safe enough there."

I relocated to that spot in the hopes I might escape without touching any more corpses for the rest of the night.

The devil laughed at me.

"You suck," I told him.

"You're almost as delightful as my daughter. Also, your plan to invoke my name in creative ways to piss me off, summon me, and set me loose on that fool? That's almost as good as my daughter wanting to misspell my name in glitter to make me show up at her whim. It would have worked. This is better. It sets the wheels of fate in motion, and it defines some futures that were, until now, uncertain. Watch closely, Anwen. Humans never learn."

When the first of the corpses clawed free of the ground and the skeletons poured from the catacombs, I understood why Eoghan disliked screams.

Director Hammel's took on a rather shrill quality. None of the dead bothered to hurry, although they didn't shamble like so many movies claimed. They walked with a purpose, shedding dirt, decaying flesh, and rotten clothes as they went. They remained silent while the director continued to waste precious air with his screams.

The devil stood with me, and as though bored with the whole thing, my dog wandered off.

I wasn't brave enough to dodge through the horde of the dead to follow him. Gordon shrugged and trailed after the animal.

The dead avoided both, opting to focus their attention on their prey.

Azrael sat on a nearby tombstone and patted it. "This is the grave of the woman he desires. I peeked."

Like the other graves, the soil was disturbed. "I guess it's a good thing he won't really be able to tell which one she is, isn't it?"

"It would serve him right, but you are right. There is no way for him to know which corpse is hers."

Director Hammel fled from the undead, and Azrael lifted his perfect hand and snapped his fingers. A shimmering dome of green and gold snapped into place over the cemetery. "There. That'll keep things contained until his very soul remembers why he should leave the dead to their rest. It wouldn't do to wake all the humans for this nonsense."

"I don't know, those assholes all knew Old Man McGregor's wife killed him, and they don't even care," I grumbled.

The devil stretched his wings, rolled his shoulders, and after a few moments, he shrugged. "Your call, Azrael."

"This matter is best kept contained. The souls I called upon are mischievous in nature."

"And the woman's soul?" the devil asked.

"You could look for yourself."

"It's best if Anwen hears it from you, who is a facet of death. I will peek into her future if you gaze upon her current fate."

Azrael relaxed. "You already looked upon her soul, haven't you?"

"I am a most curious being."

I shook my head at the devil's antics.

"The woman has been reborn to a new body. She is but a child now, and she lives in a happy home. Her mother reads to her while she is safely tucked into her warm bed. Her father will read to her next until she finally sleeps. She has a cold, which heals, but she is having trouble sleeping right now."

I smiled at that. "That sounds sweet."

"She will be rewarded in her new life, for the universe has ways of repaying its debts," the devil said. "He will not disturb her again —nor will he cross paths with her in any of her futures." With a rather malevolent grin,

he added, "I will be making certain of that. I
plan to have great fun with him when it is
time for him to make his appearance at my
gates."

"What will become of him?"

"You'll see," the devil promised. "For now,
have a seat and watch. I'd say you won't get to
see something like this ever again, but you do
live in Sunset, Alabama. You haven't seen
anything yet."

THE DEAD PLAYED a game of chase with Director Hammel, who scrambled to keep away
from them. He stopped screaming, figuring
out he needed to spare his breath if he
wanted to avoid capture. Every time he
tripped over a hole in the ground or stumbled
into a gravestone, the dead toyed with him.

They loved scuffing his shoes.

I laughed so hard my head hurt and I
cried, but I couldn't stop myself.

The dead really loved scuffing the bastard's shoes or tugging on his clothes to trick
him into believing his end was nigh.

Azrael yawned; while I could no longer
see his head, I could hear him inhale, and he
made no effort to mask his boredom. "Are
you sure I can't just remove the shroud, Lucifer? This is tedious."

"You're supposed to be a compassionate
being."

"I haven't had breakfast yet."

"You haven't had breakfast in a few thousand years. You'll survive for another few hours without having to annihilate any innocent mortals who happen to come by."

"I see why *He* kicked you from the heavens. You're insufferable. It's just a few mortals."

"I don't want extra work sorting mortals today."

"They're just a few mortals."

The devil sighed and shook his head. "They're a few mortals you would have to shepherd due to your involvement in their deaths."

The angel grunted. "It might be worth it."

"There was a carving in the catacombs depicting angels, but he couldn't see them. Why couldn't he see it and I could?"

That caught their attention, and I could feel the angel's gaze fall on me. "Had he seen that image, he would have been erased from that world and all others. It is not meant for human eyes."

"But I'm a human."

"Are you?"

I blinked, and my brows furrowed. "Well, the DNA tests say I am."

"But are you, really?" The angel chuckled, and his laughter reminded me of a wind chime disturbed by a restless breeze. "If you were human, those carvings would have erased you from that world and all others. What you are is best left for you to discover. The journey is as important as the destination. The destination itself is of no importance. Everything you are is about what you do to get where you are going. Where you go is nothing more than a place to rest before you begin your next journey. You would do well to remember that. All journeys end, but all you need to do to begin a new journey is to take a single step forward. Death is but the conclusion of one journey and the beginning of the other, as is the End of Days. That end is also another beginning and the first step of a new journey."

"But he seemed pretty concerned about the End of Days," I said, pointing at Lucy.

"That is because the End of Days is a great deal of work and little play for him. It's a war as much as it is a conclusion of all things for this world before the next begins. His journey neither begins nor ends there, for he will be among the first born in the new beginning. It will be nothing more than the blinking of an eye for him, and that annoys him. He is a true immortal, little one. When the End of Days reaches its ultimate conclusion, it will be very much like a first step into that new journey for him. Rest is not his for the taking, and while the other seeds of life slumber and wait for their new beginnings, his will be a restless spirit."

The devil grumbled, and he stomped a foot. I realized he'd abandoned any attempts to appear truly human, exchanging feet for cloven hooves. Blue fire smoldered in cracks in the ground.

Director Hammel screamed, and I twitched at the shrill sound, checking in on the bastard.

He stood on a gravestone, and one of the undead had decided to take a bite out of his shoe. Attempting to kick the undead off did no good, as every time he managed to detach the skeletal head, it hung on while the rest of the body continued to move and restored itself. I covered my mouth and giggled. "That's rather awful but also hilarious."

"If this were a zombie apocalypse film, he'd be infected right now, and you'd have to put him out of his misery by the end of the film," the devil replied with laughter in his voice. "This is only an echo of the misery he's inflicted on others, yourself included. I'm sure you'll start feeling guilt over his misfortunes soon enough. If it makes you feel better, he helped hide evidence that old man you so like was helped to his grave."

I scowled at that. "I get he's annoying, but why would so many work so hard to hide his murder? That's not even fair."

"More people like his wife than like him, and mortals are foolish creatures. They forget the good even the annoyances do. Well, most annoyances. That one hasn't done much good. But, you'll need him in the upcoming days. Don't break him until he's finished his final purpose."

"What is his final purpose?" I asked.

"While that's a most excellent question, some things are best left for you to decide—and you already know the answer if you stop to think about it for a while. It'll be obvious soon enough. Ah. There's your male. You should leash him. Azrael, do keep an eye on the children while they finish their play. I have work to do preparing a proper welcome for that one."

"Only because you're going to be particularly welcoming to that one will I do as you ask of me," the angel replied.

The devil vanished, leaving some smoke and trails of blue fire on the ground in his wake.

I turned on my gravestone to discover Eoghan and Gordon approaching, and both men looked rather miffed. "You found Eoghan!"

"That wasn't difficult, although your dog ran off. I knew where he was the whole time. We can find your dog later. He's rather swift."

"Well, he's a stray. He's collared and my number is on it, so if someone picks him up, they'll call me or just bring him to the house. It'll be fine. I'll just put food out for him and hope he comes back for his supper. He might just have been scared off by the undead. I'll have to admit, I thought about running for a few moments, but then I was told this spot was safe, and so I stayed put. It's been safe so far, so I'm pretty all right with this. I can't buy this sort of entertainment, and I've never seen anything quite like this before."

Eoghan sighed. "You cannot stay out of trouble, can you?"

"It seems not. I hope you can tolerate his screaming. I'd say I'm sorry he's screaming, but the jackass deserves it, so I'm not sorry at all."

"Angelic justice is a brutal thing. Remind me not to stir your ire. You do not play around. I can tolerate these screams. They are earned. Someone brought Lady Luck back to your home along with your things. Cecily asked me to call her as soon as you're found, although I think we shall wait until our angelic company departs."

"Why would I depart? I live here." Azrael pointed at the entrance to the catacombs. "I will take up stewardship of the Book of Life in the meantime."

Right. The book. I held it out to Eoghan. "I thought this might be in your language, so I wanted to show it to you when I found it."

Eoghan's expression turned neutral, and he took the book from me, and like Azrael, he stroked his fingers across the cover. "Yes, this is written in my native language. I know this book well."

"That you do," Azrael agreed. "You've changed little since I last saw you. You are called Eoghan in this age?"

"So it seems."

Azrael said something in a different language, his words almost musical in how he spoke them, each intonation sliding into the other with a dancer's grace. Eoghan listened, he smiled, and he answered.

I'd been right. Having someone speak to Eoghan in his own language mattered, and I turned to Gordon. "How did he handle news I'd gotten clobbered on the head and dragged off?"

"As we were unaware you'd been clobbered on the head and only aware you'd been dragged off, better than he would have reacted had he known you'd been clobbered on the head before being dragged off. He was quite displeased."

"Can you clarify that for me?"

"He's probably debating if he wants to wade into that mass of undead and add to the screaming."

Great. I'd have to figure out how to cool his temper. "Well, I'm mostly fine. I'll be totally fine once this headache goes away."

"I wish you the best of luck convincing him of that. He is also rather displeased he could not come riding to your rescue as is proper. He wanted a horse for this purpose."

I thought about that, as I'd never been able to afford a horse and liked them. "Can he put that idea on hold? I like horses."

Gordon chuckled. "He was rather displeased to discover your back yard was not sized for a horse. We had been discussing that before we received word you had been kidnapped. I'm sure he would not be bothered by planning such a thing should you enjoy it."

Hell yeah, I'd enjoy it. "I'm enjoying those vengeful dead scuffing Director Hammel's shoes, too."

The angel and Eoghan continued to speak, and the pair ignored the mayhem on the other side of the graveyard. Director Hammel lost his shoe to one of the undead, and they tossed it around in a demented game which resembled a mix of soccer and football. Gordon observed the chaos, and he raised a brow. "That's quite a lively gathering involving such a high number of corpses. Did he raise the entire graveyard?"

"I think so, and Azrael said he had asked mischievous souls to handle the work."

Director Hammel lost his other shoe, and one of the skeletons ran off with it, crouched, and chewed on it. Another joined in, and they tugged on it with such enthusiasm it broke in half.

His socks went next, and when the skeletal fingers went to work on his pants, Director Hammel dove off the gravestone and ran like the devil had taken chase. He broke through the throng of skeletons and collided with the green and gold barrier surrounding the cemetery.

Azrael turned, stretched his wings, and spoke a word. The undead halted, turned, and marched away from the beleaguered man. One by one, they returned to their graves, and the dirt settled over them. When the last of the bodies settled into the ground, the angel spoke another word, and green light washed over the ground, restoring the grass and flowers.

"It is finished," Azrael announced, and he vanished.

The barrier encasing the cemetery came down, and Director Hammel fled into the night.

THIRTEEN

Can I kill them?

I RETURNED the Book of Life to the catacombs, closed off the entry, and called the police using Eoghan's phone to report Director
Hammel had been behind my kidnapping and
that he'd brought me to the cemetery. I
glossed over many of the details, although I
did say I'd been dumped into the mausoleum,
and I had escaped with a little help from
Eoghan and Gordon, who had been searching
for me.

The cops made assumptions, and I allowed them to maintain their false beliefs.

It was a lot easier than trying to explain
how the devil and an angel of death had descended on Sunset, Alabama and turned the
place upside down.

The sun crept over the horizon when the
police finally allowed me to go home, and I
took the quickest shower in my life before
sitting down at my kitchen table to make
friends with a honey rock. I woke in bed with

no memory of how I'd gotten there, and Eoghan sat at my feet, holding out a plate of sliced melon. "Eat this so you don't try to eat me, please."

Eating in bed hadn't been something I'd done since I'd been little, primarily because I'd never had anyone to bring me anything to me. Once in the kitchen, I could never justify sitting anywhere other than the table. My stomach growled, and I accepted his offering. "Thank you."

"You sat at your table in the morning, flopped, and mumbled about your precious honey rocks before passing out, so I brought you to bed. You've been asleep for six hours, and Cecily suggested I wake you up and get something into you so you don't starve, as it was unlikely you'd had anything after you were grabbed. Director Hammel is still at large, and he is being charged with murder, attempted murder, kidnapping, concealing a murder, and a long list of things involving the death of my caretaker. It seems Azrael visited the police before returning to the catacombs to make it clear they should address certain matters."

"Address certain matters?"

"Regarding Mr. McGregor. He is, in case you were curious, fishing at the river and rather enjoying his unlife. It seems his business is still unfinished, but he's in no hurry to move on to the next life. A priest attempted to lay him to rest, and he laughed and said he might listen to a higher power, but he had no intentions of listening to someone who didn't mind his murder."

Poor Old Man McGregor. "That's different. Usually they move on when the priest comes."

"He has a strong will and he died before his rightful time. When his rightful time comes, he will head to his next life on his own unless someone convinces him to leave early. That's the doing of the node. The node seems to understand the proper time and place for life and death." Eoghan frowned, and deep lines creased his brow. "The Book of Life may be responsible. I never believed it'd be *here* of all places."

"Is it the node?"

"No. It's certainly an object of great power, but it's not one of the nodes. I don't know where those are at. I fear Director Hammel may know, however—even if he doesn't realize what he has. Attempting to break a universal law could bring disaster to everyone, and what he perceived as a success will forever be a failure."

"Azrael said his wife would be forever free from him."

"Angels cannot lie. Even I know this truth. They cease to be angels should a falsehood leave their lips. Circumstance can change, but that would not change that they had spoken the truth at the time of its speaking. At that point in time, he believed this to be true. It probably is."

"The devil said he had plans for Director Hammel."

"That would explain the angel's confidence. How are you feeling?"

I devoured the first of my honey rock slices, sighing happily over its delicate sweetness. "Much better now that breakfast is a honey rock."

"Your head? Gordon said you'd been hit in the head."

"It's all right. It aches a little, but that's it." I ate another slice of my honey rock. "He wanted to know about you."

"I hope you told him I was his death in the flesh."

"I went with mostly honest with a side dish of setting him up to underestimate your general willingness to kill him. I cooperated because I didn't feel like giving him any excuses to kill me."

Eoghan made a thoughtful sound in his throat. "That will do. That was wise of you. Good work."

"You asked the devil for help."

"I demanded help, and I refused to bargain with him. And while I am appropriately grateful for his assistance, I owe him nothing, not even a favor."

"You can still be nice to him."

"I intend to be cordial."

I expected that was the best I'd get out of Eoghan. "Have you seen my dog?"

"While I have heard about this animal, I have not seen him personally. I will let you know if he shows up. The food that was put out for him has been pilfered, likely by said animal."

"You don't like my dog?"

"I haven't met your dog. I have no problems with dogs. I like dogs. I will tell you should I see the stray. Your neighbors were inquiring why Director Hammel might want you. I was rather displeased with their tone."

Ah. Yeah. I could understand that. "Well, he's a known entity. I'm the local dropout who couldn't even manage to leave Sunset."

"Things are about to become more complicated for you."

I tensed. "How so?"

"Sunset is being invaded by a rather heavenly host, and they have taken much interest in the cemetery, the catacombs beneath it, and Azrael's awakening. This, unfortunately, has resulted in the angels paying us a visit."

Shit. "There are angels here?"

"The devil is here, too. They have taken over the kitchen, which is why I opted to bring you your breakfast. I thought you'd appreciate eating in peace."

I needed another nap, a hit of pixie dust, and some painkillers. My honey rock would have to serve as a substitute for all of those things, although I could hit up some of the painkillers. The pixie dust would make me a menace to those who could wipe me out of existence with the wave of their perfect hands. "How many angels?"

"Two archangels, the devil, and that angel and incubus who had visited us before."

I struggled to process the presence of two archangels in my home. "Which two?"

"Michael and Gabriel."

I gulped. "And Azrael? Is he an angel or an archangel?"

"He is an archangel as well. He is likely in the catacombs checking on all of its many residents and making certain they have not been disturbed."

"There are three archangels and the devil here? In Sunset?" I gulped, and to console myself with the insanity, I ate another slice of my honey rock. "But why?"

"You'll have to ask the devil. He brought them."

Somehow, things had gotten even more complicated. "And Director Hammel?"

"I suspect his meddling with forbidden magics is why they are here. He has put things into motion—dangerous things."

"Well, waking Azrael probably counts as one of those dangerous things."

"You would be right. Azrael isn't the only one to awaken, and Director Hammel will regret his choices before this is done."

"You," I guessed.

"You would be correct. I am not nearly as

kind a being as Azrael, as you will learn as
soon as I get my hands on Director Hammel."

A week ago, I would have been concerned.
Now, the thought of the bastard facing the
consequences for his actions made me smile.
"I look forward to it."

"I will do my best to keep from disappointing you, then."

A BLUE-BANDED ARCHANGEL sat on my table
with a scarlet-banded one, and something
about them unsettled me. An uncomfortable
feeling grew in my chest, and I halted in the
doorway, debating what I should do about
the sensation, if I could do anything about it.

"It is the influx of divinity," one of the
archangels announced. "It shall pass. Stay
there until you adapt if you would like."

Lucy waved at me from his seat at the table. "The blue one is Michael, the red one is
Gabriel, and you've already met Dimitri. His
incubus is prowling the street in search of
trouble, and Azrael is admiring your truck.
He is discovering the toys of this age are
amusing, and that might keep him awake for
a while."

"Nice to meet you, I think."

The angels laughed, and the devil grinned
at me.

Eoghan leaned against my refrigerator,
crossed his arms over his chest, and scowled.

"What brings the devil, three archangels, an angel, and an incubus over? Had I known an entire heavenly host would be visiting, I would have at least tried to clean first."

The devil leaned back in his chair, balancing it on two legs. "We're here to discuss Sunset's fate."

Uh oh. "That does not sound promising. What do you mean by Sunset's fate?"

"That director has put some things into motion that cannot be stopped. He has awoken the fates, he has summoned death itself to Sunset. Both have consequences. Death had already begun awakening in earnest. Add in the node here, and it was inevitable, I suppose. Some things are. Using the Book of Life contained some of the consequences, but not all. Sunset's fate can still be altered, but it will require work on your part."

"On my part?"

"We have rules we must follow—the universal laws. Mortals are often cheerfully unaware of the universal laws. Few immortals can bend said laws. Death is one of them, but even Death cannot break all the universal laws—only a few."

"Wait. I thought death was one of the universal laws. You can't raise the dead and bring them back to life.

"No, not precisely. Death, the event, is not the same as *Death*, the being. Death is a being of three parts. Azrael is one of those parts."

The devil leaned to the side and hollered, "Azrael, come be useful."

The archangel representing death appeared in the kitchen. "You have a lovely truck, Anwen. Would you permit me to ride in it soon? I would like to try this."

"Sure. I don't mind taking you for a drive."

"My many thanks, Anwen."

Life had become strange, and I wondered what the town would say about me taking an archangel for a ride in my truck. "Death is a being of three parts. Azrael is the best known of them. He shepherds souls as a being of law and order. Then there is the neutral version of Death, who welcomes all."

I sucked in a breath. "Eoghan had mentioned death being neutral."

Eoghan scowled. "Azrael and I do not see eye-to-eye on this matter."

"You can't see eye-to-eye with him. He's hiding his head," I replied.

The devil burst into laughter. "Yes. All angels hide their heads. There is a good reason for that. To look upon the face of an angel is to look upon *His* face, and that would result in the destruction of the mortal form. *His* face is only meant for those who have moved beyond this realm—and those who look upon *His* face cannot remember it here."

I frowned, remembering the carvings in the catacombs. "But wouldn't that make *His* face the face of humanity? The angels look human. The carvings looked human. His skull was human, but an old human—he lacked a sphenoid."

The devil's sly smile chilled me. "Your Eoghan lacks a sphenoid, too."

That caught my attention, and I straightened, regarding the antique with open curiosity. "Let me feel."

"Pardon?"

"I want to feel your head."

Eoghan scowled. "What nonsense is this?"

"Just humor her." The devil rose and approached Eoghan, waving for me to join them.

I did, stepping closer to the archangels. The unsettled feeling remained, but it didn't strengthen.

Eoghan heaved a sigh and tilted his head towards me. "I do not know why I'm agreeing to this."

"It's not worth the fight, and it proves many things." The devil patted Eoghan's shoulder. "It establishes some things for her."

I touched above Eoghan's eye and applied pressure enough to feel the shape of the bone beneath my fingertips, moving to the temple towards where the sphenoid would be in a modern person. My fingers located a slight ridge marking where the frontal bone extended beyond where it would in someone like me, a *homo sapiens*. "Oh."

The devil took hold of my hand, placing my fingertips near my temple where I'd located the ridge on Eoghan's skull. "Feel."

"There's..." I frowned, giving my skull a rub to discover I had a similar ridge to Eoghan's. I'd rarely rubbed my temples; I'd been told early I could die if I damaged that portion of my skull. I'd learned later in life my parents had been bullshitting me, and it took quite a bit of force to kill someone with a blow to the temple. "That doesn't feel right."

"It doesn't feel right if you were *homo sapiens,*" the devil agreed. "That is why your DNA record is unusual. It's because you are not *homo sapiens*. But because the CDC lacks DNA records for what you are, they could not match the missing fragments of your DNA. As your arm was injured rather than your head, they had no reason to do a scan of your skull. Had a scan of your skull been done, it would have been discovered you lack a sphenoid. That would have led to some studying on the CDC's part, especially as both of your parents are *homo sapiens.*"

Great. I'd gone from weird to weirder. I rubbed the odd ridge I'd never noticed lurking beneath my skin. Had I never noticed it, or had I assumed everyone had the same ridge? "How do you know this?"

"I am who I am, and I am known to cheat as often as possible. It is one of the perks of being the Lord of Hell."

Right. I danced with the devil. I should have known. "Does Gordon have this same ridge?"

"Of course not. He's *homo sapiens*. His

sphenoid is present. Do not ask me why hu-mans evolved to have an extra bone in their skulls. Evolution is a strange thing, and *He* sees no need to circumvent nature's intent for all *He* is a controlling divine. Most of the heavenly host enjoys controlling everything within their domain. I enjoy how much it vexes *Him* to keep his promise to humanity, for them to retain their free will even beyond the End of Days. Humans are delightfully re-bellious children."

If I wanted a straight answer out of the devil, I'd have to ask him directly. "What is the third aspect of Death?"

"Life beyond," the devil answered. "Azrael ensures the natural order of the universe through death is maintained. The second facet ensures death is there for all. The third is the release from death, and is considered to be the kindest of the three facets; without the third aspect, there would be no life beyond death. In truth, Azrael is less of a shepherd than the third aspect. As far as the aspects go, Azrael is the one who interferes with mortals. The other two aspects exist, although the second aspect is the one that gets the worst reputation of the lot."

Eoghan scowled. "Azrael picks and chooses."

The archangel snickered. "I do pick and choose. This is a truth. I safeguard only the souls deserving of *Him*. I am *His* mercy in a mortal's final hour. Some may say this is a cruel thing for those who have not earned *His* regard. But it is not a precise truth that I often interfere with mortals. Like the other aspects, I merely need to exist for my work to be done. But I do have more freedoms than the others. This is not a bad thing. Death could continue on without me, although it would bring unnecessary hardship to worthy souls."

I figured Eoghan's age and his beliefs put him at odds with the archangel, and if given a chance, I'd throw the two together to watch them posture. "Director Hammel wanted Eoghan to bring his wife back to life. Wait, no. I think he wanted the magic involved in wakening Eoghan to accomplish this."

The archangels cackled their laughter, the devil joined in, and if Eoghan rolled his eyes much harder, someone would have to pick his unconscious body off the floor.

"What's so funny about that? I mean, it's not a *bad* idea. There had to be a lot of magic involved with waking an antique from a bazillion year slumber. And he wanted to raise the three dead in the catacombs. The ones you invoked, Azrael."

If looks could kill, Eoghan would have escorted me directly to my grave. "A bazillion years? An antique?"

"Well, you are an antique. You're a nice antique, but you're definitely an antique."

Yep, I'd be joining my stray in the dog-house as soon as I got him one.

"The fates," the Archangel of Death replied. "I invoked the fates from their slumber and released them on this world. They are not what mythology believes; Atropos is not a fate representing death. She truly represents the end of all journeys. Conclusions. Death is an end of a journey, but it's also the beginning of one. It is but a moment in a mortal's life. Clotho is the fate he could make the most use of, as she could spin for a new soul a match for the woman he desires. She won't, though. Every soul is a piece of art, and she celebrates their every flaw. Lachesis would merely snip his thread to draw the attention of one of the aspects of death. Technically, she comes close to violating the universal laws, but she knows her art well—and she knows precisely how to snip a thread to keep from unraveling the whole tapestry of life. They are displeased their hard-earned rest has been disturbed. It was not supposed to be their time. I have tangled their precious weave. But they will also be pleased with me as soon as their annoyance wears off. I have ushered in many new possibilities this era, and they are all creatures who thrive on such possibilities."

If I kept trying to make sense of what the archangel told me, I'd develop a migraine within the hour. "I don't think Director Hammel understands who the three in the catacombs are," I admitted. "I had no idea they were the three fates."

The devil snorted. "No, Hammel is a rather ignorant fool. He is so determined to reach his goal that he does not care who or what he destroys in the process. I love some good, wholesome destruction, but there is a time and a place for all things. He has no regard for anyone other than himself. I look forward to my time with him in my many hells."

Right. "I guess that leaves me with my last question."

"Really? Your last one?" The devil grinned at me. "You are an everlasting fountain of questions. I give it less than five minutes before you have another one. It is your nature to question things."

I scowled. "What does it mean for us now that all of the aspects of death are awakened?" I considered how the devil addressed the director, and I decided I liked slicing off his title. It transformed him from an authority to something far less than what he'd once been. "Will Hammel's actions hurt us? Us being the world in general."

"And while that is technically two questions, it took two questions to the one you really want to know, so I'll let it slide," the devil teased. "Hammel, in a strange way, has helped more than he has harmed. He had the greatest capacity for harm, but that future didn't come to pass. He has the potential to bring harm still, but it is an unlikely fate. What he has done is finish my daughter's work and has restored death, both the event and the being, to its rightful order. My daughter merely halted what could have become the absence of death, something that would have ushered in the End of Days. It would have taken the end to allow for new beginnings. All life needs a seed, and the fate she prevented would have stopped death itself—and prevented rebirth, too. Her actions allowed death to awaken now."

Eoghan's eyes narrowed. "Who sought the absence of death?"

The devil shook his head. "They're either dead, converted, or enduring eternal torment at the hands of vengeful mummies. They are beyond your reach now."

Grunting, Eoghan went to the refrigerator, pulled out one of my honey rocks, plunked it onto my cutting board, grabbed my knife, and slammed the blade through the melon, slicing it in half. My brows shot up at the ease he'd cracked the damned thing open. With terrifying accuracy, he took his temper out on my favorite treat, and when he had sliced it into edible portions, he grabbed a plate, loaded it up, and put it on the table. "These are Anwen's. Should you try to touch them, I will cut your hands from your wrists and feed your blood to Gordon."

Okay. The archangels, the angel, the devil, and anyone else in my house needed to leave so I could make an attempt to lure the antique to my bed.

The archangels snickered.

"Patience, Anwen," the devil chided.

I didn't want to be patient. I wanted my honey rock, and I wanted to forever evict myself from the pool of unwanted virgins. I reached between Michael and Gabriel to snag a slice. "Honey rocks for breakfast, and more honey rocks for second breakfast. This is how to live life."

Eoghan smirked.

As long as he provided honey rocks, he could be as smug as he wanted. I could handle anything when I had honey rocks to enjoy.

"I recommend a greenhouse, sun lamps should you decide to live in a place that is not conducive to year-round musk melons. Keep the seeds. She is a threat to the local supply." The devil pushed the plate closer to me. "You need the extra calories. There's one more thing we need to discuss before we can depart and leave you to your business. The nodes here will be a problem for you."

Eoghan grunted and went to work cleaning my cutting board and knife. "We need to find them and make certain they are safeguarded."

"One is easy enough to find. It's a static object, and it's quite good at disguising itself. When you find it, you'll likely come to the conclusion I've already reached: some things are best left alone. The Book of Life can protect itself—and I would like to watch someone try to violate Azrael's chosen sanctuary now that he's awake. Call for me, Azrael. Such things can't be missed."

The archangel snorted. "I will consider it."

"He loves me," the devil informed the other two archangels.

They sighed.

Understanding archangels did have heads made it a lot easier to accept that they could sigh. The normality of their heads would baffle me for the rest of my life, but I'd get over it eventually.

Michael turned towards me. "It amuses us that humans expect anything other than that. Man was made in *His* image—and *He* was made in the image of man by the universe itself. Why would we angels also not be a reflection of this?"

"Why did the one skeleton in the catacombs have odd thumbs and an extra toe on each foot?" I asked. "Angels don't, but you also lack in a sphenoid."

"Human curiosity is such an interesting thing. The one you looked upon is the one modern humans call the first creation. That's not quite accurate, but it's what humans like to believe."

My eyes widened. "You mean Adam?"

"I do."

"Eve wasn't with him." There'd been others with him, but they'd been from other places. "That's sad."

Azrael patted my shoulder. "Just because their earthly remains do not reside together doesn't mean she's not with him. Their seeds of life have been replanted many times, and they always find one another in life. Her earthly remains have long since departed, returned to dust. His are interred as an eternal reminder of what had once been, safe within those catacombs. One day, come visit the catacombs, and I will teach you of all those who reside there. They are the true history of this world. You would make an excellent custodian of the grounds."

According to Eoghan's expression, he did not appreciate the archangel attempting to edge in on his turf. "No attacking the Archangel of Death, Eoghan. I'm not sure I would have the time to take up that duty. I have made other commitments."

"You could easily handle both, and your antique would enjoy your ventures into the catacomb. You would be welcome there, Eoghan."

That caught Eoghan's attention. "I would be?"

"Of course. It's as much of a sanctuary for you as it is for me. We may not see eye-to-eye on many matters, but we can cohabit the same space. I'm sure she'll be amused by our relentless bickering."

I turned to the devil. "Can I kill them?"

Lucy snickered. "You would miss them both were you to do such a thing."

While that was true, I still scowled. "Can

we redirect this conversation back to the nodes?"

The devil grinned and showed off his perfect teeth. "Technically, it is one node, one thing of power, and a person."

"The Book of Life being the thing of power?"

"Correct."

"There's a person who is a node?" Eoghan asked, his tone dismayed.

"The person is a person, not a node. The person *is* touched by the node, which is where the confusion is coming into play. The person is a conduit."

Eoghan's expression relaxed. "Ah. Conduits are a different matter entirely. Mostly harmless."

"Unless you drop them on a node and piss them off," the devil corrected.

That made the antique's eyes widen. "That could be quite dangerous."

"Why could this person be dangerous if they're near a node and angry?" I asked.

"Conduits often amplify the power of other people or things. Anger is often a trigger for a conduit's abilities awakening. Your Eoghan can be a conduit in the right conditions, as can Azrael."

The Archangel of Death shrugged. "It happens from time to time, I suppose. And we do not discuss Eoghan's abilities as a conduit should he be triggered. I find it reprehensible at best."

"That is because you're a being of order and he is not," the devil replied.

Okay. If they wanted me to restrain my curiosity, they were not going about it the right way. "Can we discuss these abilities, please?"

"So polite," the devil cooed. "I expect you'll get to see his powers for yourself soon enough. The first time he witnesses someone bring harm to you, he will manifest. That is his nature."

"Is he that dedicated already?" Azrael asked. "I try not to think of him in such a fashion."

"You need to join a triad and get laid," the devil complained. "He absolutely hates when she screams above all others."

"I will enjoy holding this over your head for the rest of eternity," Azrael announced.

Eoghan heaved a sigh. "She deserves respect. She truly does not fear death."

"And he finds he does not find this lack of fear to his liking," the devil added.

"I wish I could strangle you and plant your seed of life in the heart of the void so it might never bother me again," Eoghan spat.

"You'd miss me."

With a grunt, Eoghan stormed out of the kitchen.

"So grouchy," the devil said when he was gone. "How long do you think it will take for him to figure it out, Azrael?"

"Without help? An eternity. With help? A

lifetime or two. She's going to need help convincing him to join her in her bed as she wants."

That didn't bode well. "What sort of help?"

Hmm. Maybe I shouldn't have asked that with the devil in the room.

"Handcuffs might work," the devil replied. "You'll have to give him a demonstration of how they can be used for mutual enjoyment. Alternatively, I can just ask my wife to spread the joy in town one night soon after having one of her friends lure Gordon away. He needs to learn there are better ways for him to feed, and she can partner him with an incubus so they can hunt together. Vampires are typically incapable of relationships and love, although Gordon is exceptional. Azrael?"

"You want to ask me to do something forbidden." The archangel clamped his wings. "The universe…"

"It's not one of the laws, and we both know it. The eldest have learned."

Azrael straightened. "Have they?"

"Indeed. It would just take a nudge and a release of death's cold hands to turn them into beings as capable of love as any human. The younger would have much to learn, but they could once again bear complete souls."

"You have grown into a disgustingly philanthropic creature since the last time I walked this world."

The devil shrugged. "Those who sought to

circumvent death made many vampires through forbidden magic, and it would help balance this world a little. The balance is important. A vampire here and there wasn't an issue, but they're not just one here and there anymore."

Azrael's form shimmered, and for a moment, I caught the shadowy shape of his fully formed head through the shroud enclosing his head. "She walks through the valley of the shadow of death," Azrael announced.

I loved everything about that phrase, especially the weight of truth in the archangel's voice.

"One day, she will see through the shroud in its entirety," the devil agreed. "Anwen, it's a little early for you to be staring upon archangels with prying eyes. You already figured out the key secret of their visages. You have some left to learn, but you'll figure it out on your own, I suspect."

I shrugged. "I haven't fallen over dead yet. I figure I probably should have in the catacombs when I saw that carving. I know I'm not a perfect person, and that's what angels are, right? They're what we might have been, and that is what kills us—that we can never match what we could have been if only we were perfect."

"This is the truth," Azrael said.

"I haven't had this much fun since arguing with your little girl about destroying cities," Gabriel said. "She's not going to figure out what truly matters despite the hints you've been dropping. It is a place her thoughts simply will not go. Either tell her or don't, but nudging her will not work, just as it hasn't worked on any of the others who have walked similar paths. Be kind, Lucifer."

The devil grinned rather unrepentantly. "I can't help it. It's my nature. I was born bad. Being kind is such a drag. Don't ruin my fun. I get so little of it."

Yep, the Lord of Lies was spouting bull-shit, and even I could tell.

As calling out the devil wouldn't make a difference, I considered the situation for a few moments before saying, "I walked through the valley of the shadow of death when Gordon bit me. I stepped on both sides of the wall dividing the living and dead. I figure that's why I saw those carvings. I was neither dead or alive for a while, right? So I can see things I shouldn't as a result."

"Ah," Azrael said, and he relaxed. "I under-stand now."

"I told you when you read from the Book of Life," the devil replied, his tone smug. "I told you in no uncertain terms what had hap-pened. I'll admit, I cheated a little and peeked. It's good to be me."

"I didn't think to check," Azrael confessed.

"You trusted me, the Lord of Lies, with critical information. Most would call that a mistake."

"Heaven help us all," Azrael muttered.

Only one question remained I could ask, and I wasn't sure I wanted to know the answer. "Who am I, then?"

"I will not tell you, but I will give you the key you need to answer the question on your own," the devil replied. "You are the day to his night, you are the yin to his yang, you are everything he is not, he is everything you are not. You are the alpha to his omega."

"I'm the alpha to his omega? The beginning to his end?" I asked, something about the phrasing almost as unsettling as the presence of so much divinity in my kitchen.

"Just a facet of it," the devil replied before he vanished in a cloud of yellow smoke that reeked of brimstone.

FOURTEEN

This is like the start of a bad joke.

TAKING Azrael for a spin in my truck was the most normal part of my day. The Archangel of Death rode in the bed, standing so he could look over the roof and enjoy the wind. Eoghan claimed his usual seat, and Michael and Gabriel crammed into the back of the cab. Dimitri had wisely fled with his incubus husband to return to their wife.

"This is like the start of a bad joke," I said, debating where I'd take my unusual passengers. Through the heart of town might do. If I was going to be the focus of the rumor mill, I wanted to give them something worth talking about. "There's no punchline, though."

"Well, we could stand in a line and punch people if you'd like," Gabriel offered.

"Once upon a time, I'd believed angels were supposed to be kind beings. I have learned this is not the truth."

The archangels snickered, and Gabriel

replied, "In some ways, we're rather human, aren't we?"

"You're annoying," Eoghan grumbled.

They laughed.

"Stop picking on the archangels, Eoghan. They're our guests."

"They're contaminating Lady Luck."

I joined the archangels laughing. "It's just a ride in the truck for a while, Eoghan. They're not contaminating Lady Luck. Be nice. Just be glad the other one went back to causing trouble elsewhere. He'd fight with his brothers in the back because he can—or he'd be riding in the bed with Azrael to help scare half the town. Hey, you two archangels. I'm going to dump you at the cemetery with your brother before I go home. I'm going to have lunch and go back to bed, as my head still hurts."

"I will lay the groundwork of healing for your head at the cemetery, but you will want to go to your bed. Eoghan, you will want to keep a close eye on her. You can call my brother should you have questions. She will be fine, but her behavior may be unexpected. Holy fire does strange things to humans of all variants."

"I'm just glad I don't have extra toes or longer thumbs. I like my thumbs and toes just as they are," I said, debating on where to take my unusual passengers. "There's not much here outside of the cemetery and some farms."

"Perhaps you could show Eoghan where you grew up. Where you started is as important as where you are and where you're going," Gabriel suggested.

Huh. As that made sense and my parents were probably headed back to Las Vegas already, I headed across town to the ratty old farmhouse they'd gotten from an estate sale for a pittance. The hundred acres rotted, as did the building, which had never counted as a happy home to me. I put the truck into park at the end of the driveway, eyeballing where my parents tended to park their old beaters.

Neither vehicle was anywhere to be seen.

"They are not here," Gabriel announced. "And no lock can defeat us. Entering such a property breaks no angelic law."

"I don't have a key," I admitted. "They never gave me one as a child, and since they keep asking for money, they can't afford another mouth to feed anyway."

"Such sad humans."

That was one way to put it. Shrugging, I put the truck back into gear and pulled down the driveway and parked near the front doors. Time hadn't done the place any favors, and nobody had bothered with the lawn since I'd left. Sighing, I shook my head. "Well, it's not quite like how it was when I was little and my parents took advantage of eager child labor to keep the place somewhat presentable."

"It's decrepit," Eoghan said, and he

frowned. "It has potential, and it saddens me to see it like this."

I liked Eoghan thought the place could be something worthwhile. "I used to love this house."

"You still do," Michael corrected. "You do not love the people who live here, but you do love the house. It is where your heart has lived for most of your life, and your heart remembers."

Damn. "There's not much I can do about that."

"Of course there is," he corrected, and he got out of my truck. "Show us your home."

"What do you mean by that?"

Azrael hopped out of the bed of the truck. "He means Eoghan has much wealth, and the humans who created your seed of life desire wealth. He would not at all miss the wealth he would spend to secure this home and bring it to its proper glory, and they would peacefully leave you be, as he would write in such a clause into the agreement for the sale of the home."

Deep lines furrowed Eoghan's brow, but then he smiled. "I've changed my mind about you, Azrael. I might almost like you."

"I will forever vex you, but we shall vex each other on good terms, much like our beloved fallen brother insists on vexing us at every opportunity but we love him all the same. It is not a bad way to live."

"Don't push your luck."

I giggled at their posturing and shook my head. While they investigated the front yard, I checked on the back to discover even more natural destruction. Once upon a time, there had been a back yard. A year of growth had transformed it into an impassable jungle. "What the hell? Did they spray the whole thing down with fertilizer to help it along?"

Azrael joined me. "Hardly. You might want to have a new house built. This one is not long for this world." The archangel pointed at the foundation, which had crumbled to the point of having holes leading into the basement. "That is not how it should be."

I sighed. "Yeah. The damned thing is coming down around their ears. They wouldn't get anything for the house here, but they might get something for the land."

Azrael turned and shouted, "There's space for your horses, Eoghan."

That got the antique on the move, and he strode over. "My willingness to pay for the land has increased significantly. How much land is good for horses?"

"There's a hundred acres. It used to be a farm, but the farmer got old and died, and he didn't have any family left, so the town sold the place off at auction. My parents bought it back when they were much younger and hadn't pissed their money away."

Eoghan's brow furrowed. "Azrael, is the node *here*?"

"*He* moves in mysterious ways," the Archangel of Death replied.

"You asked for a ride in the truck because you knew she'd take us here," Eoghan accused.

"Yes."

The antique was not impressed with the archangel, and he braced his hands on his hips. "Won't that bring Hammel here eventually?"

"Should you and she be found here often, yes. This would be a good thing to have happen."

I liked the old house and its many acres just as much as I liked the house I rented. I wondered if I could have it all thanks to Eoghan's hefty paychecks

"Who the hell knows where my deadbeat parents went this time," I grumbled.

"The blue-feathered menace over there can help you with that," the devil announced from behind me.

I shrieked at the unexpected arrival of the Lord of Lies. "Would you stop that?"

"No. It is far too much fun to pop in at my whim and scare the liver out of you. I love watching your antique get all snarly every time you make noises he doesn't like."

"He is the devil, Anwen. You can't expect him to be a kindly spirit even part of the time," Azrael chided.

Right. I dealt with a bunch of winged ass-holes out to cut a few years off my lifespan. I took a few moments to breathe, considering my options. "All right. I see I've been doing this wrong. What do you want us to do so we can just get to doing it? That's what's going on, right? You have something you think we should be doing, so you're maneuvering us so we do it."

"Isn't she cute, Azrael?" the devil cooed.

I debated kicking the devil in the shins.

"I value my feathers, which her antique would pull out should I answer that question. You know how long it takes to regrow our feathers."

The devil snorted. "It's instantaneous."

"I do not find you all that amusing."

The devil grinned. "Ah, but you do find me somewhat amusing. You love me, but as I'm a most wonderful brother, I won't force you to admit it right now. Eoghan, she's absolutely correct about her suspicions, but playing our game directly benefits you. You want what can be found here. You want that Hammel fellow out of your way and escorted to my many hells, which would be a consequence of you acquiring this property in a peaceful manner, and you will gain other benefits by making this your main property. You can then turn the other home into a haven for your vampiric friend so he might be able to build a family of his own in a peaceful way. That was her idea, by the way. I am merely stealing it and presenting it on her behalf, as she would fail to move beyond thinking it."

Eoghan regarded me with a raised brow before giving the devil his attention once more. "As you are determined to make this a reality, just tell me how much I should pay in the correct currency, what terms I should make on the purchase, and how to go about this."

"Anwen's parents can't pay their property taxes because they have spent their money on poor choices. Their various vices. It is their nature. There is something to be said for them. Their example showed Anwen what *not* to do with her life, and she has done well despite the obstacles in her path. Her parents will lose the property within a month should they not acquire the funds. By purchasing it now and paying off their owed taxes, you will be able to acquire the property and building, free of debt, for a hundred thousand dollars. However, two hundred thousand will purchase you permanent peace, as her parents would move a rather notable distance away using the excess money. Tragedy will eventually catch up with them, but that tragedy would occur in either case. They are not wise people. The only difference is that the tragedy of their choosing would happen a little later in their lives with the more expensive option. This will weigh far less heavily upon Anwen's shoulders as a result. I seem to have more lawyers than I know what to do with. I will gift one to you for this matter, as doing such things annoys my brothers, as it goes against my most cruel and evil nature. Annoying them is the only payment I need for this."

I could think of a few things that would ensure there were no accidental debts with the devil. "I will require a coffee date with your wife as payment for putting up with you."

"My darling would love that. She doesn't often return to the mortal coil without me, as she has some odd misconceptions about her role as my wife. For some reason, she seems to think if she leaves my presence while here, she will land herself in a great deal of trouble. Her troubles ended long ago. Of course, I may have neglected to tell her that to keep her close to home. I do love when she gets bristly. I keep telling her she can go where she pleases, but for some reason, she doesn't believe me."

I could think of more than a few reasons why that would be. "Well, your title *is* the Lord of Lies."

"True, true. It's like people take that seriously. I only lie when it directly benefits me."

"Wouldn't smart mortals always take that seriously?"

"You don't. You stop to think about whether I am being honest or not. It confuses you every time you realize I am being an honest being—but you do consider my every word in search of the lie. My lies are of a more subtle nature. I do lie, though. That is my nature."

I could believe that, but I always questioned if it was truly his nature—or his duty.

"You're catching on."

"Since you're being so forthcoming about the future, what can you tell us about Hammel's plans?" I asked.

"That is not something I will tell you. It's something you'll have to discover on your own," the devil replied. "You already have the pieces of the puzzle in your possession. You merely need to put them together in a way that makes sense. You know that the node is here somewhere. You know that it is an object. You also know that it will attract your prey here. You know your prey's motivations. You can do what you want with him. You have just cause, and all you'd have to do is tell an angel you'd been kidnapped by him to turn any charges into self-defense, especially should he come onto your property causing problems—another reason you would be best off purchasing the property. With a little angelic assistance, the sale could be processed within a few days."

Two hundred thousand could buy a future, and it seemed so little for so much, although before Eoghan, such a sum would have been an unobtainable wish. "Why is the house worth so much here?"

"They kept refinancing the property to pay for their vices," the devil replied.

Of course. My parents would. "To the point they have a mortgage and owed property taxes amounting to a hundred thousand?"

"Correct."

Why wasn't beating sense into my parents legal? "Dare I ask how much the house cost them? I knew how they got it, but I didn't know how much they paid."

"Oh, twenty thousand."

I slapped my forehead. "Those braindead idiots!"

"It could be worse," the devil soothed.

"Okay. I'll bite. How could it possibly be worse?"

"They could cut a deal with that Hammel fellow about you. You might hate them, but you're a gentle being, and they are your parents. Oh, Eoghan?"

"What?" he replied, and he scowled at the devil. "Unless you're telling me my two hundred thousand prevents that from happening, I don't want to hear it."

The devil laughed. "Yes, it will prevent that future from coming to pass. It will make other futures come to be, but those are consequences you will find easier to handle. And now that I've meddled enough to annoy my heavenly brethren, it's time for me to get home to the missus. I'll tell her I've made a poor bargain involving her, and as soon as she's done educating me on the errors of my ways, I'll send her over for coffee, Anwen."

The devil disappeared, and I rolled my eyes over his antics. "Okay. Which one of the archangels do I talk to about talking to my idiot parents and getting them out of my hair for the rest of my lifetime if at all possible?"

Michael raised his hand. "I'll volunteer. This is more fun than I've had since Lucifer thought it was a good idea to adopt a sphinx."

"What's wrong with sphinxes?" I asked.

"Oh, nothing's wrong with her. She just makes it her mission in life to try to kill her father when she's not doting on her husband, who happens to be a kelpie."

"Kelpie? What's that?"

"Kelpies are demonic horses," Eoghan replied with a scowl. "A rather nasty species, really."

"This one is fairly benevolent. He's a saltwater variant, and he only has interest in dragging his wife to the shore so they can make little babies. He hasn't had any luck yet, but I give it a year or two before he catches her off guard and I get a little niece to spoil. I suspect it'll happen around the same time he teaches her how to swim, as she's rather hopeless around water. They'll toss more fillies than they'll know what to do with, as my brother has a wicked sense of humor and no dignity. They'll get a son eventually, but only after his gem of a daughter threatens to castrate him if he doesn't stop meddling with her husband."

That poor woman. "You're all aiming for her to have kids, aren't you?"

"It's a joy in our long life. My contribution will be swimming lessons, I believe. He is very protective, and he will not take her into the water until he's confident she can swim—but every time he gets her near the shore, his common sense abandons him, so the requirements for them to produce a child are never met."

I laughed at the thought of a being as powerful as an archangel lowering himself to teaching a woman how to swim so he could have a niece. Then, as I wanted to get on with the rest of my life sooner than later, I said, "Let's assume I want this over as quickly as possible with as little interaction with my parents as possible. How would we accomplish that?"

"I will present an offer to them for the property including a payment on all owed back taxes, get their signature, and pay for it in cash, with an immediate closing date following the final approval of the sale. I will be your legal representative for the transaction. While Eoghan's name would be on the official documents, it's minimal work to have ownership become joint after the finalization of the sale. The bank will add a day or two, but this is no concern. Should you add in an agreement that you will handle anything left on the property, and that the price includes them moving out sooner than later, you should find the keys in your possession within three days."

I could work with three days. "And in the meantime?"

"Go home, relax, and don't go on any evening trips to purchase furniture."

Right. Buying bookcases had gotten me into trouble once already. "I think I can manage that."

"Eoghan, you should keep her amused at home. You should use your masculine charms to accomplish this," Michael suggested.

Michael went to the top of my list of archangels I liked.

According to Eoghan's expression, he believed the archangel had lost his mind. "Pardon?"

"Right. Forget I said anything. Anwen, my dear, I will discuss this matter with Darlene before your coffee date—and I'll pay a visit to her to make sure she's clear on what the actual situation is. I'd rather my brother not come to his demise at the hands of his wife. He's bored, and when he gets this bored, his wife does sometimes manage to beat him into submission—and it really makes a mess of his hells when he's on bed rest for a few months because he angered his wife."

What the hell could his wife do to the devil to put him on bedrest for that long?

"You really don't want to know the answer to that question. It's terrible, and being the devil, he even likes it. But there is nothing scarier in all the hells than the devil's wife running the place."

"I should be more surprised by this than I am," I confessed.

"I propose you start looking into your dream home on the internet." Michael stretched his wings and gave them a shake. "Work on that with Eoghan. Build a future on the rubble of the past, although you will want to thoroughly investigate the house before you demolish it. It would do you well to show Eoghan your past, too."

"But why?"

"So you can let it go, of course. These things have a way of clinging if you don't air them out."

"I'll take that advice," I promised. Letting go would do me a lot of good—as would moving on.

"That's a girl. Now, run on home. I'll pop in to get the appropriate signatures as needed, I'll work with Lucifer's precious little attorneys making certain they are ironclad, and I'll even make sure no one signs their soul away in the process. It's annoying when souls get signed away in basic paperwork."

"Thank you for that."

"You're welcome. Good things will come, so just bear with this a little longer."

FIFTEEN

Taking the advice of an archangel
seemed wise.

TAKING the advice of an archangel seemed wise to me, so I took Eoghan home, set up the laptop at the kitchen table, and browsed real estate sites for houses while he sat with me, marveling at the modern designs. I learned three key things about him during our browsing.

He loved modern homes, he loved anything that could be turned into a barn for horses, and he fell in love with the idea of living on a ranch. The ranch made sense to me; he could ride and check on his herds and reach back to his roots despite being separated from them by thousands of years.

I preferred the larger farmhouses, the kind that could grow up to become a plantation manor with a little work and a few extensions.

Gordon joined us after nightfall, and we huddled around the laptop trying to make sense of the real estate world and how someone might have the perfect house built where an imperfect one stood. Gordon pointed at a massive log cabin that fringed on being a mansion. "You should get something like that."

I clicked on the house's picture on the real estate site, winced at its multi-million price tag, and did my best to ignore that element of the home. The exterior took the log cabin motif to extremes. The interior began rustic and transitioned to modern in places like the kitchen, the master bathroom, and the small movie theater and bowling alley in its basement. I whistled. "That's insane."

Eoghan pointed at the picture of the movie theater. "What is this room for?"

"Watching movies. You know that television we bought?"

"I do. The annoyance came over and showed us what it was, and he turned on a movie so we could be amused while waiting for news, as we would otherwise create trouble inappropriately. Once the movie was over, he suggested we should visit the cemetery."

The devil would be the death of me at the rate he was going. "What movie?"

"The Land Before Time."

Wow. The devil was truly ruthless. "Did you enjoy it?" Neither man would look me in the eyes, which made me giggle. "You totally enjoyed it." I bet they cried, too.

I did, always.

As I could be a nice person when I wanted to be, I didn't press them about it, clicking to the picture of the bathroom, which had an oceanic theme. "This is nice." I clicked to the next bathroom, which had a clean, elegant, and modern theme and a jet tub I could spend the rest of my life in. "This is nicer. I want a bathroom like this."

"What's so special about it?" Eoghan asked. "It looks nice enough, I suppose. I like the ocean theme better, though."

"The tub includes massagers in this one." Checking the notes, I gave a breakdown of the insane luxuries, including a heated floor, a ceiling shower, and everything a woman needed to pamper herself. "All it's missing is a place to put my books when I'm not reading one."

"Books and water do not mix," the antique announced.

"They do when you're using a waterproof electronic reader. I just haven't been able to afford one. As soon as I feel I can, I will buy one to add to my glorious book collection. And my book collection will be better than the town's library."

That wouldn't be hard; the town's library was located within a mobile home and contained fewer than five hundred books. When I'd been in middle school, I'd read the entire collection, and when I'd asked if there would be more coming in and been told no, I'd realized why everyone left Sunset.

Damn it, I already wanted to go back to the bookstore and buy more books for my fledgling library.

"Ah. Yes, that reminds me. We retrieved your new bookcases, and they are in the basement for now. We weren't sure where you wanted to put them," Eoghan said.

"My new house needs a library. A big one. It must be the best room in the house."

"I will not argue with you over this. I have enjoyed books since their invention, although initially, a disturbing number of them were exclusively religious texts, which annoyed me. Works of art, but not subject matter I wanted to spend all eternity reading. I was quite pleased when texts shifted from religious and non-fiction to fiction. Fiction is delightful."

Well, keeping Eoghan amused wouldn't stress me much. I'd take him to the bookstore, and once we exhausted the local store, I'd run him to one of the cities to the larger ones—or introduce him to online shopping.

His bank accounts might run dry if I showed him the wonders of online shopping.

"Do you think buying the property is a good idea?" I asked, clicking to check out more pictures of the ridiculous mansion and the wonders within it.

"Of course. Your expression told me so," Eoghan replied.

"My expression? How so?"

He chuckled, leaning back in his chair.

"When you drove to it, and it came into view, you were tense and wary. Upon realizing your parents were not present, you relaxed and smiled. When you realized how much it had fallen into ruin in such a short period of time, your expression once again became tense. Its state made you unhappy. The property makes you feel, and that is important. Some of the emotions are not good, but some are. That is important. There is also room for horses."

Right. Eoghan liked horses. "I have no idea what's needed to keep horses."

"A stable," he replied. He gestured at the laptop. "Let's search for one of those."

Oh boy. I recognized a lost battle, so I searched online for what made a good stable, and we wasted more time looking at stalls, the equipment needed to care for a horse, the cost of care, and how much horses cost. I whistled at the price tags of the animals, which ranged from as much as a month's rent to costing more than my parents' home.

"I have a pair of horses for you," the devil announced. "My wife has informed me if I do not give them to you for bothering you so much, she will surely find a way to kill me this time."

I hadn't even managed to call the devil's wife yet, and she was already out for the devil's blood on my behalf?

I loved her, and I only knew her name.

"How did Darlene find out Eoghan wanted a horse?"

"My wicked brother told her. Did you really have to involve him? My wife has taken over our bedroom and bathroom to make herself pretty for your play date. She's wearing her spots, and I wasn't invited to count them. I was invited to make sure the house sale went through, but my brother is currently—"

"—has taken care of the preliminary phase of the sale," Michael announced, also from behind me.

Why did archangels and their devil of a brother insist on manifesting behind me?

"It's more fun that way," Michael admitted, and he reached around me to set a stack of papers on my table. "As I'm a most benevolent being, I have managed to streamline the sale of your home to be concluded by this evening. It will cost an additional fifty thousand dollars to complete the signing as soon as signatures are ready, but the bank manager was willing to play ball for a fast-tracked sale. It amuses me how legalities can be dodged with the right monetary incentives. It also helped that your parents were willing to abandon everything in the building. It seems they have already removed everything they perceive to be of value from the property."

Huh. "Is hell freezing over, Lucy?"

"It often is. My wife loves her air conditioning. She is a snow leopard, after all.

There's even a room in the house that has snow year round for her enjoyment. I figured if I wanted to survive my marriage, I needed to cater to her special needs, and snow leopards without snow get very pissy. Pissy kitties like hurting people. Usually me."

"I wonder why," I muttered.

Michael snickered. "However much fun it is to watch my brother lose verbal spars, there are a great many papers to sign. Eoghan, to simplify matters for you later, I have taken the liberties of making you and Anwen joint owners of the property. I have also taken the liberty of inquiring with neighbors regarding additional acres, discovering you can add an additional seventy-five to your property, and that property includes a barn in tolerable condition for the housing of your horses until you have made your main home habitable. That will take sixty days to close, but I have secured it for you for a hundred and fifty thousand, which is above market for this area. The couple is older, and the property has become too much for them to readily manage. To them, this offer is a miracle."

"Mr. and Mrs. Smithy?" I asked, aware of the older neighbors, who'd tried their best to be kind to me despite my parents.

"Yes, that is the couple."

"They're nice people."

"Nicer than most here," the archangel agreed.

"Is that a good purchase, Anwen?"

"For your horses, yes. Your bank accounts won't miss the money, either."

"Understatement," Michael muttered.

I jabbed the archangel with my elbow. "If you're wanting to build a future with horses in it, the extra acres will give them a better home along with enough room to do whatever else you want, including operating a farm if you'd like."

"I would not enjoy a full farm, but I do enjoy a garden."

"You'll have more than enough space for a garden," I promised.

"Then we will do this. Show us where to sign, Michael."

It took almost an hour to go through all the paperwork, as Michael had to teach Eoghan how to sign his name and read the important clauses to him, explaining what they meant. It amazed me the antique approached the task with infinite patience, showing no sign his lack of understanding of English bothered him.

I supposed it had become a way of life for him, having to navigate a world without understanding the written languages every time he awoke. That bothered me.

The devil patted my shoulder. "Don't worry yourself over such matters. Within a year, he will be reading every book he can get his hands on, and you will find the easiest way to keep him at home will be to provide him with a new book."

Huh. Catching a man and keeping his attention might be easier than anticipated.

"It's all about having the right bait," the devil agreed. "I'm sure my wife will help you with the finer points."

I hoped so. "What's the next step?"

Michael helped Eoghan sign the last of the paperwork before stacking it in a neat pile. "I will go secure the rest of the signatures and issue the payment for the property, which will be processed by the bank immediately, as you are paying them quite the sum to do so. The tax payment is also being submitted and verified by the bank to streamline that portion of the purchasing process. I will come back here within the next hour with the keys, which is when you become the official owners of the property. I recommend you stay here at night to sleep and wait around for Director Hammel to come to you. It won't take him long to learn you have purchased the property; the Smithys will make certain of that."

"How should we deal with him?" I asked.

"However you see fit. We can't do everything for you. This amuses us, which is why we lend our aid. Although, I suspect Azrael will become a nuisance until this business is finished. He dislikes when his rest is disturbed. See, Eoghan? You have common ground with my brother. You both dislike being roused from your slumber."

"This is not a good thing."

"It's a great thing," the devil replied, and he stretched. "Try to get along. You are equally important to nature's flow, and it wouldn't do to upset the ladies—and my lady? She's already upset. If you keep Anwen happy, you might actually make it through this era somewhat intact." With a pop and the stench of damned brimstone, Lucy vanished.

Michael laughed. "For the Lord of Lies, he is a disgustingly honest fellow—and he often offers good advice. That is wisdom I would take seriously, Eoghan. Do yourself a favor. Tell the devil's wife that the devil is a lucky man to have a woman like her. It'll help you get through the next few days of your life without earning a beating from the Queen of Hell. And don't make the mistake most make."

"What mistake?" I asked.

"She just looks nice. She partners so well with my brother because her capacity for evil is only matched by her capacity for good."

AS PROMISED, I held the keys to my childhood home within an hour. The familiarity of them, once hanging from my parents' keychains, drove home how much had changed in a few days. Obtaining financial stability shocked me, but holding the keys of my childhood felt more like a miracle than any-thing else that had happened since I'd offered my arm to Gordon, expecting to die in the basement of the funeral home.

"There wasn't a third set of keys," Michael said.

"There never was." My parents had never believed I deserved them; if neither were home and had locked the door, I'd been ex-pected to sit outside, amuse myself, and wait. I'd spent many an hour under the boughs of a weeping willow doing my homework or reading my text books, waiting for them to come home. I couldn't count the nights I'd slept beneath the stars for that reason.

"I hadn't looked into the reason why," the archangel said, his tone heavy with remorse. "I apologize."

"You did no harm. They are memories." I considered those old experiences and how they'd shaped my present. "No, they aren't bad memories. They're just difficult ones."

"How are they difficult?" Eoghan asked.

"I never had keys to the house. My parents expected me to wait outside if they weren't home. By the time I dropped out of high school, they were almost never home. They usually locked the door. I did what I could, but that was the way of it."

"They sound like cruel people."

"She is everything they are not—and she is that way because she decided she would not be like them." Michael closed my fingers over the keys. "These are both the end and the beginning of a journey."

I understood what the archangel meant; I would continue the cycle by giving Gordon the extra keys to my little rented house—a house Eoghan wanted to purchase only because I liked it.

A week ago, I wouldn't have believed for an instant so much could change in a matter of days. In some cases, my life had changed in a matter of hours.

Michael leaned over my shoulder, using the laptop to pull up a listing of a log cabin. "This model has much of what you wish, and it will be trivial for the manufacturer to add the things you want, and a second installment can be converted to be a rather nice stable for Eoghan's horses—and your horses, too. You won't be able to share space with him without having a horse or two of your own."

"The devil is giving her a horse," Eoghan grumbled.

"He is giving you both horses, and you will find them amusing. He is giving you four horses, which will keep you sufficiently busy. Perhaps they will help you with a certain matter."

Hammel. I wrinkled my nose. "Is it too much to ask for him to just bugger off?"

"Some things you must handle yourself. This is one of them. We have meddled as much as we can. These are insignificant things we have done."

I gestured at the papers and the laptop. "This is not insignificant!"

"To us, it is. It is but the faintest ripple in even your life. Humans always fail to remember most of life's inconveniences will pass, often sooner than they believe possible. I recommend you try to get some sleep and look at your life with fresh eyes in the morning."

Michael disappeared, and I grunted at the archangel's abrupt departure. "I feel like I'm missing something important, and I don't know what it is, and that's starting to really annoy me."

Expressing my frustration helped.

"I'm missing something, too," Eoghan admitted. "I suspect we'll figure it out when we locate the node. They tend to be wells of power *and* insight—or at least every one I've encountered. But who knows? Well, beyond those busybody archangels and the devil."

I waited for Lucy to show up, but the kitchen remained devoid of the Lord of Lies. "How about you, Gordon?"

"I think I've mostly figured it out," the vampire confessed. "But I'm not fully certain, so I'm not ready to share my theory yet. I believe it'll be confirmed soon enough—and if you don't figure it out on your own, I'll explain my theory. I could be wrong."

"Is it detrimental to any of us?"

"No, I don't think so. It's just strange."

I'd lived and breathed strange since beginning my work at the funeral home. "Then it'll keep for a few nights. I'm ready for bed. Gordon, should Hammel show up, drain the fucker dry. Just do it on the front lawn and when the police ask, request an angel and tell him you were acting in defense of another."

Eoghan laughed. "I love how you are finding a way to get away with premeditated murder *and* feeding our companion properly."

"Is that feeding him properly? Gordon would be sacrificing his stomach for us. Hammel can't be good for his digestion."

Both the vampire and the antique considered my words, and as one, they nodded their agreement with my assessment.

I smiled and headed to bed, wondering what tomorrow would bring.

SIXTEEN

Fire can purify anything.

I NEEDED to take my sense of curiosity, stab it in the back, dump it in a hole, fill the hole with acid, and wait until it was reduced to an oozing puddle, and bury it. Had I been wise, I would have hired a demolition crew to handle my parents' house.

My parents were a lot of things, but they could smell a good deal just as well as I could smell the rotting garbage and dead animals in the basement. Garbage removal cost in town, something that annoyed me on a good week, and my parents' solution to the problem was to turn the basement into a landfill.

Death was too good of a fate for those bastards.

"Well," Eoghan said, pinching his nose closed before braving the steps, which creaked beneath him. In his other hand, he wielded a flashlight, which he pointed at the refuse filling the once large but barren concrete room. "I recommend fire. Fire can purify anything, even this."

"Burning it is illegal," I replied, heaving a sigh over my misfortune. Eoghan's light revealed the decaying corpses of several raccoons, which had likely fallen into the basement from a gap in the wall to die. Of what, I couldn't tell. Water dripped from a leaky pipe overhead, and it was only a matter of time before the ceiling caved in. "I wonder if I could convince the government to give me an exception. I think you're right. Purification by flames is the only choice."

"This is vile."

"Ain't that the truth. I'm glad we left Gordon at the other house. Nobody deserves to see this. It's a health hazard. Get back up here before those stairs collapse. I am so sorry I thought we should check the basement first."

"Well, at least we know what the smell is," Eoghan replied, and after a moment of hesitation, he retreated to me, and he shuddered. "Your parents are despicable beings."

"Now they're somewhat rich despicable beings. Rich enough to not bother me for a while at least."

"Money well spent, if this is at all a reflection of their souls."

I considered the garbage and rotting raccoons. "I think it may be."

"I hope the rest of the house is not as deplorable. We might need to call upon the heavenly host to deal with it should it be much worse. Will any sane human of this era accept money to deal with this mess?"

"Surprisingly, yes."

"Is money that scarce in this era?"

I shrugged. "My parents certainly think so."

"I do not believe they are good examples of humans in any era."

"I'm not arguing with you, although I probably should. They are my parents, however bad they are at being parents."

"They are two humans who indulged in lust and produced a child. That doesn't make them parents. I would say the evil horned one is a better parent, especially compared to them."

"The evil horned one?" the devil complained, manifesting in the hallway at the top of the stairwell. "That was a most excellent attempt at avoiding my attention, Eoghan. I must give you that."

Eoghan sighed. "You again?"

"Me again. It's one of my charms. How do you like the house?"

"I want you to light it on fire after we make certain there's nothing important left in it," I grumbled.

"Well, I am the devil, and I care nothing for mortal laws, and I can incinerate it to its foundations with a single snap of my fingers. Snappity snap! I could be talked into such a thing."

"I will say nice things about you to your wife," I offered. "She might not kill you when I'm finished."

"That is a very convincing argument, I must admit."

Yep, the devil was whipped by a cat. "Has she relented about permitting you to count her spots?"

"No," Lucy whined.

"Stop upsetting her, and maybe she'll let you count her spots."

"But she gets so lively when she's annoyed with me. If I am particularly evil, her tail poofs and she hisses at me."

"You only have yourself to blame," I replied, gesturing for him to get out of the way so we could escape the basement. "This place is even worse than I thought it would be."

"Yes, it does seem to be rather odiferous, and there are corpses in your basement."

"If there are more corpses than the raccoons, frankly, I don't want to know about them." I considered the house, where my parents might leave anything of value, and headed for their bedroom upstairs. Like the basement stairs, the steps creaked. "Eoghan, stay down there with Lucy. I'm not sure they'll hold your weight. No wonder they weren't here. They were probably waiting for the place to come down around their ears. What did they do to the house? It wasn't this bad a few years ago, I swear."

"The roof leaks. By leaks, I mean there are more holes in it than roof," the devil replied. "A storm tore it up and they didn't bother to fix it. You didn't check the roof yesterday—or any of the other times you've come around here since you moved out."

Huh. He was right. I hadn't bothered to look up. "Well, that sucks."

"Demolition will be much cheaper for you should you put in some honest effort to convince my wife she should let me count her spots."

"That's all I am promising, and it's not my problem if she refuses."

"Bargain made. Is this afternoon good for coffee?"

"If she's coming here and wants to sit in the back yard, sure. You can play waiter and bring us coffee and treats. Pampering your wife may help encourage her to allow you to count her spots."

"People keep telling me that, but I'm the devil. I have a reputation to maintain. Do you know how much pride I lost when I had to get on my knees and beg?"

I raised a brow at that, doubting the devil could be brought down to his knees by anyone. I climbed the stairs, and the devil teleported to join me in the hallway. "I don't want to know. Why are you following me up here?"

"When the floor collapses in the one room up here, I figured I would earn some gratitude from your man, who is pacing downstairs, well aware you are walking around in a death trap."

Okay. I could take a hint. I turned around and headed back down the stairs. "If there's anything useful in any of those rooms up there, fetch. I'll toss in a few extra nice comments to your wife, including how you spared me from falling through a floor today."

The devil laughed. "I am pleased to note you are developing a sense of self-preservation. Well done."

Eoghan raised a brow. "You believe him?"

"I really don't want to find out if he's yanking my chain. I would—"

Crack.

"I'm okay!" the devil called out.

"I see there is wisdom in your path of caution. I apologize for doubting your acceptance of his claim."

I giggled. "When a being who can look into the future at his will tells me the floor will collapse after informing me the roof has been trashed and the entire house is rotting, I'm going to believe him. I'm not stupid."

"You present a valid point. I will pay penance for my unfortunate mistake and general lapse of common sense."

"I will think of something good for later." I tiptoed to the front door, careful to avoid the trouble spots we'd identified when we'd first entered the house. "I have to tell the devil's wife really nice things about him as payment for dealing with this house. This is the easiest bargain I've made in my life. I will sing his praises once he torches this damned thing so it doesn't bother me again."

"Closure is a most valuable gift."

Yes, it was. "And burning it to ash will save on the demolition fees."

The devil popped into existence beside us, and he held a moldy jewelry box in his hand, offering it to me. I recognized it as my grandmother's from my father's side. I frowned, as I thought the precious box had been lost years ago. I took it, opening the lid. The hinges snapped off from neglect, and I cringed at having broken it. Inside, my grandmother's most prized possessions glittered in the sunlight, the silver tarnished, the gemstones dusty, but everything intact despite the box's horrific condition. "I thought this was gone."

My grandmother, right up to her death, had bothered with me, building me the swing in the back and teaching me how to play. She'd also helped me with my schoolwork, laying the foundation for my ability to budget and survive in a world that cared little for me.

Over the years, I'd forgotten about her; she'd died shortly after I'd turned nine, and her ghost had visited me so I'd know the truth my parents had refused to tell me.

She'd been one of the last ghosts I'd seen before the incident in the hospital.

Her jewelry had disappeared sometime after her death.

"When the departed have a strong enough will, anything can happen. It's rare for ghosts to manifest in such a way. She hid the jewelry box in the wall of your bedroom, hoping you would one day inherit the house that is rightfully yours. She lingered until your father inherited her box, and then she spirited it away. As I intend to leave not even ash behind, I would have ruined her plans. Nothing else here has a weight or presence associated with it."

Later, I'd cry for the old, sweet woman.

The devil patted my shoulder. "Her seed of life has since been replanted. She found heaven to be dreadfully boring and bullied her way back to the mortal coil."

I smiled at that. "You're going to have a terrible reputation if you keep this up."

"I maintain my most horrific reputation among those who deserve it. I've no interest in having your soul."

"Hey! What's wrong with my soul?" I waved the broken lid of my grandmother's jewelry box in his face. "If you don't give me an excellent answer, I'm shoving this up your ass and telling your wife to add ten years to her ban on you counting her spots."

"She is a vicious being," the devil complained to Eoghan.

"You act as though this is a problem, and I find nothing problematic about this at all."

I sat on the grass, which was in dire need of being cut, and checked on every piece of jewelry in the box, which included a lot of rings with large stones, which I assumed were beloved but otherwise worthless glass baubles, the kind of stuff I'd wanted as a child but my mother had never gotten for me.

I'd clean them up and treasure them.

"They're not glass," the devil announced.

I frowned, staring at the many rings, necklaces, and bracelets crammed inside. "What are they then?"

"Most call them diamonds, rubies, sapphires, emeralds, peridots, opals, moonstones, a few variants of quartz because she thought the colors were pretty, and so on. They're real stones. Like you are inheriting them, your grandmother inherited them, and her grandmother before her inherited them. These tend to skip a generation as they go down the line, often hidden away for a granddaughter to find. It's a family tradition. I am a terrible being, peeking into the past at my whim."

"Am I supposed to reward you for this information?"

"I would really like to count my wife's spots tonight."

I laughed. "How did you get into the doghouse, anyway?"

"I wouldn't let her steal your dog and take him to my many hells for a while."

Eoghan scowled.

I eyed Eoghan. "Why are you scowling when we're talking about my dog? You haven't met my dog yet, have you?"

Lucy smirked.

Eoghan lashed out and punched the devil in the nose. "If I could, I would kill you right now."

My mouth dropped open. "You punched him!"

"He deserved it."

"I really did," Satan agreed. The Lord of Lies and possessor of too many titles for me to remember rubbed his face. His nose bled blue fire. "Maybe you should do that again. My wife might actually take pity on me for a change."

Without waiting for any other invitation, Eoghan popped Lucy in the right eye. "I will never reject such a kind offer. Thank you. Would you like your left eye to match your right one? You'll need to halt your regenerative powers should you wish to garner any sympathy from your wife."

"No, that's quite all right. Thank you. I think that's enough."

"Are you sure?"

"Quite sure, thank you."

"Why did you find that offensive, Eoghan?"

"He likes his secrets and enjoyed when you scratched behind his ears."

My eyes widened. "*You're* my dog?"

Eoghan sighed. "I truly hate you, Lucifer."

"He is. I told you, Anwen. All facets of death have converged on Sunset, and who better to judge the state of death than Death himself? He would be the best person to know about Death; he is death in the flesh— one of three parts who can exist in the flesh. Azrael is the second. I'm sure he'd just love to—"

Eoghan slammed his fist into the devil's gut, a perfect hit to the kidney if the devil had human organs.

Apparently, the devil did, as he choked out a gasp and doubled over. Then, as the antique wasn't finished bringing the devil down low, Eoghan rammed his knee into Lucy's groin. "Maybe your wife will thank me for that one."

Ouch. "I think he's paid for his sins for a while there, Eoghan."

"What she said," the devil gasped out.

Without any hesitation, Eoghan clobbered the back of the devil's head with his elbow. "But are you truly certain about that, Anwen?"

I thought about it. "You know, if you beat him sufficiently, I'd be forced to feel pity and sympathy for him, which I would have to share with his wife. I should go to the grocery store and get something for a picnic. There should be a nice place in the back yard we can use. Just don't beat him so much he can't be useful and keep his word to remove the house and save on the demolition fees."

"I'll keep that in mind."

I took my grandmother's jewelry box and headed for the truck, leaving the devil to his fate.

I BOUGHT TOO MUCH FOOD, acquired a weed eater and enough gasoline to run it, a blanket to make picnicking cozy, and everything else we'd need to have a nice afternoon in the back yard. A pair of mountain bikes later, because I'd always wanted a bike and someone to ride with me, and I headed back to my new house to discover Eoghan beating on the devil still with an audience of a hybrid snow leopard wearing a form-fitting blouse and a pair of jeans. She bounced on her toes and clapped, her tail poofed as the devil liked.

"I haven't had this much fun since the last time Kanika seriously tried to kill you," she said with laughter in her voice. "What did you do now, you big idiot? Death is trying to kill you, and he might even get away with it if you keep pushing his buttons."

"My name is Eoghan," Eoghan replied.

"But you're Death."

"So? I am also Eoghan. Azrael is Death as well, but he is also Azrael. I'm sure the third facet also has a name, which isn't Death." Eoghan kicked the devil in the back of his heel, earning a yelp. "Must you be so difficult, Lucy?"

"Yes. He can't help it," the snow leopard

replied, and she snickered and pointed at her husband. "You're getting your ass kicked by Death."

"And you like it, you cruel wife," Lucy complained.

"Of course I like it. Every time I try, you just laugh at me and say it tickles. You enjoy it. You aren't enjoying this beating."

I shut Lady Luck's door, hauled the groceries out of the back, and set it down nearby before getting the weed whacker, filling it up with gas, and starting its motor. "All right, Eoghan. He's been beaten enough. Please watch my grandmother's jewelry box. I have a back yard to slay. I can't picnic in a jungle. Lucy, get rid of that eyesore of a house, make sure the cops don't have a problem with your demolition services, and take care of the drinks. If I didn't get the right food, bring whatever you think is better with you when you come, but be aware you will be eating my offerings at the risk of Eoghan beating the sin right out of you."

"That would be quite the feat," the devil's wife replied, grinning. "Can I watch?"

"Absolutely."

"I love you. I'm Darlene."

"Anwen. You ever use a weed whacker before?"

"No, I can't say I have. Before I took pity on the layabout over there, my neighbor took care of the edging in my yard. I did use the push mower. It was fun enough."

"This is far better than a push mower." I marched around the house. "Don't breathe near the hole. The basement is nasty, and it's the primary reason I'm having your husband torch the whole damned thing."

"I could smell it from the driveway." Darlene tapped the side of her nose. "It's sensitive. Too sensitive. I really need to convince him to change the stench of hell. If I wanted to smell sulfur all the damned time, I would've moved to Yellowstone. The geysers are prettier than lava fields."

I bet. "When was the last time you let him count your spots, anyway? According to his whining, it has been at least a decade."

Darlene skipped along beside me, and her tail fur smoothed. "A month. He's been a very naughty devil, and he hasn't been naughty in the right ways. I'm sure he'll learn to say he's sorry one of these days."

"I will not!" the devil called out from behind us.

"Then you'll be counting my spots in approximately never, asshole!"

No wonder the devil had been willing to do so much for so little. He'd need a miracle to get out of the doghouse with his wife. "Do you fight often?"

"We're supposed to not be fighting?" Darlene grinned and waved her hand to dismiss my concerns. "He gets worried when I act all lovey dovey with him. It usually means I want something, and when I want something, it usually involves him having to do something embarrassing, such as confess his eternal, undying love for me in front of his devilish horde."

The devil popped into existence in front of us, stretched out his wings, and leaned forward to get nose to nose with his wife. "Never again, you."

I considered beating the devil with my weed whacker but thought better of it; his hard skull would break my new machine, and I needed a cleared yard so I could have a picnic. "The house is still standing, Lucy. Get your ass kicked by your wife after you've done your chores."

"Maybe she should run your hells, babe. She's bossing you around, and you're even going to do what she wants. It stinks. I'll consider an exemption from your spot-counting ban should the house be properly demolished without creating any legal problems for her or Death."

"Eoghan," I corrected. "I'm still having trouble believing that part of things," I admitted.

Eoghan strolled over. "Which part?"

"You can transform into a black dog and you didn't tell me," I complained. "I could have pet you anytime I wanted, and you hid it."

The devil snickered. "You can conquer her with a mere promise she can pet you at her leisure, Eoghan. Not only does she love dogs, she adores you as a dog. You're already ahead of the game. It's good to be the Black Dog of Death, isn't it?"

Heaving a sigh, Eoghan bowed his head. "Why is killing you forbidden?"

"You'd miss me."

"I really wouldn't."

"You would."

"Boys," Darlene warned.

To my amazement, both men shut up.

"Okay, how did you do that?" I demanded.

"I merely taught mine the truth of the situation: I have what he wants, and if he upsets me, he doesn't get what he wants. The other one is smart enough to understand if he upsets me, Satin over there will get pissed and he'll have a real fight on his hands. I'm just using my authority. You have it, too. You'll see."

"Satin?" I asked.

"Our daughter's favorite name for him. He scarred the poor girl for life once after wrapping some nitwit up in a fortune of fabric and lighting him on fire. She copes with having seen her father in all his glory through odd nicknames and other strange coping mechanisms. She's got enough divine blood in her that she isn't wiped out should she get a peek of his face, but she shies away from the memories. For good reason. The first time I got a look at him, he had to take drastic measures because I wasn't born with divine, demonic, or devilish blood—and angelic blood won't save you from that, not that I have a scrap of angelic blood in me."

"I try not to think about that," the devil admitted.

"He's a big softy, and don't you listen to his lies," Darlene ordered. "The house is still standing, my dear. It stinks. Get rid of it, go calm the locals down once you're done, and don't you dare forget my coffee."

"Should I just grow coffee in our back yard?" The devil glared at the decaying ruins of the house. "Fine. I'll take care of it. Spots, my darling. I wish to count them."

"If you want to count spots, you need to earn them. Shoo. I get to play with a weed whacker, and I can't do that with you in the way."

The devil spat a few curses at his wife, who waved him off until he teleported away. "He's so high maintenance."

That he was.

Blue fire engulfed the house, although no heat washed over us as I expected. I watched with interest as the flames brightened, crackled, and died away, leaving a rather large hole in the ground. Not even the foundation remained, not that there had been much of a foundation anyway. Blue flames belched from a section of the front yard, marking where the septic tank had once been.

The devil reappeared. "You needed a new septic system anyway. You'll thank me later."

"I'm thanking you now. Thank you, Lucy."

"Spots, Anwen. I need my spots."

"Go calm the locals, and I'll ask your wife really nicely to relent and allow some spot counting." Then, as I could be as much of an asshole as his wife when I wanted, I stepped on my toes and patted his head. "You'll be okay, Mr. Devil."

"You're evil," the devil replied before he disappeared again.

"I think he likes me," I said, waving my hand in front of my face in an effort to clear the air of the brimstone stench.

"He likes my spots, and he's just using you to get access to them," Darlene replied.

"We'll probably survive. Shall we go teach the back yard a lesson?"

"Absolutely."

SEVENTEEN

I will bring severe injury to any who
try to take a piece of mine.

DARLENE LIKED MY WEED WHACKER, and
judging from her enthusiastic destruction of
every rogue plant to cross her path, she
needed more than coffee to get her through
the rest of the day. "Hell must be tough. I
don't think those plants are going to bother
anyone ever again."

"It has its moments. It's been busy lately."

"I can't even imagine how hell could be
busy, what hell being busy entails, and how
that results in you venting through aggressive
weeding of my back yard."

"He asked the asshole to come over."

"The asshole?" I asked, glancing at
Eoghan.

"Not that asshole."

"Hey," Eoghan complained. "Why am I an
asshole? I haven't done anything right this
moment to earn such a thing. I am very deliberate when I wish to be a most arrogant
asshole."

Nice. He'd been working on his sense of humor. "It's accumulative."

"Since when?"

"I decided that right now." I grinned at him. "And you were truly an arrogant asshole when we first met."

"There's a good reason for that," he reminded me.

Darlene dove for the next section of weeds to be leveled, and I removed the slaughtered weeds to clear space for the blanket and picnic basket. "While true, you about scared a few years off my life."

"I still won our wager," he replied.

"If you had spots, I'd say ban him from counting them," Darlene said, treating the weed whacker like a scythe. "Withholding spots is an excellent tactic. I'm sure you can come up with something. Perhaps freckles?"

"Alas, I do not have freckles he could count."

"Such a pity. I'm sure you'll come up with something appropriately alluring."

"Why are we killing the plants here?" Eoghan asked.

"We're going to picnic, and we need a cleared space to picnic. This space has been selected. Wait here." I headed back to the truck, loaded up on as much as I could carry, and dragged it over to the chosen picnic location. Three trips later, I went to work laying out the blanket on the space Darlene had cleared away. "It's not perfect, but once the back yard is properly maintained, we can just come out here, toss down a blanket, and enjoy ourselves."

"I see." After a moment of hesitation, Eoghan joined me on the blanket. "And we do what?"

"Eat food, talk, and be merry. That sort of thing. Mostly, we eat. If we're lucky, we'll get some entertainment to go with the food." I dug through my food purchases and revealed a cutting board and three honey rocks. "It's not a picnic without honey rocks."

Darlene killed the motor on the weed whacker, set it down, and stared at me as though I'd lost my mind. "You got one cantaloupe per person?"

I shrugged. "I'm certainly going to eat one by myself, and I will bring severe injury to any who try to take a piece of mine. I made the purchase with the safety of others in mind."

She laughed. "And I thought I was bad about coffee. That's adorable." She brushed the grass off her clothes and joined us on the blanket. "Picnicking in any one of the hells isn't really an option, although I might have to make a nice space in my snow lounge to do this. He'll hate it, and as such, I'll love it."

The devil popped into being, and he held a tray of iced coffees, which he offered to his wife. "What are you doing to our house now?"

"Figuring out how to picnic," she replied,

smiling as she accepted the coffees. "You had no idea what they wanted, so you got everyone what I like?"

"Precisely. I'm the Lord of Lies, not the Lord of Putting in Extra Effort. You should know this by now, my darling. The only one I put in extra effort for is you, and I do so grudgingly and with the expectation of my good behavior going towards permission to count your spots."

To some, love looked like roses and sweet nothings. To others, it was bickering and posturing with secret smiles.

To my amazement, I found the devil's odd brand of love to be far more genuine than the pretty lies.

The devil winked at me. "Just for that, I have good news for you."

"Must you always read people's minds?" Darlene complained, reaching across the blanket to smack her husband's leg. "You're so bad."

"In this case, yes. She thought something complimentary about me. You know I need to be praised, my darling. I'll surely expire if I don't receive sufficient attention and an opportunity to count your lovely spots. I am ruthlessly using Anwen to secure my opportunity to count spots tonight."

"You're obsessed." Darlene squared her honey rock on the cutting board and slammed the poor knife through it, chopping it in half with no sign of effort. "Just handcuff them together and cheat."

"They don't have appropriate living arrangements for that quite yet, darling. We don't want to traumatize their vampire friend."

Eoghan raised a brow, but as he looked more amused than alarmed, I decided to say nothing and pretend they weren't discussing how we should be spending our time together.

Then again, I thought dragging Eoghan to my bed would be a very good use of my time.

I had more problems than I could shake a stick at, but in good news, the decrepit ruins of my parents' house wasn't one of those problems.

Darlene scowled and eyed the hole that had once been my parents' house. "You make a good point. When you cheat, the couple does tend to embarrass anyone who knows them for a few days. But they'd like it."

"You can also cheat, my darling."

"You cheat better than I do, and I'm displaying my spots for you right now."

"I do find the presence of spots to be highly encouraging. You should encourage me."

"You promised me entertainment today. Until I'm properly entertained, I am not sharing my spots with you."

"But I want them," the devil whined.

"So needy. Entertainment first. Those are the rules."

"That implies I get to count spots today."

"If I'm properly entertained, you may count spots."

The devil pilfered one of the honey rocks, cracking it in half with his bare hands. "Today is a good day. Your entertainment will arrive soon. The first part of the entertainment will be here shortly after Anwen finishes preparing her treat."

I waited for Darlene to finish slicing her honey rock before I went to work on mine, and as I was a generous being, I cut Eoghan's up for him at the same time. "I like how the entertainment is waiting for me to have a snack."

Michael, Gabriel, and Azrael popped into existence behind the devil. Gabriel fisted his hand and smacked his devilish brother upside the head. "You're trouble. Why must you always create trouble?"

I nibbled on my honey rock and observed the entertainment. Darlene did the same, and the tip of her tail twitched. Her ears remained forward, which I translated to mean she enjoyed watching her family's drama.

Eoghan snorted and ate his share of honey rock, shaking his head.

"It's fun," the devil replied.

I laughed at that. "If you expected any other answer from him, you need to go sit in the corner and adjust your general expectations."

"You're meddling. Again. You're toeing the lines. Again. Why must you do such things? *He* has noticed, and we're supposed to make sure you don't create more trouble. *He* told us to keep you company to make sure you don't do something foolish. Again."

"*He* loves my antics. The stuffy believers just don't like me, so *He* has to pretend *He* hates me."

The Earth was not of sufficient size to contain the devil's ego.

"You're luring the one who seeks to circumvent death here. On purpose. To do what?" Gabriel demanded, and he crossed his arms over his chest and stretched his wings. I assumed the wing display was meant to intimidate. The devil laughed and waved to dismiss his angelic brother's complaints. "Lucifer, can't you be serious?"

"I am being serious. This is the most efficient solution to the problem, and it permits me to meddle to the fullest extent possible. If I permitted things to play out in their natural course, it would take weeks to accomplish the same goal. This way, I also get to enjoy a picnic. It's been a while since I've enjoyed a picnic. My wife is also enjoying the picnic, too. You know how I feel about anyone interrupting things my wife enjoys."

"You're whipped," the devil's wife informed him. "By me. I like that. It hasn't been that long since I let you count spots."

"It's been too long."

Eoghan leaned towards me and whispered, "He could have counted her spots an hour ago and it would have been too long for his liking."

Lucy heaved a sigh. "I see how it is. I was being helpful. Can't I be helpful without everyone doubting me?"

"Absolutely not," all three archangels chorused.

I laughed and went back to eating my honey rock. "Hammel is coming here, then?"

"He'll be here fairly soon," the devil replied. "I sent a minion to tell him what he wants is here. Which it is."

Crap. I'd forgotten about the node. I twisted around to stare at where my parents' house used to be. "We didn't incinerate the node, did we?"

"We?" the devil replied.

"I told you to do it, and you did it. Therefore, we applies."

Darlene snickered. "You're right, you goof of a husband. I *do* like her. Anwen, we're going to need to picnic and have coffee again soon. I haven't had this much fun in a while."

I liked the sound of that, so I nodded. "I can probably convince Eoghan to tolerate your husband. They can keep each other amused while we enjoy coffee."

"Men are a lot of work, aren't they?"

I pointed a piece of my honey rock at Eoghan. "My initial impressions of this one involves a lifetime of potential frustration."

That earned me a scowl. "Pardon?"

I ignored the complaint in his tone and took a bite of my melon.

Eoghan grunted but didn't say another word.

"Men, particularly husbands, are constant sources of frustration. As he is not yet your husband, you can trade him in for a different model if he doesn't live up to your expectations. Once married, especially to the annoying immortal types such as these two men, you tend to be stuck with them. I was thoroughly tricked, and now I have to make the most of it. My spots are a most effective tool at keeping him tolerable. If he isn't tolerable, he doesn't get to see the spots let alone count them. They're an effective disciplining tool."

The devil sighed. "They really are. I like those spots too much for my own good."

"You're a pest," Darlene informed her husband.

"But I forgot about the node. Shouldn't we know where it is *before* he gets here?" I asked. "Won't it be problematic if he acquires it?"

"It weighs about six thousand pounds. It's not going anywhere, Anwen," the devil replied. "And it's not like knowing where the node is will help him. Nodes have power, but what he wants is an impossibility. This node isn't like some, which are basically magical batteries. This one takes potential and gives them life—in the right circumstances. It *could* give him the raw magical power required to accomplish his goals, but it would break the universe, and that sort of thing is annoying. Anyway, he had his chance, and he squandered it. More accurately, he didn't realize he had his chance. The Book of Life is outside of his reach, the fates are off doing whatever they want, and the facets of death all have a rather strong dislike of him. You did put the Book of Life back where it belongs, Azrael?"

"It's fine. The mausoleum, as Anwen thinks of it, is properly warded against mortals wandering into it. That won't stop the perceptive, the determined, or the divine from paying it a visit, but you won't have random townsfolk walking in at their whim."

I frowned. "Wait. What do you mean by taking potential and giving them life?"

The devil reached over and pressed his finger to my nose. "You're a potential. Every mortal—and immortal—is a potential. Your seed is a potential that has the opportunity to grow in the right conditions. In your case, your potential bloomed as the universe intended, with the node aiding the efforts. You no longer need the node to reach your full potential; its work is done."

"It's depleted, isn't it?" Eoghan asked.

"Not quite, although Azrael's little display at the cemetery used up most of the excess power it had. It will spend the rest of this emergence recharging, after which you'll find this property suitable for remaining awake until the next emergence."

Eoghan sucked in a breath. "That's a pretty powerful node, Lucy. I'm usually among the first to go dormant."

"I would say it's less powerful and really good at its one trick. Your Anwen has been grooming it for most of her life without knowing it, and things she likes, it will like—and she likes you. Your range won't be too far outside of Sunset when this emergence collapses, but I think you'll find the restrictions tolerable."

I'd been doing *what* to the node? I tossed a melon rind at the devil, smacking him in the head with it. "I have not been grooming anything!"

"Wrong type of grooming," Darlene said with laughter in her voice. "He means you've kept the node company, and it likes you. That's all. He wasn't trying to be a pervert this time. Usually, he does—but not this time. That might be a miracle."

The devil rubbed his forehead where I'd hit him with the rind. "You're such a pervert, Anwen."

My face flushed. "I am not!"

"You're the one who assumed I meant you were sexually grooming and potentially assaulting a node."

I grabbed my next slice of honey rock, devoured it in record time, and flung the rind at the devil. "You're *evil.*"

Rather than allow it to smack him in the head again, the devil caught the projectile and set it on the cutting board. "And you have good aim with those melons. You should save some of that as ammunition for when Hammel arrives."

"Why would I at all share my honey rocks with him? He might get to enjoy the juice should I hit him with the rind. I should go collect rocks to throw at him." I grunted. "What am I supposed to do when he gets here? Should I just call the cops and let them deal with him?"

"You have two facets of death here who would be more than willing to aid you with today's activities."

"Darlene, make him deal with the asshole. I don't want the asshole ruining our picnic," I whined.

The snow leopard tossed her head back and laughed. "You don't like beating around the bush, do you?"

"Not if he's…" I frowned and considered my weed whacker. "Is it possible to kill someone with a weed whacker?"

"Yes," the devil replied. "It is absolutely possible to kill someone with a weed whacker, especially if it has been imbued with holy and devilish fire."

I turned to Eoghan. "Have you ever killed someone with a weed whacker before?"

"Until today, I have never seen a weed whacker, so no, I can't say I've killed someone in such a fashion."

"We could kill him with the weed whacker," I suggested.

"I see you are not very concerned about Hammel's fate," Eoghan replied.

"The fucker tried to kill me. Turnabout is fair play, and I've decided I'm meaner than he is. I'll go back to being shy and nice later, after he's gone and stops trying to kill me. And he kidnapped me. Two strikes. Three strikes, he's out—and coming to my property, probably to try to either kidnap or kill me again, is definitely the third strike. I have better things to do than worry about whether or not he is going to try to kidnap or kill me again. Or hit me over the head. Or try to feed me to a vampire."

"Or try to feed you to me," Eoghan added, his tone amused.

Darlene snickered. "She wouldn't mind if you—"

The devil reached over and covered his wife's mouth. "He's thousands of years old and very formal, my darling. However willing she may be, let's not fluster him. That said, Azrael could officiate things to make the next part of her life easier."

"Bed her, wed her, and plan to stick around for life because she won't let death have you, Eoghan," Azrael suggested.

"She doesn't get a say..." Eoghan's eyes

widened, and he gave the archangel his full attention. "You can't be serious."

Azrael shrugged.

As the antique wasn't getting a straight answer out of the archangel, he turned to the devil. "You can't be serious," he repeated.

The devil smiled. "I am often serious when I do not appear to be. It is one of my favorite lies."

"It really is," Darlene muttered.

"I married such a cruel woman. Me. The devil. Brought low by a woman's spots."

"Being brought low sometimes gains you access to those spots you so love. You'll probably survive. It'll be a near thing. I'll just have to take you home with me and keep an eye on you during your severe illness and your recovery."

"Can I interrogate him before you take him home?" Eoghan asked.

"Of course. If you beat him, he can cry about how he was treated so poorly and requires my love to survive. Watching him brought low is one of my joys in life."

"Explain yourself, Lucifer!" Eoghan demanded.

"I didn't have anything to do with this. It's the universe's fault. Blame the universe. Azrael, tell him I'm right."

The archangel once again shrugged. "As I cannot lie, I must report he is indeed correct. The universe is to blame for this. The universe planted the seed, the universe provided the conditions needed for the seed to grow, and your awakening has less to do with the magic of this era and more to do with her presence than anything else. More specifically, the first time she approached death's door in earnest, you awoke. That began the moment that vile human set her on the path that should have led to her death. Instead, she got you. I'm not sure which fate is worse."

Ouch. I grinned at the archangel's disgusted tone. "That was just mean."

"But true."

I loved archangels. They redefined what it meant to be an asshole, but they were so damned honest about it. "How do you feel about using a weed whacker to kill off a jackass who tried to break the rules?"

"I would be quite pleased to offer some holy fire to the cause. I would lower the shroud so—"

"No," Darlene said, and she pointed at the archangel. "You keep that thing where it belongs!"

"That thing is my head."

"Keep it where it belongs."

The devil's soft chuckle drew my attention to him, and he reached over, snagged his wife by the waist, and dragged her across the blanket onto his lap. "I'll cover your eyes, my darling. It won't hurt you to see him. It won't even hurt your new friend, although her reaction to beholding the heavens is more curiosity than anything else."

Darlene's tail, which had puffed, warned me the incident of seeing her husband's face had left a mark. "That's not fair."

"Don't be worried, Anwen. She wasn't born able to look upon the heavens without consequence, and while she's capable of withstanding it, her soul remembers."

Azrael circled the blanket and stroked his hand over Darlene's hair. "I can erase the memory if you'd like. *He* is only willing to meddle so much."

"*He* just likes when I owe *Him*," the devil complained.

"Why do you owe *Him*?"

"When my brother here slipped and she caught a glimpse of her husband in his full glory, *He* planted just enough divinity within her soul to allow her to survive. It was not without consequence. Her soul has since been converted, but she still remembers, as her mortal soul is still hers—it is simply more divine and demonic in nature than human."

Darlene scowled, and she hid her face against her husband's chest. "I'm not a coward."

"No, you were mortal. Most mortals are immediately slain for beholding the heavens," the archangel replied.

Even Michael and Gabriel, who remained silent spectators, fidgeted.

"And since I'm not precisely mortal, I can see you as you are," I guessed.

"Precisely," Gabriel said, and he sat nearby,

reaching over to pick up one of the uncut honey rocks. "This is a divine soul—or a soul that is more than mortal. The outer rind is what protects those of us with it from the reality of an angel's existence. Or *His* existence. Comparatively, humans lack the protective rind. They are beautiful but fragile. Divines are less beautiful, but we have the strength and defenses they lack."

"You consider yourself to be less beautiful than humans?"

"Humans are every possibility. That is a thing of beauty. We angels are set in our ways, and change is rare for us. Yes, I consider us to be less beautiful than humans. But they are also frustrating beings, and there are times I do not at all mind they reap what they sow."

"Angels are assholes," Darlene muttered.

The devil kissed the top of his wife's head. "That we are, my darling. Would you like to use the weed whacker on that foolish mortal? I know how you enjoy some wholesome carnage."

She shook her head. "Anwen should come into her own, but make sure your fire hurts extra. The jerk deserves it. I like existing."

"So do we all. I shall make sure her weed whacker becomes a suitable tool of justice."

"That sounds so wrong coming from you," Michael complained.

I laughed.

EIGHTEEN

This really isn't an efficient weapon.

I'D SEEN enough trauma pass through the funeral home to recognize Darlene lived in the past, present in body only. The devil served as a quiet anchor, listening to his brothers discuss their options while waiting for the final player of our twisted game to arrive. Instead of guilt over planning to kill someone, I prepared the weed whacker, removing the protective shield designed to prevent people from turning it into a lethal weapon.

A gun would have done the job better and more humanely, but I didn't own a gun and had no idea where to get one. Well, I had a good idea where to get one, but I'd have to go rob my neighbor's house. He wouldn't miss a few of his guns. Hell, he might not even notice I'd taken one—or ten—of them.

"This really isn't an efficient weapon," I confessed. "A gun would do a better job. And a quicker job. It would probably do a cleaner job, too."

Gabriel joined me, and he touched the weed whacker. The cord burst into blue and white flames. "You will find this contribution to be helpful. His death is both necessary and symbolic. It must be at your hand, too. At your hand means triggered by an action you take. In this case, be it choosing to stand where he will reach his ultimate end, by taking this weapon you're fashioning and slicing his throat with it or shooting him. For the record, letting the devil do your work would be the most merciful way to kill him, although you will find this weed whacker more efficient than you thought possible. Anything else will prolong that human's suffering, which you would not enjoy."

"Why must his death be at my hands?"

"You cannot grow into your true self without witnessing a death you ultimately hold responsibility for. Only then will you reach your full potential. It must be a deliberate death, one of your choosing. Essentially, a murder, although this is a deserved one. You will understand soon enough. And Eoghan?"

Eoghan scowled. "What?"

"Do try to control your impulse to protect her from what she is, even should his soul scream—or he startle her into screaming."

"I hate the screaming," he muttered.

I frowned, considered what I knew about Eoghan and his secrets, and asked, "The souls scream upon death, don't they? And you can hear them. It's not the literal screaming that bothers you."

Eoghan sighed, and Gabriel patted my shoulder. "He strongly dislikes when you scream, although he doesn't dislike your screams for the same reason he dislikes most screaming. He is concerned you will suffer. He fails to remember you are an entirely unique entity, embodying everything Azrael and he do not."

"I don't understand," I admitted.

"You will soon enough. Try your weed whacker out on your yard to amuse yourself —and to understand the power you currently wield." Gabriel turned to Eoghan. "None of your overprotective whining."

"Why do you think I'm going to whine?"

"You are male and you are invested, but most importantly, you are male. I present my brother as a prime example of what it means to be annoyingly male. However, if you wish to see the devil in all his glory, you would merely have your lady stand somewhere over there." Gabriel pointed behind the devil. "This Director Hammel would step within his reach and find himself directly escorted to my brother's many hells. It would also fulfill the condition she holds responsibility for his death. She would merely choose her weapon wisely."

Weed whacker or the devil, weed whacker or the devil. How much did I truly hate my former boss?

Huh. I hated him enough I couldn't find any disadvantages in allowing the devil to deal with the fool should he at all threaten the snow leopard—or come within reach of her. "I'm a terrible person, aren't I?" The archangels laughed, and I started the weed whacker. "Bring it on, you winged menaces."

"So vicious," Azrael said with laughter in his voice. "Are you sure you're ready for an eternity with her, Eoghan? I could save you."

Eoghan picked up a slice of honey rock, raised a brow, and partook of my favorite treat. "I am finding the current situation to be pleasing."

"Of course. You discovered there was, in actuality, a soul you did not want to slip from your grasp. Frankly, your bellyaching over it was becoming obnoxious. Not even you can circumvent what we are."

I realized the true reason so many had believed I'd struggle with Eoghan.

He understood he would live forever.

He understood I would not.

"You will now," Azrael promised. "But yes, that was a factor, and an important one. He will still resist your attempts, but he will do so for the love of the game rather than the fear of what he once believed was an inevitability. His is a gentle soul no matter how he postures. Think of it this way. You are a gift from the universe, one meant for Eoghan as much as you're meant for humanity and this Earth's many creatures. You serve a purpose, but you were created as a mercy. The universe is many things, but it loves its children—and Eoghan is one of its beloved children. It didn't put sufficient thought into being stuck with him permanently, but even the universe has its flaws."

"Azrael," Eoghan warned.

"Eoghan," the archangel mocked. "You are always so annoying about life and its inevitable conclusion. Even I am capable of understanding the desire for companionship. That is my role, after all. I am a companion through death. You are the welcoming arms of death. You are no different from me beyond how you go about your purpose."

"One day, may you get exactly what you deserve," Eoghan growled out from between clenched teeth.

"He means a wife and a demon to go with her," the devil announced. "I can help you with that. I know some excellent incubi who will make even better fathers, and I even have a few defective ones who crave loyalty running around. I'm just not sure how that keeps happening. I should beat it out of them one of these days."

"Please, no. I have seen this wife." Azrael pointed at me before pointing at Darlene. "I have seen that wife, too. Why would you wish such a thing upon me?"

The devil laughed. "Because wives are wonderfully fun, even when you wish they didn't hurt. My wife is a delightful creature, and in reality, I will count her spots for her benefit this evening, however much I will enjoy my manly duties. For all she postures, she enjoys when I count her spots. By nature, she is an affectionate creature, but she had always been taught she could not seek out such affections, as it would require the sacrifice of her pride. She is a work of art, beautiful because of her flaws."

I realized the woman had passed out on her husband's lap, and she purred in her sleep. "That poor woman. Is she all right?"

"I do not want to erase what has become an integral part of her, although I wish it would not hurt her so much to remember," the devil admitted. "There are some things even I cannot do."

"When young Anwen witnesses death in the flesh, she will be able to close and open that door and make acceptance an easier thing for your kitten," Azrael promised. "*He* understood the necessity of what she endured, but it is not *His* duty to finish healing her soul. You will find your role in the matters of death to be mostly enjoyable, Anwen."

"I will?"

"Yes, you will. You will see soon enough. Test your weed whacker, and see what holy fire can do."

Curious over what sort of tool my implement of lawn correction had become, I moved a safe distance from the picnic blanket, revved the motor, and gave it a test swing.

The grass ignited, and a wave of blue fire stretched out in an arch. Back before my parents had turned to drugs and other vices for happiness, the back yard had been a favorite place of mine, with neatly trimmed grass and the scattered trees standing tall, proud, and full of life, with the tallest oak sporting a swing for my enjoyment.

The yard from my memory returned, although the flower beds and gardens would need to be replanted. The holy fire left dark soil in its wake, ready for my attention. The flames engulfed where the house had once stood and stretched into the front yard, halting at the property line and extinguishing at the street.

"That is so cool," I blurted.

Gabriel chuckled. "I am many things, but I enjoy when I can transform a house into a home, and this yard was more of your home than the house itself, was it not? Holy fire is many things, but it is a tool of creation. My fire linked to your memories and brought many of those memories back to life. It is a form of healing blended with a form of destruction. Some of my brothers and sisters are even better at this art than I. We all have our purpose."

I killed the motor of the weed whacker and hurried across the perfectly trimmed grass to the giant oak, its swing, and the big, dark rock I had liked using as my launch plat-form. It took a stick or pole to bring the swing to my rock, but I'd loved the thrill of jumping off.

My mother had thought of it as a death trap. My father had provided the stick and a little rope with a loop so I could pull the swing to me without wasting hours of time struggling with the task.

I'd believed they had loved me then.

While the holy fire had cut the grass and restored the yard to rights, the swing was long gone, and not even scraps of its ropes remained. I climbed onto the rock and sat, giving it a fond pat.

Gabriel followed me. "Did you spend much time here?"

"There used to be a swing here, so yeah. I did. I'd stand here and jump onto the swing."

"That's the node," the archangel informed me in a whisper.

I frowned, shifting on the rock so I could stare at its dark surface. "Really? This is it? It's a rock."

"Correct. It's a rock. It's a boring although rather large piece of quartz. And it is the power that human desires—and it cannot even do what he wishes. Mortals can be such troublesome creatures. You should return to your companion before he gets angsty, as he knows that human comes, and he does not want you far from him. He will be even more anxious because he does not wish for his burdens to be yours. He forgets the role of your aspect."

"What *is* my role, if I am as you believe?"

"New beginnings—the life that comes after death. You are also the mercy of death. You represent everything beyond death's doors. Azrael shepherds the good. Eoghan is the facet of death who welcomes all. But you? You're the one who guides souls from death back to life. Until now, your role has been handled by the universe itself, until mortals broke the chain. The devil's daughter brought much death through her choices, but because of her, you could reach your potential now, and thus, the chain is restored. Without her, the node would not have sparked your awakening into your profile—and those who had tried to circumvent death would have caused the universe itself to turn its back on this Earth, beginning the End of Days. Because of you, the circle of life continues. Eoghan and Azrael both merely need to exist for their power to manifest all over the mortal coil. The same applies with you and your power. But, you pay a dear price for that. For you, and for them, there is no end. You, like the universe, are eternal. And that is why Eoghan often sleeps. He will sleep less with you at his side—and he will find the screaming to be lessened with your presence."

It took me a few minutes to think through the ramifications of the archangel's statement. I would worry about the rest of my life and the lack of its end later. "But how could the devil's daughter have done such a thing? Did she come here?"

"She didn't have to. She just had to be at the right place at the right time. That's all. Because she was at the right place at the right time, other events were put into motion that led to that Hammel human attempting to circumvent death, which woke your potential. The universe no longer needs to replant the seeds of life. You do that just by existing. But that's also a price you'll ultimately pay, the same price Azrael and Eoghan pay. The End of Days will come and go, and you three will persist. After the End of Days, Azrael will sleep while waiting for the rebirth of the angelic host. He will no longer be an angel then, but rather an essence. You will likely shed your mortal form as well. Like Eoghan, I think you'll find the form of a black canine pleasing, although you may go the feline route simply to annoy him."

I laughed at the thought of being a cat just to annoy Eoghan. "Do I have a choice?"

"Of course, although you will find the black dog's shape easier for you to master due to the number of myths surrounding the form. It is a symbol, and such symbols have power."

"Can we make it work for so long?"

"Until death do you part does take on an entirely new meaning when you will never cease to exist—and never is a long time. I suspect you will both sleep between the more boring eras, as that's what the true immortals tend to do. And when the End of Days comes to its ultimate conclusion, you will be the light in the dark. The universe will provide the new world, but it is your hands that will replant the first seeds of life in the next existence. But yes, with enough courage and strength, you could make your eternity a glorious thing. You two fit together. He will find comfort in your presence, for you will make the passage from life to death an easier burden. The dying find peace when their souls recognize there is life beyond. You will find peace and comfort in his presence, as you know there are none Eoghan rejects. I pity the souls of those who stir your ire."

"That sounds a little farfetched to me," I confessed.

"You will understand soon, although you've scratched at the surface of it."

I could think of one thing that might fit a scratched surface involving death. "The boundary. When Gordon bit me. Is that what you're talking about?"

"Yes, that was the moment where you touched your true potential. Gordon has become special because of what you are."

"How so?"

Gabriel rolled his shoulders and leaned against my dark rock. "What do you know about vampires?"

"Well, according to the CDC, when a vampire dies and is brought back, someone else's soul takes the body. They keep the body's original name, but the person the vampire was is gone. True resurrection is an impossibility. Some speculate the new soul is often like the old person, but the truth remains: the original soul is gone."

"In reality, the original soul is bound to the comatose body and is considered lost until the vampire is destroyed. That soul slumbers, dormant. Some misguided fools, the ones' my brother's daughter stopped, were circumventing the universe's price for that sort of immortality and knocked everything out of balance. The vampires they created were using imprisoned souls stolen from the vampires to fuel other undead. They were creating a situation where multiple awake souls occupied one body. Not all vampires have a dormant and a conscious soul. The original vampires swapped souls with each other, as their creation was an act of pure love and tragedy. There are no imprisoned souls with them. They are different because of that. Their offspring are also different." Something akin to regret laced the archangel's voice.

"What's wrong? Why do you sound so regretful?"

"The day the first vampires were created was the true beginning of this Earth's end. They bent the universe's sacred rules about death. *He* finds them sad, but they are also *His* beloved. They were a mistake, but they were —and still are—a beloved mistake. If all vampires were like them, many things would be different. But all vampires are not like them, until now. Until Gordon."

Crap. I'd done more than just meddle. "I made a mess of things again, didn't I?"

"No, but you may have inadvertently undone the damage done so long ago. I will not look into the future of the next risen vampire to discern the nature of that soul, but it would be a good thing for this world should only one soul be bound to one body. It is a damnation, Anwen. The soul that becomes the vampire leads a cursed life in many ways —and the captive soul is damned to limbo until the vampire is destroyed. While the original vampires broke the laws of the universe in a fashion, they also followed the laws as well. One body, one soul."

Ugh. "But I thought only one soul can occupy one body. Vampires have two souls?"

"That is correct. When Gordon was made during the emergence, his true soul was trapped, dormant and held hostage in limbo while the damned vampiric soul controlled his body. The soul is bound to the body but drifts in the eternal void that makes up the universe itself. It is neither here nor there. It is part of that body yet separate. There are two souls, one that is ultimately lost in slumber, and the vampiric soul, which is yet another tragedy in the tragedy that is a vampire's existence. You untangled the pair of souls bound to Gordon's body, allowed the vampiric soul to return to its rest while waking Gordon's true soul and returning it from limbo. He remains a vampire, but he is not like the others of this age. You may be able to restore other vampires to their true souls, too. If the original soul has not been destroyed, you can unite them and set the vampiric soul free."

I narrowed my eyes. "You keep saying freeing the vampiric soul. Why?"

"Unlife is as much of a blessing as it is a curse. The vampire's active soul is usually suffering through damnation of some sort, enduring punishment for their sins. You have given Gordon a great gift, and you did so for no other reason than desiring what was best for him and his soul—and returning his true soul was what was best for him. Eoghan hates hearing the screams because he hears the broken hopes of the dead. You are his mirror, and you bring hope wherever you go. There is a reason the dead rose and sought you out here. You care, even for the lowest of them."

I grimaced. "Like Old Man McGregor."

"He is an excellent example."

"I feel sorry for him."

"That is because you are a being of compassion. That is part of your role in the cycle of life and death. It is the universe's sense of compassion that makes it bring renewal after death. You embody that compassion. It is the same reason you were willing to work with Eoghan despite the harshness of your first meeting with him."

"Huh. And here I just thought I was attracted to arrogant assholes."

"That is a factor in your behavior," the archangel replied.

"I'm a mess, aren't I?"

"You are as you need to be."

"Why do I have a weird skull like Eoghan and Azrael? I wasn't born in the same era."

"Modern humans are not compatible with older species of humans. For the universe to partner you with him, it had to make you in his image—in that you are the same species of human. Were you a modern human, you could share the same bed, but you could never share the same bed and produce a child from your union. This gives you that option, and long-lived species tend to wish for children down the road to add flair to their lives. For you, being a parent will be a hard but rewarding journey."

I understood. "We will have to watch our children die."

"You will. But they will move from one life to the other with no fear of what it means to die. I expect Azrael will shepherd them to your Eoghan, and you will send them beyond the boundary in as much comfort as you can. It will be a sad thing, of course. Death is for those left behind—but the reward of having them is worth the pain of their loss. But you will take those souls who hurt the most in their prior life and give them a taste of what it means to be cherished. You will be fine." The archangel turned, and aware he did have a head, I suspected he observed something in the front yard beyond my view. "The human comes. I recommend you stand close to my brother, doing so knowing you lure that one to his end. My brother will feel better handling the duty of ending that one's existence, and Eoghan will rest easier knowing you didn't take holy fire and use it on a mere mortal. He finds holy fire disconcerting."

"Why?"

"It makes the souls scream."

Ah. "Poor Eoghan."

"My brother will be merciful—for now. But when he is taken to my brother's many hells? My brother will erase mercy from his definition. That human has earned every moment of suffering. Then that soul will be balanced once more and returned to the mortal coil to be planted again."

"I don't have to actually do anything for that to happen, do I?"

"Exist," the archangel replied.

"My job seems deceptively easy."

"You are about to learn the truth of it. Choose how you wish this to end."

"Is the devil's hand the most merciful here?"

"Yes, I would say so. Death will be swift—swifter than how you would do the job yourself. Your Eoghan has no interest in mercy at this point in time."

Right. "Isn't he supposed to be neutral?"

"He does not do well at being neutral when it comes to you."

I considered that and shrugged. "If the bastard touches Lady Luck, I'm shoving the weed whacker up his ass and killing him that way."

"Fortunately for everyone here, we will not need to witness such horrors today."

"Are you sure?"

"I am certain."

"Instead of a scythe, can I keep the weed whacker?"

"You just want your lawn to be easy to maintain," the archangel accused.

"Well, yes."

"If you were to invite my brother to picnic here with his wife, we would surely show up to tease him, as it is a joy in our long lives. It seems fair if we were to help you with your lawn care should we be here for such a picnic."

"Bargain made!" I marched to the devil to stand behind him, setting the head of the weed whacker on the ground. "Hey, Lucy?"

"Yes, Anwen?"

"We should have a picnic once a week so I can make Michael and Gabriel help me mow my lawn."

"As such entertainment cannot be purchased, consider it done. Darlene will enjoy that. Even an hour among friends is a balm on her soul."

Gabriel sat beside his brother on the blanket. "I think you will find your beloved's soul will have little need of any balms in the future."

"But she likes it."

"You can still do it. You're the Lord of Lies. Lie as you are inclined to do."

The devil glared at his brother.

"He comes," Michael announced. "Do let it play out, Eoghan. Remain a neutral witness. Do not make a mess of a good thing being stubborn and male."

Eoghan scowled. "I do not like this."

"You were not supposed to like it. Let her fly. And should she fall, then it is the appropriate time to tear the annoying human male rival apart and help him on his way to visit my brother's many hells."

The devil cleared the picnic blanket and eased his sleeping wife off his lap. "I love when my brothers are reduced to encouraging me to bring murder and mayhem to the mortal coil. This is even better than Christmas."

"I feel like you're now using your wife as bait so you can murder someone." Then again, did it matter if the devil used his wife as bait? As long as she slept through the murder, she wouldn't care—and I didn't want to find out how the snow leopard reacted to being woken from a trauma-induced nap.

"Yes, I am. I do enjoy a good murder. I'm just using you as an excuse to be able to participate in a legitimatized murder. Which is entirely your fault, as you're not stopping me. You could if you wanted. As for my wife, she tends to rampage, and if I'm not fast enough with my murder, she'll steal my kill and shred the body by the time she's done with him."

"I see you two are well matched in general brutality."

"My wife sincerely enjoys winning. I enjoy winning. It's a constant battle. Eoghan, you would be wise to let the woman win from time to time. It makes her less eager to try to kill you."

"Perhaps if you would set aside your egotistical ways for five minutes, she may not wish to kill you," my antique replied.

"While this is true, we would have a great deal less fun, and I enjoy fun. My wife? She makes much of my life fun. One day, you'll understand. I think you already do. She will test your patience. She will make you like it, too."

"You're a menace," Eoghan announced.

That the devil was, but rather than point out he announced the obvious, I smiled, shook my head, and waited for the former director to arrive so I could focus on what the rest of my eternal life would bring.

NINETEEN

Few souls have a hard alignment
with the forces of good, evil, order, or
chaos.

THE INCIDENT in the cemetery had broken
something in Hammel, and the once proud
man walked as though he'd taken up the
weight of the world on his shoulders and
found the burden impossible to bear. Something in his eyes, however, put me on edge.

"You see his approach to death," Michael
whispered in my ear despite his place seated
on the far side of the picnic blanket. "That
something is the boundary between life and
death, which is reflecting against the deepest
parts of his soul. He has sealed his fate
coming here."

"Put your head back on its shoulders
where it belongs," I complained. "That's just
awful."

The archangel laughed. "It is just some
magic, Anwen. My head is where it belongs. I
am simply opting to project my voice into

your ear at a whisper rather than agitate the fool behind me."

The fool caught sight of me, and the man's expression darkened.

A smart woman would have run. I hid behind the devil and grabbed hold of the weed whacker's starter in case I needed to take a few swings.

Eoghan tensed, but he remained seated, a honey rock rind held in his hand. Given enough motivation, I believed he might find a way to weaponize it. I could think of a few ways I could put a honey rock rind to good use. First, I'd use the end to gouge Hammel's eyes out before attempting to insert it up his nose to scramble his brains. Assuming the rind couldn't penetrate into the skull properly, I would have to try to asphyxiate the bastard with it.

From there, the various possible insertions of honey rock rind took a dark and twisted turn.

"This is all your fault," Hammel snapped, striding over. At his side, he wore a gun.

Did everyone in the damned town except me have a gun? On second thought, they probably did. Nobody in Sunset liked being told what to do, and guns offered the illusion of authority.

Hammel was definitely the type to want to maintain his authority.

The gun was a problem, although I had good reason to believe the problem wouldn't last long. The devil's gaze locked onto it, and I recognized when Lucy transformed from family man to the beast capable of bringing ruin to the world if he escaped his chain.

A single twitch towards the gun would end Hammel's life, and I saw no need to prevent the inevitable. No, however satisfying trying to scramble my ex-boss's brains with a honey rock rind, I'd take the quick and merciful route.

I'd stand up for myself first, though.

"Nothing that has happened here is my fault. It isn't my fault your wife died. It isn't my fault you can't bring back the dead. It isn't my fault you're a cheap bastard. It's also not my fault you had no idea what you had in your basement. It's definitely not my fault you can't listen to reason. I suppose it is my fault for putting up with your abuse for so long, but I didn't have a whole lot of options in this one-horse town."

Thanks to Hammel, that had changed.

"Abuse?" My ex-boss snorted. "You should be grateful anyone would take an uneducated waste like you."

Hammel opened his mouth to continue his verbal assault, but the devil went from seated to pouncing, his hands and feet transforming from human to claws and hooves. Lucy's form rippled, and the horned beast of legend drove the wayward man to the grass. Bone crunched, blood spurted, and death came, not at a scream, but on the sigh of a final exhaled breath.

The devil vanished in a cloud of brimstone, taking Hammel's body with him when he went. Something remained, a haze in the air as though something I couldn't quite see lingered, waiting.

"That is the imprint of a passing soul," Gabriel explained. "This is what you need to witness."

I'd seen ghosts before, but the mirage before me lacked the same presence and substance of the incorporeal dead.

Eoghan sighed. "And, as expected, the coward screams."

I heard nothing. "Does he?"

"I would scream, too, if my brother had his claws dug into me and dragged me to hell," Michael confessed. "It is not a pleasant journey. The soul is gone already, but this is an echo of its passage. Azrael has turned his back on this soul, for this soul is not worthy of such comfort or companionship in death. Eoghan would rather not deal with him, but he will—once the soul settles a little."

"And what about me, then?"

"Be patient."

"They need to accept their death before they can move through the boundary in full," Eoghan said, setting down the honey rock rind and giving the hazy apparition his undivided attention. "Like you, I don't truly need to do anything for a soul to move through the boundary. I just get to listen to them scream most of the time. That happens when someone dies close enough for me to witness, and I become aware of the soul's passage. Sometimes, the departed seek me out when they struggle to go beyond on their own."

"And what about the ghosts?"

"What about them?"

"Why do they linger?"

"They had a good enough reason to stay, I suppose. They can leave if they want. Nothing holds them here but themselves. That is what I am. That is why I am here."

Azrael chuckled. "For all he is a vengeful creature at times, your Eoghan has never denied anyone their rest. There are those who have been barred through other ways, but that is no fault of his."

"Except me," I muttered.

The archangel laughed at me. "Oh, he would have broken his rules for you, of that I have no doubt, but it is the universe itself that makes us as we are. We cannot die for we are death. You'll get used to it."

"I still don't understand what I'm supposed to have witnessed here. It's a shimmer."

"Just wait a little longer," Azrael soothed. "While the soul leaving the body is instantaneous upon true death, the souls linger somewhat before fully crossing the boundary. It takes some time for it to move on. When it does, you'll understand."

"I have determined archangels enjoy being as vague as possible."

"We are often told we are assholes," he replied in an amused tone. "Here. It begins. My brother is shackling his latest toy, and the rest of the soul is being pulled into whichever hell has been chosen for him. Perhaps the universe means to take the merciful route with your awakening. But this seed of life forms while the soul pays for its crimes in life."

The haze dimmed, fading until all that remained was a tiny speck. A hint of something, a faint chill in the air, reminded me of the presence of ghosts, although much weaker.

The chill possessed a cutting edge, as though someone dragged a frozen sheet of paper over my skin. I hissed and recoiled.

"It is not a pleasant seed, is it?" Gabriel asked, and he heaved a sigh. "You feel its potential. Cold, unyielding, and hard. But even these seeds must be replanted. That is the intent of the universe. For as long as there is good in the world, there must also be evil. For as long as there is chaos in the world, there must also be order."

"His next life begins with that seed?" I asked, considering how something so tiny could become a person—a person capable of so much harm.

"Your life began as such a seed as well, and the universe took much care with your planting. You won't plant every seed. But you have the option to plant the seeds. You could take this seed, put it in a box, and then find the right people to give it to. An infertile woman may become fertile with the right seed. And a corrupted, cold seed can become warm with the right planting. Go on. Cup it in your hand. You won't hurt it."

"So I shouldn't hit it with the weed whacker a few times first?"

"I would not."

I regarded the last remnant of Hammel's life, heaved a sigh, and put the weed whacker down. I stepped around the picnic blanket so I wouldn't disturb Darlene, who slept through our conversation with no sign of waking. The closer I got to the seed, the colder the air became. "It's really cold."

"That is a consequence of the life he led. In life, he was not what anyone would call a good man. He sometimes did good things, such as providing you with food when your paycheck was not enough to cover your costs, but he did not do it for any care for you. It would have cost him more money to find someone new, and he would have had to pay them better. He knew this. Even his good deeds were motivated by greed."

"Won't he be just as bad if he's replanted like this?"

As one, the archangels shrugged, and Azrael joined me, took hold of my hands, and pulled me close enough to envelop the seed between my palms. He released me and

patted my shoulder. "Right now, the seed re-
flects its origins, its previous life. Right now,
his soul faces the consequences of his actions
in life. When his punishment has concluded,
you will find the soul will warm until it is a
more neutral entity. Few souls have a hard
alignment with the forces of good, evil, order,
or chaos. Nurture is as important as nature.
As you are what you are, you can choose to
keep this seed safe in your custody until it is
time for it to be replanted—and by the time
he has been brought back into balance, you
will understand how you can manipulate the
seeds of life."

Eoghan grunted. "You're going to give her
ideas, Azrael."

"Yes, I am. That is my intention. She needs
to learn her role, and while you are neutrality
and I am considered the more benevolent
face of death, she must learn all of her role,
which has as much capacity of good as it does
evil. And sometimes, evil and darkness is
what needs to be planted. And that is what
she must be prepared for. The light cannot
shine without the darkness, Eoghan. This is
the way of the universe. She is the one who
can bring light to the darkness—and create
darkness so the light may shine. I'm sure
you'll have some glorious arguments over
some souls she opts to keep in her custody
until she decides what to do with them. If
you're particularly unlucky, she might even
cherry pick the souls of your offspring. I ex-

pect you'll find yourself the father of abused souls. She is the type. She cannot save everyone, and she recognizes this, but there will come a point that she can save one, so she will. And she will seduce you to do so."

I opened my mouth to protest such a plan, spent a moment to think it through, realized the bastard asshole of an archangel spoke the truth, and snapped my teeth together with a clack.

Azrael laughed at me.

"You are a feathered menace. Are you sure you are not the devil's henchman?"

"I assure you I am not. I am merely honest. What will you do with that seed, Anwen? This is but the first of many choices you will have to make about the nature of souls and balance within the universe. This is what you are. Do not mind Eoghan. He has opinions."

"I can do whatever I want with his soul?"

"You can. The only part of its fate that has been sealed is that you will decide how it is replanted upon conclusion of his punishment."

The devil reappeared in his human form, sat on the picnic blanket, and gently gathered his wife, settling her on his lap with her head resting against his chest. "I enjoyed that."

"That didn't take long." I clasped my fingers together so the seed couldn't escape from me. "You have his soul, but I have his seed."

"Yes, that is how it works," the devil confirmed. "When the seed is ready to be planted, the soul will return to it from my hells. The seed won't become fertile until the soul has been brought back into balance. Right now, the seed has too much of a capacity for evil. If we were in an era of good, you would consider planting it to bring things back into balance—but for now, he should enjoy my hospitality. View the seed as the spark that brings life, and it holds the soul when life is ready to be made. The seed is not, technically, the soul, but it is only compatible with the soul it belongs to. It's complicated. The universe typically is."

"What am I supposed to do with his seed?"

"You could make him a her in the next life. Seeds lack gender. Souls also lack a gender, although when souls are partnered, they tend to keep their original genders. So, let's assume you and Eoghan partner, and you were mortal, which you are not. Should your seeds be planted again in a future life, you would remain a female, and he would remain a male. Forcing that human to be a woman in the next life would be a fitting punishment."

"You're already punishing him. Isn't the point of you punishing him to make it so I don't have to?" I peeked between my fingers, and the seed stayed nestled between my palms. "Why isn't it trying to escape?"

"It can't. It lacks a soul right now. For the most part, it is an inanimate object." Lucy chuckled. "For the most part."

"Why was 'for the most part' so important you repeated yourself?"

Eoghan snorted. "He's the devil. That's why."

"I'm hurt, Eoghan," the devil whined.

"Are you even capable of being hurt?" Azrael asked. "Interesting. Have you truly fallen so far?"

"Now I'm really hurt. Stricken low by my cruel brother."

The archangels laughed.

"Focus," I scolded. "What am I supposed to do with this seed?"

"Put it in a box, carry it in your pocket, and do whatever you want with it. Just try not to lose it," the devil replied. "I'm sure you could find it again, but it's so annoying when you lose a seed of life you've been holding onto for a while. I have a few I need to plant I've misplaced, and when my wife finds out, she's going to spank me."

"You just want me to spank you," Darlene mumbled. "You're noisy. What'd you do now?"

"I'm always noisy, disturbing your naps. You naughty kitten, gorging on so much melon you needed a nap. I lost one of the seeds I was supposed to be keeping an eye on."

The devil amazed me, behaving as his title warned, lying to his wife to protect her from her memories.

"Idiot," Darlene grumbled. "If you make

me look through the house again, I'm banning you from my spots for three months."

"That's too long. The seeds are stupid, and you don't even like the assholes who own them anyway. Don't ban me from your spots for three months over a few nasty souls nobody wants anyway."

"Touch her on her shoulder," Michael's voice whispered into my ear. "Then you will see the darkness of those memories—and you will learn a little more."

I held Hammel's seed in one hand and patted Darlene on the shoulder. To disguise my motivations, I said, "I'm sure he's just yanking your chain. Anyway, I have more melons if you want to gorge on them again. They're that good, aren't they?"

The feeling of soft, melting ice greeted my touch, with one spot colder than the rest. The boundary between life and death lurked within her, and I fought to keep my eyes from widening.

She somehow still stood in the valley of the shadow of death and hadn't quite been able to step away from it like I had done when I had approached the doorway to the afterlife.

"Precisely. That is precisely what ails her. When she remembers, she draws closer to the boundary, but her soul understands it is not yet her time. It becomes afraid. It tries to protect her the best it can," Michael whispered, and I got the sense his words were meant for me alone. "*He* could not guide her fully back. All he could do was ensure her survival. No one can take back what death has claimed except death itself. It is against the laws of the universe. But this is your domain, for you are death, and she has not fully faced what it means to meet you, Azrael, or Eoghan. You can guide her through that valley and take away the shadow from her. And, if it pleases you, the seed of life you bear can carry that burden for a while until it is ready to be planted. A fitting punishment, and one that will ensure this seed forever flinches from attempting to bring the dead back to life. It will not be difficult for you to guide her. Shoo her away from the boundary. Wave your hand if that helps."

"Yes, they are that good," Darlene replied, and with a happy purr, she snuggled against her husband. "I can't help it I'm a cat. I like to nap."

I suspected the wear and tear of her soul hovering close to the boundary of death tired her more than anything, and I concentrated on the boundary and the feeling of her soul. As I liked the idea of shooing her back to where she belonged, I imagined doing just that, sending her away from the boundary and back to the comfort of the unlikely soul waiting nearby rather like an eager puppy.

I understood, then, why Lucifer had first been called the Lord of the Morning, an archangel representing the light.

He radiated light and warmth, which only grew brighter when Darlene's soul ventured closer to his.

It didn't take much to have that trapped part of her scampering back where it belonged.

And, as Michael had suggested, I shooed the darkness that had clung to her into the seed in my hand. The shadow lurked, a spot colder than the rest within the seed. In time, I would shoo it away, too. I could only hope I could identify when the time was right for the seed to escape another facet of its punishment.

"Just like so," Michael whispered. "It is finished," he said in a normal voice. "Enjoy your spot counting tonight, brother, try not to annoy death in all its parts too terribly much, and do attempt to keep your word about fixing this hole you have made."

The Lord of Lies chuckled. "I always enjoy when I can count my wife's precious spots. I'll see about the hole after I have enjoyed counting her precious spots. I *always* enjoy counting my wife's precious spots. It may as well be a universal rule."

"That's because you're a pervert," Darlene said, and she stretched with a yawn. "That was a nice nap."

"I am glad you enjoyed your nap, my darling. And as for my perversions? Of course I enjoy my perversions. They're so entertaining. While you were napping off your gorging, I took care of some unpleasant business and helped a new guest to his accommodations. Once I have finished counting all of your beautiful spots, you can go play with him. I put your favorite toys outside of his cell for you. It's been a while since you've gotten to toy with one of the naughty souls."

"If you're trying to secure more spot counting, it's working."

"I am. Pure selfishness on my part," the devil lied.

I'd seen a glimpse of the devil's soul, and for her, he was nothing but a light in the dark.

"And now you understand," Michael whispered in my ear. "My brother is a blessing, however much that annoys *Him.* For all my brother fell, his fall became one of *His* greatest gifts to mankind. My brother's fall bought mankind its freedom."

Huh. That one had gotten missed by the history books.

"Indeed," Michael replied.

I'd need a lot of time to think about that mystery of the universe.

"Maybe you all should go home," I suggested, waving the angelic and devilish congregation away with my free hand. "I am going to clean this up, head back to my house, and figure out what to do in the meantime. I also have plans for the rest of my honey rocks."

"Of course you do," the devil replied with

laughter in his voice. "You are a shameless addict."

I laughed. "I really am."

"They are quite good. I find them pleasing," Eoghan admitted. "They are a pleasant and harmless vice."

"Then you will enjoy helping her to grow a garden of them in the back so she can enjoy them at her leisure. Perhaps you should build a greenhouse so she can enjoy them year round." The devil smiled and kissed the top of his wife's head. "And with that, I will pay you a visit another time. I have much to do tonight."

The pair disappeared, and the angels followed the devil's lead, leaving us alone. I opened my hand to regard Hammel's seed with a frown. "I really don't know what I'm supposed to do with this, Eoghan."

"Take your time thinking about it. It's going to be just about an eternity before the devil is done with that one. Deserved, if you ask me."

"Did he scream a lot?" I asked, aware Eoghan had already commented about Hammel's departure.

"For a rare change, I liked it," Eoghan announced. "It is well enough he will have many long years in the devil's care for his deeds. My memory is long. I do not feel he suffered enough in the transition for his crimes."

"You can't torture the seed anymore than it's already being tortured." To make sure

Eoghan didn't do anything nefarious to the seed, I put it in my pocket.

"I like that you admit the seed is being tortured," he confessed.

"It seemed fair at the time. When an archangel seems to think it's a good idea, it probably is. Still, poor Darlene."

"Did you see her soul?"

"See it? No. I felt it. She had wandered near the boundary, and it is a cold place. I'm not sure if I want to see the boundary again. I've been there once, and feeling it is bad enough. Her soul doesn't stray near the boundary anymore."

"And now? Is her soul restored?"

I smiled. "I think she'll be just fine. The devil has a pretty nice soul for a bad guy. It just took a little shooing to get her to go where she belonged. I suspect her soul is enjoying a lot of snuggling right now. He's surprisingly warm, bright, and gentle. I guess he hasn't lost all of his original nature, has he?"

"Souls rarely do for all they are balanced before returning to life. But they can change with time, given the right environment. I've seen the darkest souls cross through the boundary to live their next lives as remarkably good beings. It can happen."

"And where I help plant this seed will help determine if it happens, doesn't it?"

"It's not an easy burden to bear."

I shrugged. "Somebody has to do it."

"Right you are. I suppose it was only a

matter of time before the universe tired of doing the job. It hadn't taken the universe long to tire of death, creating me. Shall we relocate this picnic to your other home? It seems we have to think about what we should build here."

I knew exactly what we would build on the property: our future. Smiling, I went to work cleaning up the picnic. I saved the weed whacker for last, and blue fire danced along the handle, covered my hand, and infiltrated the pocket containing the seed. As far as I could tell, nothing had changed about the seed, but I couldn't be sure.

For a brief moment, I swore I heard an angel's ringing laughter, but I spotted no sign of one of the divines nearby.

"Angels are assholes, Eoghan."

He laughed. "Did you just figure that one out?"

"Not really, but I thought I'd let you know anyway. Let's get out of here."

TWENTY

I'm going to need a manual on how
to seduce an ancient antique.

THE POTENTIAL for life lurked around every
corner, waiting in the oddest of places. I
spotted another seed of life in Lady Luck, just
chilling on the dashboard until it could bring
its soul back to the mortal coil. I buckled in,
regarding the tiny grain of light through narrowed eyes.

"You see something," Eoghan observed,
clipping his seatbelt into place.

I gestured to the dashboard. "There's a
seed of life there."

"Perhaps it seeks an opportunity to bring
a soul back to the mortal coil."

"In my *truck*?" I blurted.

Eoghan examined the cab with interest.
"There is sufficient space for such an en-
deavor. It seems like it would be a challenge,
but I could find interesting ways to make use
of these belts."

Okay. I stopped and considered the cab
for a while, too. I could understand how

the belts could be used in interesting ways. After learning the truth about Eoghan's nature, I suspected I would be the one using the belts on him if he insisted on remaining stubborn. "I'm not sure I want a voyeur just sitting around watching what I may or may not do with a seatbelt."

"It's not really sentient. It's just seeking opportunities. They tend to show up where there are opportunities."

"In my truck?" I demanded again.

"I don't see why not. I've participated in my fair share of seductions in carriages. This is not that much different from a carriage. It's far more comfortable, too."

I refused to become jealous over some woman who'd died hundreds of years ago, although I made some assumptions on the having died hundreds of years ago part of things. "Were you the seducer or the seduced?"

"A little bit of both, really."

Well, that didn't help my general cause any. "You're going to have to help me out here, Eoghan. Either I'm going to need a manual on how to seduce an ancient antique, or you're going to have to step up your game... but not in my truck."

"Why not in your truck? It possesses many horses, and I find this appealing."

Of course. I'd purchased his dream truck, and I had to admit, she had a certain appeal.

"Not in my truck yet," I replied, shaking my head at the insanity of it all.

"Yes, it would be a bit much for a first seduction to take place in such a location. Carriages make excellent seduction spots for later in a relationship."

"Or with a paid lady of the night?"

"While I have met many a lovely lady of the night, I have never bedded any of them. I require more dedicated attention. I do not share well."

Neither did I. "Having witnessed your behavior, I readily believe you are not very good at sharing."

"Some things I am willing to share. A honey rock, for example, is something I would share with you."

"Well played, Mr. Olin. Very well played."

"Only a blind fool would not notice your adoration for those melons. I will take the advice given to me and plan a way to provide you with them year round. I may have to hold your prized melons hostage. Appropriate affections paid out would result in you receiving a melon to enjoy."

Well, if he was trying to seduce me in my truck, he went about it the right way. "Keep talking."

He chuckled. "If I keep talking, I would be forced to reduce you to begging, and while this is a lovely truck, it is unsuitable for such an event."

I swiped the seed of life off my dashboard

and put it in a different pocket so Hammel's seed couldn't bother it. "Does your magic let you see the past circumstances of a soul?"

"That is more of your power, once you learn to use it, but I can to a certain degree. Some souls have stronger imprints of their pasts than others."

Hmm. I retrieved the seed and held it out to him. "What can you tell me about this one?"

Eoghan placed his hand over mine and closed his eyes. After a few minutes, he grunted. "She had a difficult life and a worse death. The seed probably perceived you as a safe place and manifested here."

I found it odd the universe could be so uncaring yet compassionate at the same time. "Do I want to know how difficult?"

"No, you don't. It is best if you do not pry too deeply into that soul's past. It would be best if she slept without remembering."

"Has her soul been resting a long time, then?"

"I can't tell you that. I can tell you that she lived during a time of war and plague. There were still horses, but there were also odd horseless carriages. I cannot tell you much beyond that."

"That sounds like World War I. A bad flu happened at the very end of the war, and when the soldiers all came home, they brought the illness with them. A lot of people died." I couldn't remember if magic had yet swept through the world or not then. Magic had changed everything, but some things remained the same—including humanity's need to kill each other for money, power, and position.

"Yes, she had a soldier. He had returned home to her broken. If the disease hadn't killed her, he would have. I get the feeling she believed, right up to the bitter end, she could fix him. Perhaps she could have. War ruins people. It changes them. But love can be a very powerful thing. She did not live long enough to find out."

I grimaced. Even in small, backwater Sunset, violence infected some homes much like a disease. In a way, I'd been lucky. My parents' abuses hadn't extended to physical violence. They'd found other ways to torment me.

Perhaps her hope he'd improve had been why she'd stayed—and influenza had spared her from a long and bitter road.

I hurt for them both. "That's so sad."

"Before the war, he had been kind and gentle."

"That makes it even sadder."

Eoghan nodded. "She hadn't screamed when she died. She'd been too tired. Hers is a gentle soul by its nature."

It amazed me he could sense so much from the seed. "Will I be able to do the same as you can?"

"In time, I'm sure. It took me a thousand

years to sense the seeds at all. You're seeing them right away. Perhaps in time you can learn parts of my magic, just as I have learned parts of yours."

"And Azrael?"

With a huff, Eoghan shrugged. "I don't want to talk about him right now."

"What do you want to talk about, then?" I closed my hand around the woman's seed and returned her to my pocket. "I'll figure out what to do with her later."

"Generally, if you want the seed to go away, just ignore it for a while. It'll go where needed. If you want to keep it around, you need to express the intent to keep it. Most put the seeds they want to keep in a box to symbolize their intent to keep it. The seeds are mostly inanimate, so once someone has laid a claim, they tend to stick around because they're not really intelligent enough to wander off despite being capable of doing so."

Life was truly complicated. "Okay. I'm just going to drive us to the house and deal with this another day.

Eoghan chuckled. "That's one way to handle the situation. If that makes you happy, then we shall do that."

I gave myself a few minutes to think over my situation, focusing on my odd relationship with Eoghan, my unrelenting attraction to the egotistical antique, and my utter lack of experience with men. "I've been told you're going to be challenging to seduce, which is

accurate, as I've never even attempted to seduce a man before."

"I already told you before, all you have to
do is beg," he replied in an amused tone. "You
seem quite stubborn, so I expect this will take
you a very long time."

I considered that. How did he define beg?
Would a simple please work? Saying please
sounded like begging to me. I'd be willing to
say please. I'd even pull out a thank you afterwards, as I had some manners and even knew
how to use them. "I don't like begging, but I
will say please. I'll even put on something
pretty when I say please. I'll have to go buy
something pretty, but you're paying me good
money to stick around, so I can afford to buy
pretty things. We'll have to take a field trip to
the city for that, because there aren't many
good stores here. If you're really nice to me,
I'll let you help pick out the pretty things."

"You're already beautiful. You do not need
to try to make yourself pretty."

I smiled at that. "But pretty would be very
lacy."

Eoghan's eyes narrowed. "May I take that
back? I seem to have developed an interest in
you making yourself pretty alongside you
being naturally beautiful."

Love, I supposed, was truly blind, as I'd
never thought of myself as anything other
than plain and somewhat boring. I'd seen
beautiful women before. I wasn't one of
them. With enough work and makeup, I

could make myself somewhat fit society's expectations for women.

I'd never liked the results—or the money required to hide my actual face beneath several layers of product.

"I will say please once and only once," I stated, starting Lady Luck's engine.

"I find it amusing you are attempting to negotiate. I see I have much to teach you on what it means to beg. I look forward to slowly and meticulously educating you on this subject. It seems only fair, as you need to teach me your language."

I backed my truck out of the driveway, at a loss of what I was supposed to say, do, or think. "Should I be concerned?"

"You'll enjoy it, so no. Beyond a lack of sleep, you have nothing to be concerned about. As what I have planned for you will take a great deal of time, you'll have to wait until our home is properly built. We wouldn't want to disturb your neighbors. That would be rude."

"I'm not exactly a loud person."

Eoghan leered at me. "When I'm done with you, you will be."

A BLACK DRAGON covered in opalescent scales lounged out on the roof of my house with his tail wrapped around the building. My neighbors gawked at it, and when I pulled the truck into the driveway, the dragon snorted smoke.

"Oh. It's Yuless." Eoghan flung the seatbelt off and dove out of my truck before I had a chance to kill the engine, a hand keeping the door propped open. "If you break her house, you'll repair it and everything inside. And you'll upgrade everything while you're at it."

Well, at least Eoghan cared about my house and possessions. My life had taken such a sharp left turn out of normality I appreciated *someone* understood the basics of survival, which included having a home.

The dragon snorted again, and more smoke poured from its nose. "You were always slow to get out of bed. I was told there's a woman."

Well, I did count as a woman. I turned the key in the ignition and sighed, giving Lady Luck a pat on her dashboard. "I'm not sure my life could possibly get weirder." Delaying wouldn't help, so I got out of my truck, closed the door, and circled the vehicle so I could shoo Eoghan away and close his door, too. I locked it, and my truck beeped to notify me the alarm system had engaged. Then I went to the back to unload everything. "There's a dragon on my house, Eoghan."

"Yes. His name is Yuless. He's almost as old as I am, he's far more annoying, and he loves using houses as his bed. It makes him feel special. One of his favorite hobbies is to annoy me." Eoghan sighed. "Please don't break her house. She is quite fond of it, and she's already had a house broken today. She does not need a second home of hers broken quite yet. Anyway, if you break the house and endanger our vampire companion, I'll be most displeased."

"The vampire is fine. He is dozing inside. I startled him when I paid a visit, but he said you were out with your woman. At that point, I couldn't just leave a message and head home, so I opted to wait. The humans are quite distraught I have taken up temporary residence here. They amuse me. The one likes that little weapon of his a great deal, and he thinks his threats are anything other than amusing. I helped myself to the first one he pointed at me. It tasted delicious. Good metal, aged wood. There might be a hole in the house, but that is not my fault."

"Jeff, you didn't!" I complained, turning around to face my neighbor and stomping my foot. "Where are your manners? Or better yet, where is your common sense?" Pointing at the dragon counted as rude, but I'd deal with the consequences of that later. "Did you fail to notice he is a dragon?"

"He invaded your property."

"He isn't doing anything wrong."

"He shouldn't be there."

"He's a dragon, Jeff. I figure he can go any-where he wants. In case you had not noticed, he is large enough to swallow you whole. You're lucky he only ate your gun! You'd probably tickle while kicking and screaming to his stomach."

"She's not wrong," the dragon announced. "I prefer my humans charred, but I might make an exception for a particularly annoying one. What do you go by in this age, old friend?"

"Eoghan. The lady is Anwen. I thought it would be fair to warn you that Azrael is up and about."

"I have been warned. I've been told of your woman's role, too. You must be pleased."

"An ignorant fool thought to sacrifice her to me. I've accepted his offer with much glee. He was corrected on his misconceptions, but I am keeping her around. She's unfortunately independent, and she wishes to earn her keep, so she is taking on the role of caretaker."

"Your caretaker will require a caretaker. What became of yours?"

"Murdered."

"A sad end to a loyal, good family. I'm sorry."

Jeff spluttered. "Anwen, what is the meaning of this?"

"It seems Eoghan is friends with a dragon, and the dragon has paid us a visit. Put your gun away. It's rude. Be hospitable for once, please."

"He ate Betsy!"

"Well, you shouldn't have pointed Betsy at him and fired her. You can buy a new Betsy from Walmart. She cost you less than two hundred dollars, and she's the firearm equivalent of a cheap hussy," I replied, allowing some of my scorn into my tone. "She was the cheapest damned double-barrel your money could buy."

"Anwen," Jeff whined.

"Jeff," I whined back. "Put the damned gun away and leave my guests alone. Don't make me be callin' the cops. For pity's sake, what does a woman have to do to get some peace around here?"

"Move to a different house," Eoghan muttered. "One without neighbors."

I almost laughed at that. "Eoghan, be nice."

"I don't feel like being nice. He put a hole in your house."

I snorted, wondering if I should tell him a tiny hole counted as dinky damage compared to the shit my parents had pulled over the years. "That's nothing some spackle and elbow grease won't fix as long as he didn't take out a wire, a pipe, or a window."

The dragon pointed at something on the second floor with the tip of his tail. I sighed at the hole in the siding in my damned bedroom. "This is where it hit."

Well, as the house hadn't burned down and my bedroom light was still on, I figured the bullet hadn't done any real damage.

"I swear, Jeff, if I find holes in my laundry, I'm going to come over there and beat you with your own damned guns."

"I didn't mean to hit the house!"

"How could you miss the dragon almost as big as my house? If you don't know how to point the damned thing, don't shoot it! Look at him, he's as big of a target as the house."

"Like you could do any better."

"It'd be a fifty-fifty, and I ain't shot a damn gun in my life."

"Your papa done did you wrong, girl. He shoulda taught you to shoot when you were just a little thing."

"The only damned thing my papa knows how to shoot is crack. You know that, I know that, and the whole damned town knows it. If you're going to go being insulting, at least be creative about it."

"You've gotten quite a mouth on you," Jeff snapped back.

Before I could reply, Eoghan said, "I recommend you take your ill-humor somewhere else. Upsetting her means upsetting me, and unlike her, I am not nearly as inclined to be nice. If that isn't a stern enough deterrent, you are not friends with the dragon. I am."

The dragon chuckled, and smoke coiled from its nose. "I am very old friends with him, yes. I would also be quite offended should you upset his love."

My face flushed, as neither one of us had gotten to the point we'd declared love had anything to do with our relationship. Lust certainly did, and I enjoyed that we developed a friendship to go with it.

But love?

The dragon snorted smoke with a hint of flame. "I'm a telepath, little lady. Just because you're almost as blind as him doesn't mean those pesky emotions that keep bothering you aren't just that. You were ill-taught what it means to love. You'll figure it out. Eoghan will help you. And Eoghan? Take your time with her. She wouldn't know what love is even if you slapped her in the face with it. You'll have to teach her. Few others have."

"We have all the time in the world," Eoghan replied, and he smiled. "I intend to enjoy every second of it."

"I feel I should warn you, my old friend, that she might just tie you to a chair and have her way with you should you take too much time."

If my face got much warmer, it would burst into flames.

"You will need much luck with her, old friend." The dragon laughed, uncurled, and eased off the roof of my house. I marveled at the dragon's precision, and he took great care to avoid damaging anything important. Dodging my truck, Yuless swung his great head to me, and he breathed in my scent. "Take care with him, little lady. He carries many burdens with him, and you will find him to be most annoying about it. Should you need any help with him, do contact me. I will send word with how you can contact me."

I retrieved my new phone and held it up. "Do you have a phone number?"

The dragon chuckled. "I certainly do. I find these phones most fascinating. A world's worth of information and wonders, available at the tap of such a tiny screen."

The dragon lived in Florida, and he gave me his phone number and address so I could drag Eoghan across the country to pay him a visit. I hesitated, wondering what his opalescent scales felt like.

"You may touch," the dragon replied.

I put my phone away, and holding my breath, I rested my hands against Yuless's massive nose.

I expected cold and hard, but the warmth surprised me almost as much as the almost plush texture. "You're soft!"

"I recently molted. It's velvet, much like a deer's antlers. The scales beneath are diamond hard—or even harder, but the velvet encourages the scales to grow faster. When I lose a scale, a new one grows with a thicker covering of velvet. When the scales are done growing, the velvet will shed. I collect it and turn it into cloth. The hobby amuses me, and I produce a great deal of velvet following a molt."

"What do you do with your scales?"

"I make things from them. It fills the time when I am away. Once they're shed, I can warm them with my fires and shape them. I have been making dishes, for I find human dishes to be amusing. Carving them into forks and spoons is a challenge. But they make excellent cutlery. I will bring a set for you. I will also include a nice pair of manacles so you can capture your man at your leisure. Would you like a chain and leash to go with your manacles?"

I giggled at the thought of chaining Eoghan with dragonscale manacles. "Yes, please. I'd love that."

"Of course you would," Eoghan muttered.

I grinned at him. "If you play too hard to get, I will not say please, but I will say thank you."

Eoghan's smile possessed a sly and wicked edge. "Will you?"

"Can I pay you to make that a rush order, Yuless?"

The dragon laughed, stretched his wings, and bobbed his great head. "Why not? Keep him on his toes, Anwen. He deserves you more than you can ever know—and you deserve only his best. Never forget that. I'll pay you a visit with your gifts and my wishes for your happy future."

"Watch it, dragon, or you'll be next," Eoghan grumbled.

"As I have from the day I drew my first breath, I wait. Should you find her, send her my way. I would be forever in your debt."

With that, the dragon launched into the air, spiraling upwards until he became nothing more than a speck in the clear sapphire sky above. "How long is his forever?" I asked.

"Only time will tell." Eoghan turned his attention to Jeff and the rest of my neighbors. "I recommend you treat your living better so your dead do not become vengeful. Start with Mr. McGregor, and may his ongoing presence be a reminder of why you should mind your manners."

After taking hold of my hand, Eoghan pulled me to the front door of the house. "What was that all about?"

With a chuckle, he clasped my hand and kissed my knuckles. "For all Azrael is benevolent, he has a mischievous nature and a grave sense of humor. I'll tell you this much, Anwen. Sunset will never be the same."

Truer words had never been spoken, and unable to help myself, I laughed. Sunset wouldn't be the same—and neither would I.

For the first time in my life, the small town had everything I'd ever wanted, and I looked forward to what tomorrow would bring.

The next novel in the Magical Romantic Comedy (with a body count) series is **A Chip on Her Shoulder**, the story of how the devil met his bride, releasing in September 2020.

Like werewolves, bounty huntresses,

and a woman on a mission? **Doggone Mess: A Magical Romantic Comedy (with a body count)** is in **Dirty Deeds: an urban fantasy collection** coming out in January 2021, including all-new stories from Faith Hunter, Diana Pharaoh Francis, Devon Monk, and R.J. Blain.

About R.J. Blain

Want to hear from the author when a new book releases? You can sign up at her website (thesneakykittycritic.com). Please note this newsletter is operated by the Furred & Frond Management. Expect to be sassed by a cat. (With guest features of other animals, including dogs.)

A complete list of books written by RJ and her various pen names is available at https://books2read.com/rl/The-Fantasy-Worlds-of-RJ-Blain.

RJ BLAIN suffers from a Moleskine journal obsession, a pen fixation, and a terrible tendency to pun without warning.

When she isn't playing pretend, she likes to think she's a cartographer and a sumi-e painter.

In her spare time, she daydreams about being a spy. Should that fail, her contingency plan involves tying her best of enemies to spinning wheels and quoting James Bond villains until she is satisfied.

RJ also writes as Susan Copperfield and Bernadette Franklin. Visit RJ and her pets (the Management) at thesneakykittycritic.com.

FOLLOW RJ & HER ALTER EGOS ON BOOKBUB:
RJ BLAIN
SUSAN COPPERFIELD
BERNADETTE FRANKLIN

CPSIA information can be obtained
at www.ICGtesting.com
Printed in the USA
LVHW092333150921
697901LV00002B/166